DRAGON SCARS

BY

AMANDA T. FOX

For information, or to order additional copies, please contact:

Beacon Publishing Group
P.O. Box 41573 Charleston, S.C. 29423
800.817.8480 | beaconpublishinggroup.com

Publisher's catalog available by request.

ISBN-13: 978-1-949472-52-3

ISBN-10: 1-949472-52-3

Published in 2022. New York, NY 10001.

First Edition. Printed in the USA.

DRAGON SCARS

Special thanks to:

Digital art by Dawn Femme

Photography by Cathleen Tarawhiti

Model - Sophia Malecaut-Watts

Table of Contents

Chapter 1

Emeline Lilian fell to her knees beside the roses, gently packing the soil against the roots with her garden glove-covered hands and smiled when the sun glistened on the morning dew still resting upon its petals in the afternoon light. She brushed a few straight, brunette strands behind her pointed ear, her golden eyes glistening in the water just behind the rose bed as she stood. Her blue summer dress brushed against her calves and her bare feet scraped against the dirt as she strolled through their small garden.

Others in her village moved from shop to shop, finishing their daily errands, or opening for business. Children rubbed their eyes as they held their mothers hands and toddled along the cobblestone walkways. Men and women bartered for goods and tried to charm one another, and a few married couples bickered about one topic or other.

Emeline shook her head in amusement. Such trivial things to argue about when there were plenty of adventures just waiting to be had out there, beyond the small village, just waiting to be discovered.

As much as her father had urged her to settle down and find love, no man in the village was interesting enough for her. Of course, she could have picked any one of them and built a family, but a loveless, boring marriage wasn't what she was after.

Most women just wanted families and strong husbands to protect and care for them, to make them feel special and wanted.

Emeline didn't need that. She knew she was special all on her own and she didn't need a man to tell her that. Even though her father was very protective of her, she didn't need anyone to protect her, either.

She bunched her fingers into her skirt and huffed a sigh as she watched a couple debate over which vegetable to eat. A little girl with a handkerchief tied around her brown hair turned away while holding her mother's hand and tucked her thumb into her mouth. Her blue eyes caught Emeline's and held, captivated.

Emeline smiled kindly and gave a finger wave. The girl smiled in return, her eyes lighting with happiness. Making sure that neither of the little girl's parents could see, Emeline reached down to a wilted flower and gave the girl a wink.

Magic tingled down her arm, trickling until it surrounded the rose, bringing it back to life and bringing it to full bloom.

Her mother finally turned away from the argument with her husband when the girl gasped in delight and followed her gaze to Emeline, whose magic had faded away. Instead of waving at Emeline, she quickly turned her child away and ushered her family away from view.

Emeline sighed as she dropped her hand and turned to go back into her home.

Nobody appreciated those who were different, just condemned them, and despite her attempts to stop it, it hurt.

Why was being different such a terrible thing?

Her father, Navi, looked up from washing dishes when she entered the modest kitchen and smiled. "I see she hasn't changed a bit in her judgmental ways."

"No, she hasn't," Emeline said sadly.

He dried his hands and held her shoulders in his hands as his kind blue gaze met hers. His graying hair seemed to almost glow in the sunlight and a kind smile curved his lips.

"They will regret their action one day, dear Ema. For now, I think it is time for another lesson. Your magic won't get better without practice."

She shook her head and grasped his forearm in support as their foreheads met. Emeline closed her eyes and her shoulders rose and fell with another heavy sigh, drawing in the scent of the ginger and spice her father always wore. "I have practiced enough, I know how to use my elven magic. I just wish the others didn't see me as a witch or some kind of abomination. I wish we hadn't moved to the human realm. I miss home, where everyone loved each other even for their differences."

He tilted her chin up and leaned back to look down into her eyes. His beautiful daughter, ever the valiant one. "We moved here because we were being hunted by demons. Elves were always the healers of the supernatural world, but without us, demons can take anyone they want off the board. You understand that don't you?"

She gave a nod of resignation. "I do. But at least with our people, I could practice my magic openly and be praised for it. Our differences were celebrated, not condemned as it is in this world."

He sank into a chair outside the kitchen doorway and looked up at her as he held her hands in his own. "Our clan was always the strongest, filled with the best warriors, and the most cunning of the elves. But the demons are on a bigger rampage than they have ever been to gain power and take over the realms, both living and dead. Now that they can walk in both worlds, it wasn't safe to stay with everyone else. We were putting them in grave danger simply by existing with them."

"I know," she said softly.

He gave a sad nod. "So we stay here. Hopefully soon, it will settle down and everything will fall into place. We could be happy here, in this little village, with its judgmental townspeople," he joked. "It's only been a few months, just give it time."

She gave a nod and forced a smile. "I will try."

He gave a curt shake of his head and stood with a deep breath. "For now, I need to prepare to go to the market tonight to sell our vegetables tomorrow. Though people tend to fear what they don't understand, they seem to love elven produce."

She snorted. "What do they think it is, if not elven?"

He turned from his strides toward the stairs and waved his spread fingers goofily with a grin as though performing a magic trick.

"Lillian produce!"

She giggled with a shake of her head and watched him go upstairs before she began to gather food for dinner.

Jasper Rogue stood strong on the cloud, his fists clenched as he watched the ship below him sail toward a new destination. His large midnight blue wings were folded against his back, falling to his knees as they waited to be opened for flight. His yellow eyes glowed in the waning sunlight, and his dark red hair almost seemed to turn brown in the shadows. A scar ran across his eyebrow to his cheekbone and a smaller one caused a white line to appear in the middle of his bottom lip. They continued to criss-cross over his chest and stomach. One long, thin scar encircled both his biceps and two more were along his wrist almost to his elbows. The scars on his back were hidden beneath a hooded cape that broke over his shoulders to cascade down his chest. Two holes broke around his wings, allowing them to sit folded comfortably on his back as he stood.

On board the ship was a captain who was holding his new wife in his arms as they talked about their days. Her brown hair flew back in the wind as they watched the sunset and her purple eyes were alight with amusement at what her husband whis-pered into her ear.

How he longed to have it…

Jasper heaved a sigh and his eyes blazed with the sad fire he felt within himself. No matter how of-ten he reminded himself that no one could ever love him, it still hurt. He longed to feel the warmth of a woman he loved tucked into his arms, where she would feel safe and warm, without fear of what he looked like. To know what it would be to love a woman with his entire being and know without a doubt that she loved him in return, regardless of the scars.

He snorted.

No such woman would ever exist.

Even his best friend, Luke, had won the heart of the one woman who could stand his existence without flinching, and he would be serving the end of his eternity in the afterlife with his love.

"Well, you've protected them, and now, I'm bored!"

Jasper growled at the grating sound of her voice. "Ana, go away."

The former demon-witch landed beside him unsteadily with her wings and almost fell over the edge of the cloud. Once one of the most powerful witches in existence, Ana Grey was a reformed demon from Hell. The darkness in her had turned her soul, but after centuries of enduring Hell, she had finally escaped. But when she helped to defeat her own mother Dawn, Lucifer's second in command, the angels had granted her the chance to redeem herself and get into Afterlife to be with her father.

Unfortunately for Jasper, this meant that she was his new charge.

Her raging red hair smacked him in the face as he pulled her back from the edge with an eye roll and crossed his arms. "I told you not to leave the castle."

"I ignored you," she replied with a shrug. "I was bored out of my mind there! I need something to entertain me, so I looked for you so I could amuse myself."

"Lucky me," he groaned.

She looked down at the couple and tilted her head. "Aw, they are adorable. Ooh, and he is one sexy pirate. Look at those arms of his! I bet he could take down a mighty beast in one fell swoop without breaking a sweat."

Jasper glared at her, his patience at an end. "Go away."

She turned her attention to him with false innocence, opening her red eyes wide. "What? I was just saying she's a lucky girl."

He blew out a sigh and sparks flew out with the air. "You aren't going away, are you?"

She smirked at him.

He expanded his wings and fisted his hands once more. "You need to get used to flying with your wings if you're going to fly with me."

She put her hands on her hips as she gave him a deadpan look. "Excuse me, but I didn't *ask* the angels to make me a dragon. Lydia and Luke said I would be rewarded for helping defeat my mother and yet here I am, a witch-dragon…thing with a lot of power and yet, nothing to do."

He scrubbed a hand over his face. "Do you ever shut up?"

She studied her nails as she frowned. "You're grumpy. Must be you're mourning your lady love." She stared daggers at him. "Well get over it. She's dead and so is her lover, which means they are happily ever after. You weren't included."

Despite his annoyance, his heart ached at her words.

Without warning, he turned away from her and fell off the cloud.

Navi had left by horse hours ago with a kiss to his daughter goodbye and a promise to be back early the following evening. Emeline cleaned up her plate from dinner and moved to start cleaning the dishes. Her mind drifted to the little girl from earlier, and she smiled to herself as she absently washed the dishes, marveling at the wonder of human children. They were so easily pleased with such little things.

Unlike the adults who scorned her for being kind to them.

Even if she wished more than anything to have an adventure, a part of her truly did want to bear children one day, to be so loved and accepted by someone that a family came naturally, one that naturally lent itself to love, warmth and laughter.

A knock came at the door before she could dip her hands into the soapy, warm water and she wiped her hands on her apron, brow furrowed in confusion. She made her way to the doorway and looked out the peephole her father had made in the door.

What she saw made her eyes widened.

It looked as though a group of people were on her doorstep, each carrying a gun or torch, and something about the way that they glowered, even at the door, made her heart jump wildly in her chest with fright. Her breathing grew choppy and she fought down panic as she told herself that it would be alright, that perhaps they weren't after her.

As politely as possible, she eased open the door and forced herself to smile through the crack. Three burly looking men turned their attention to her from the other side as she said hesitantly, "Hello. May I help you?"

"Come outside," the dark-haired one said deeply as he glared at her.

She swallowed hard as her gaze scanned over the torches in the villager's hands and unease spread through her.

"What is this about?"

"Come out or we will drag you out," the darker-skinned man barked at Emeline rudely.

She eased the door open and looked out. Every person in the village looked back at her with such hatred, and her stomach twisted into knots. Her panic was beginning to rise again and her fingers trembled on the door as she stared, wide-eyed, at the men before her.

"Why are you here?"

The two biggest men, out of patience, forced the door the rest of the way open and it slammed into the wall as she jumped back with her hands up. She started to back away fast, ready to run but it was too late.

"Please, don't!"

They grabbed her arms and dragged her out for the crowd to see on her covered front porch. The third man, the quietest of the bunch, grabbed her hair and jerked her head back, despite her protests and struggles.

"This is a witch! She has come to curse our children, our women," he announced with such hatred that venom seemed to drip from every word, his voice a low growl that caused the crowd to gasp in horror and fright.

Tears swelled in her eyes and she jerked against the strong grip they had. "I am no witch! I'm a normal woman, I swear it! Please don't do this!"

"Burn her," some of the people in the crowd cried.

"Kill her!"

"Get rid of her!"

She started sobbing and the man with her hair in his fist leaned forward, flashing his red eyes at her. "Die, elf."

Her eyes widened and she shook her head frantically as they began to pull her, kicking and struggling, down the steps and toward the town square where a circle of firewood had been piled around a single post.

She struggled anew.

"No," she protested to the other men holding her, as she tried to dig her bare feet into the dirt to slow them down, stop them, anything.

"*He's* the demon, he will burn you all! Please, listen to me!"

The two holding her flashed their eyes red and she let out a cry of alarm.

"I won't hurt anyone, I promise! Just let me go!"

With the crowd shouting and holding their torches high enough to light the square, the demons tied her to the post in the middle of a wood pile. Though she struggled against the bindings, they easily tied her hands behind the pole as though she was no more than a feather. Her cries for mercy were lost amongst the angry mob, and thus fell on deaf ears. Tears spilled down her cheeks and she yanked on the ropes, but they held strong.

Red, what she deemed to be the nickname of the red-haired demon, leaned forward and sneered at her. "When your soul joins Lucifer in Hell, you'll join the other elven healers. Your torment will be so much worse for your beauty, but you will eventually cave and work for us soon enough."

She glared at him before she ground out between clenched teeth, "Never."

She spit into his face and an inhuman growl escaped as he turned away in surprise, then back with menace. He leaned into her face and his eyes glowed a deathly red as he bared his fangs at her. "You will pay for that when we meet again."

All three turned and left the stake.

She tugged at the ropes and worked at the tie, but it was no use.

This was how she was going to die.

Another man, this one thinner, climbed up onto a stool and held his torch high as he addressed the townspeople in a shrieking, wobbling but hateful voice, "This woman is charged with being a witch! A demon from Hell, bent on destroying us all and those we love most! Today," he turned and pointed at her with such rage in his eyes, it caused her to flinch. "She will die for these crimes. We will burn her away from existence, and her very essence from this town until we are cleansed again!"

She pulled at the ropes with a cry of protest, her once bound hair coming loose around her. Tendrils of brown locks fell into her sweat-covered face as she watched in horror as the crowd cheered with joy. Her breathing was choppy, and it felt as though there was a vise around her chest that refused to let go.

The man jumped down and approached. She flattened her back against the post, her breathing picking up in her panic.

"Don't," she pleaded with him, her voice barely a whisper passed the lump in her throat. "You're making a big mistake, please listen to me!"

He held the torch over the wood, the flames beginning to lick at the branches that outstretched from the wood, as he snapped, "Good riddance, witch!"

Without hesitation, and with much encouragement from the mob surrounding her, he dropped the torch.

Chapter 2

Jasper closed his eyes at the feel of the wind on his face and the sound of nature around him, from the crashing of the waves to the birds flying alongside him. At the last minute, he opened his wings and caught himself when he was nearly to the water's surface and soared, going higher and higher until the clouds were surrounding him, enveloping him in a protective fog.

"I wish you would just get over it already."

He grunted at the sound of Ana's voice just behind him and shut his eyes. In his musings, he had failed to hear Ana following him, which meant he hadn't heard if anyone had called out for help either.

"We're heading back to-"

A shriek had him halting in the air with Ana soaring by him at full speed in surprise before she could stop herself with a curse. The sound vibrated through him and an urgency that he hadn't felt in a long time ripped through him like a tidal wave.

"I hate these wretched things! How do you stop?" She got her bearings and glanced up at Jasper, her sarcasm falling instantly into concern upon seeing his expression. "Why did you stop? What is it?"

"Did you hear that?"

Another terrified scream tore at his heartstrings, causing his chest to ache as though a vise held his heart in its rough grip, and he placed his fist there. Whoever had screamed was in a great deal of pain and somehow, she had sent that pain soaring through the air to him.

He dove, uncaring if he was above water or land. As he broke through the clouds, he listened in for the screams in the immortal realm, but no darkness drew him toward the origins of the innocent.

Reaching further with urgency, he listened in the mortal realm.

Her scream ended in a sob, tearing through him once more, and his brow furrowed even as he moved above the clouds at a speed too great for anyone to see. No mortal could be heard on this side and no immortal was permitted beyond the fog into the mortal realm, so how could he hear a woman's scream?

With his dragon ears peaked and sensitive to every sound, he heard more cries and ignored Ana as she tried to keep up behind him, her breath heaving. Occasionally, she would shriek or gasp as she failed to keep herself flying straight and under normal circumstances, he might have laughed.

This wasn't a normal circumstance.

Finally, they broke through the fog above the clouds that formed a thinly veiled gateway to the mortal realm, one that only allowed a choice few through, and he started downward, landing just behind a building in a small town that sat in the center of a valley. Somehow, he knew that whoever had screamed had come from here.

It would have been a lovely village, if not for the shadows cast by the roaring fire in the center and the cheers of villagers in the distance.

He tucked his wings beneath his cape and grunted as Ana crashed into the back of him with a grunt. He stumbled forward but quickly caught himself as he glowered at his charge, the glow of his eyes lighting the wall beside him.

She fell back onto the ground with a gasp and scowled up at him. "What are we doing here?"

He looked around the edge of the building and his eyes widened as he frowned and ignored her question.

An elf struggled to get free from the top of the wood pile, her ears peeking out from her messed, brown hair and her pleas ringing in his ears. She struggled and sobbed, watching in horror as the flames licked dangerously close to her skirt and bare feet.

So, they sought to murder an innocent immortal, did they?

He strode forward, fists clenched before Ana stepped in front of him, tucking her own wings into the folds of the cape she wore. She raised her hands up and gaped at him in astonishment as though she didn't recognize him.

"Are you crazy? If they see your wings, we will have broken the laws not only for the immortal realm, but for the Afterlife realm! Do you have any idea what the angels will do to you, what *Michael* will do to you, if they find out we've even crossed the barrier?"

"I don't care," he said as he brushed passed her. Red-hot anger coursed through him and he felt the beast within him rising along with the desire to tear the people surrounding the beautiful woman apart, piece by piece. Every sob, ever cry, every ter-rified sound that came from her lips made his temper rise higher into dangerous levels. He didn't just want to save her, he *needed* to.

He stepped forward and shoved through the crowd as he pulled his hood over his head to hide his face. Midway through the crowd, one man grunted and protested at being shuffled but one murderous look from Jasper had him stepping quickly out of the way in fright.

After a few people were pushed to the side, the crowd began to part before him, his height and heavily muscled build giving them no other choice. He reached the front and, with a deep breath that drew him backward, he blew air from his lips.

Wind whipped around the fire, putting it down to a slow burn, and blew the torches of the people around him out. Hats and scarves blew through the breeze, pushing over the people closest to the flames. The village people gasped and screamed in fear, some running for their homes for fear that he would get them next.

The woman, having scrunched against the wind, lifted her head to see what had stilled the fire and her widened golden eyes met his. Her chest rose and fell in panicked breaths and tears glistened on her cheeks. Her brunette hair was a mess around her, hanging in waves even as they curled against her face. A dress that must have been blue at one point was darkened with soot and burn marks, the edges ripped and black.

Despite the marks of the flames, she was the most beautiful woman he had ever seen. A picture of pure innocence before his very eyes.

Jasper felt something dark close in behind him and peeked over his shoulder, careful not to loosen his hood any as he muttered, "Demons."

Ana gave a nod from behind the panicking, fleeing crowd, her expression grim as she hid herself from the living in the ghostly realm, her sword drawn. It was a skill she had picked up from her step-sister, Fate, after her passing, and it only added to her own lethal set of skills.

No demon would be escaping this night.

Turning his attention back to the woman at the stake, he began to climb through the embers toward her, his boots crunching on the wood that had already turned to ash.

As he advanced, she struggled harder and her breath heaved harder in panic as she sobbed and tried to get away from him. His heart broke in his chest at what this poor woman had endured, but he stood strong as he finally stood in front of her.

She bowed her head and fell to her knees, her burnt dress blending with the wood below her. "Please," she whispered as she cried in fright, her entire being shaking. "Please don't hurt me. Don't take me to Lucifer, I beg you!"

His back stiffened and he narrowed his eyes even as he knelt in front of her. He rested his elbow on his knee and gently placed his hand on her cheek hesitantly, turning her up chin up to face him.

Her tearful eyes met his and for a moment, it felt as though time stood still.

Her cheekbones were high and red from her tears, her button nose red and sniffling, and her red lips were dried and pouted from distress. Her feet were bare, bruised, and covered in small cuts as though she had been dragged from her home and reddened burns had begun to form on her skin.

He leaned closer and she calmed a little, watching his every move as though just as fascinated with him as he was with her.

Finally, he murmured to her, "I would never hurt you, little one. You are safe with me."

He reached behind her with his free arm and ripped the ropes from her hands, careful not to further injure her braised skin.

Emeline rubbed her wrists, the bruises and cuts from her struggles now visible.

She hesitantly looked up at him, but all she could see were shadows. Still, the moonlight lit yellowed eyes much like hers, full of a strength and kindness that captured her and held her in its grasp, unwilling to let her go.

He helped her back to her feet, but she stumbled, her legs weak and his strong arm wrapped around her to steady her. Suddenly, she was chest to chest with the large man, staring into the eyes of her hero once again.

"Who are you," she asked breathlessly.

"Someone who broke too many laws because he heard your cries," he said softly.

Something crunched behind them and the man shut his eyes as though something pained him horribly.

"This is just so cute," a beautiful woman behind him interrupted sarcastically, "but it's time to go."

Jasper gave a nod and began to urge her down the pile toward safety.

Jerked from the same moment that had captured him only moments before, she gave a start and tried to push away from him. "We can't! If they know where I am, then they know where my father is! They could already have him!"

"There isn't time before more demons arrive," he explained grimly.

She twisted and fought against his strength weakly, but she was no match for him and they both knew it.

When he refused to let go, her eyes beseeched him as they watered and she curled her hands against his chest, pleading, "Please, you have to let me save him!"

One look into her eyes and Jasper gave a groan as they moved off the wood.

No man in existence could have said no to a look like that.

Chapter 3

The villagers had cleared out with only the demon's ashes from Ana's blade left behind. Silence reigned through the night and the only combat to the darkness of the night were the retreating flames from the stake.

Ana took one look at Jasper and shook her head vehemently, "No." At his stubborn gaze, she said more forcefully, "*No*, Jasper. It isn't happening."

Jasper shifted his attention back to the girl and Ana waved her hands as she shouted stubbornly as though he couldn't hear her, "No way!"

He glowered at her, his eyes glowing against the night as he held the girl comfortingly against his chest, holding her from collapsing. No doubt the emotional toll of the night was taking her energy, evident by the way her knees continued to buckle.

Ana put her hands on her hips. "How long do you think it will take for more demons to hear of their brethren's deaths? Dra-" She paused and scowled at the woman sobbing incoherently in his arms, fisting her hands at her sides as she ground out, "*We* are highly coveted by Lucifer. Word of these deaths will reach him and then we'll be hunted! Especially the-"

"Enough Ana," Jasper bellowed. "We will go after the girl's father."

The woman in his arms stiffened. "I'll go after him. I know where he is going, I can get him and we'll hide elsewhere. I promise, we can take care of ourselves."

"I'm afraid it is too late for that," Jasper said sadly. "They know your scent, they will follow you wherever you go. No matter which realm you hide in, demons have been sent for you and they won't stop until they have you."

She looked out into the darkness as she thought it over, shock on her face. The elf had been through so much this night. There was no way Jasper was going to let her go off to fight who knew how many demons to rescue her father.

She wouldn't survive it.

Ana slapped a hand over her eyes and scrubbed it down her face in defeat. "We're going after the elven man, aren't we?"

Jasper gently released the elf, testing her steadiness. "Can you stand, elf?"

"My name is Emeline," she said softly, testing her footing. "Yes, I think so."

He took a moment to breathe in her name before he spoke, the sound of it caressing his senses like a drug.

He forced his mind back to the situation at hand. "Are you sure you are up for this?"

She nodded. "I think so."

"I can't believe this," Ana said on a groan and threw her hands up as though she were the last sane woman left. "We will be seen. The angelic council will have a fit and we'll be sent to Hell for eternity. All these months, trying to be miss goodie two shoes, will be for nothing!"

Jasper scowled. "Let them try."

Emeline shook her head as though she had been struck. "Angelic council?"

He glowered at Ana, who suddenly seemed to be fascinated by the tree line. "No more talk. We get the man, we leave. End of story."

Emeline looked between the two before she said finally, "We need to go! My father could already be taken and we're wasting time talking about it. Are you coming with me?"

Jasper turned to face her, certain his features were still darkened by the night and his hood.

"Lead the way."

Emeline offered him a soft smile before she took off down a path away from the village.

Ana crossed her arms over her chest as she stomped after Jasper, grumbling. "This is so stupid. We never should have been over here to begin with, and now we're running around the *mortal realm* saving people. The girl was stupid enough to come over to this boring realm. She should have died for her crimes and you know it."

Jasper stopped and turned on his heel so abruptly that Ana bumped into his chest with a gasp of surprise. He stood tall and proud, his fists clenched at his sides in obvious anger. The muscles on his arms twitched and hardened, ready for a fight.

"She is not destined to die, Ana. We protect the innocent; that is our primary reason for being in this life. Now, enough of this childish tantrum before I find a way to tie *you* to that stake."

She smiled, sarcasm dripping from every word. "Like I've never burned before. Maybe you forgot my time in hell."

He turned away and strode after the girl, determined to catch her before she disappeared into the night. He could practically feel Ana as she rolled her eyes and reluctantly followed with mutters and curses under her breath.

Emeline stumbled a couple hours later on the path to the next village. She was wearing down, exhausted from the nights events and she knew it, but she had to save Navi. There was no telling what those demons had done to him.

Maybe they haven't found him yet, she thought hopefully.

Her mind drifted on the two beings behind her. The girl, Ana as Jasper had called her, was still muttering, but she managed to gracefully stay up to speed with him as though the hike was nothing to her.

With that thought, she was shifted to another. His hauntingly beautiful golden eyes. Much like hers, but his were darker, with flecks of brown in them, as though a fire burned there inside of him, waiting to be unleased.

Something about him fascinated her. The warmth of his arms around her, the comforting sound of his deep, melodious voice as he had assured her that she was safe. The way he had saved her and damned the consequences that could have followed. Had his charge not defeated the demons so viciously, he would surely have torn them apart.

At the top of a hill, she stopped with her eyes wide as she looked down on the town that sat close to her own. Her father stood bound on a platform, a noose around his neck as a burly, tall man read his crimes. As though sensing her stare, the man turned and for a split second, his eyes turned black beneath the torch, his incisors lengthening into fangs. As quickly as it showed, it vanished and the demon stumbled backward, fear on its face.

Emeline's brow furrowed at the man's reaction.

Why would a demon fear her?

Warmth by her right side made her shifted her attention over her shoulder at the dark figure of Jasper. He glared down at the demon for a minute before he said to her, "You will stay here."

"What," Emeline exclaimed. "I will not! My father is down there and I will not allow him to be put in the center of whatever fight you are about to start!"

"Ana, ensure she does not follow me," he continued as though she hadn't spoken, his glare deepening on the demon. The man was now stumbling through the list of "crimes," his hand trembling.

Ana smiled a wicked smile and Emeline swore she saw the girl's eyes glow red.

"And if she refuses?"

He turned a steely look at the young dragon and Ana put her hands up in surrender with a roll of her eyes.

"Oh, alright. Go have your fun and I promise, we'll both be here when you return."

With a shake of his shoulders, he threw his head back and a terrifying roar rang through the air as every muscle in his body tensed.

Emeline jumped and hurriedly scrambled away, eyes wide.

"What…?"

Before she could protest again, he took off at a run, there one minute, gone the next.

She watched worriedly as he chased the townspeople away, then drew a sword with tribal markings on it. The black etchings glowed red as he swung and two people turned to ash, their human forms giving away to their decimated demonic ones.

Ana snorted at Emeline's shocked expression. "Never seen a demon destroyed, have you?"

Emeline turned an annoyed look at her, temporarily pulled from Jasper's incredible fighting skills. "Demons rampaged my village and murdered my mother. Most of us fled, but many fell. We do not fight them, we fear them! So they had no reason to attack us!"

"Except to steal your worthless souls."

Emeline heard her father grunt and quickly turned back. Jasper had cut him loose as the townspeople hurried to get away from the fight and he dropped to his knees, weak but alive.

"Father," she whispered in relief and fear.

Jasper urged him to his feet and off the podium, then toward the hill just outside of town as people ran by him, screaming in terror.

As they drew closer, she could see the bruises on Navi's skin and the abrasions on his neck, but her gratefulness outweighed her worry.

He was alive!

Just as relief settled into her heart, terror replaced it as a shadow moved in a bush just off to Jasper's right. It was almost invisible in the darkness, but it had moved against the full moon behind them, its eyes glowing blood red. Claws ran from its fingers and when his mouth opened, the moon made his fangs appear to glow in the dark.

And it was obvious who his target was.

"Jasper," she cried.

But it was too late.

The demon jumped, it's black and red eyes glowing as it growled, and sank its teeth into Jasper's shoulder, the sound sickening.

She gave a cry of alarm as Jasper fell, taking Navi with him, and grunted, baring his teeth in pain as air hissed through them.

Jasper turned to fight at the demon as it began to claw at him and lifted his weight from Navi so he could escape. He slammed the monster into the ground, causing it to cry out and open its mouth wide enough for Jasper to pull his shoulder free of its grasp.

Navi scrambled to his feet, looking back in horror at the ensuing fight as he joined his daughter's side, his arms around her.

The demon and Jasper circled one another, the snake-like demon hissing enough for his tongue to peek out. It wasn't long before the beast charged at Jasper, slamming him into the ground hard enough to crack bone.

Jasper pushed at the demon but its sharp teeth snapped at him like a snake hungry for its meal. His hands circled around its neck even as its small arms and legs clawed at him, drawing blood from his sides.

"Go," he shouted.

Ana charged forward but Jasper threw the demon away from him and put his hand out, his hood still over his head as he turned onto his stomach, his wounds covering the ground with blood.

"No, get them out of here!"

Ana stopped and hesitated for only a moment before she reached down and took Navi's arm, pushing at him the second he was on his feet, and urged Emeline to move forward.

"Move it, now!"

"We can't just leave him," Emeline said hurriedly, digging in her heels as she looked helplessly over her shoulder.

Ana grabbed her arm and pulled the elf into her face. Her eyes glowed red and her fingernails dug into Emeline's arm. "The sooner I get you to safety, the sooner I can get back to save him," she snapped. Twisting Emeline around, she just about dragged the elf down the path. "Now go!"

Navi tugged her free of Ana's grasp, scowling at her, before he turned softened eyes toward Emeline. He put his hand where Ana had clawed at her and stroked soothingly, but nothing could ease her nerves.

"Trust her, Emeline," he urged. "She will save him."

She hesitated only a moment more before she turned and ran after Navi with Ana behind her but stopped a few steps out before she was turning back.

Jasper had saved not only her life, but the life of her father. How could she just abandon him?

Would she ever see him again if she fled?

Ana disappeared over the side of the hill, her focus on her mission, and Emeline took the opportunity to run full speed back over the hill toward the grunts and groans, her heart racing.

Jasper was laying on the ground, motionless, while the demon ripped at the flesh on his back with its claws and…scaled wings?

Was he a demon?

Chapter 4

For a moment, she was frozen in surprise, but denial hit her hard and she shook her head. There was no way he was a demon. No demon would save an elf, not at the wrath of Lucifer and his horrible tricks.

Against the odds, she knew in her heart that she could trust him.

Navi shouted in fright behind her, but she kept going until she rammed into the demon, her slight body knocking him a few feet away. The demon shrieked as it fell, unmoving, to the ground and rolled a few feet away.

Jasper gave a grunt, trying to push to his feet but his wings were badly torn and his shaking arms fell from beneath him, causing his body to crash hard into the ground.

Tears of pain filled her eyes and she dropped to her knees beside him, willing her panic to wane, even just a little. She held her trembling hands over his wounds, causing blood to soak into her skin, and reached for her magic, mumbling without realizing it, "Please work. Please help him, please, please, please!"

He went still, his chest barely rising and falling with his breaths, and it felt as though her heart had stilled in her chest.

He couldn't die! He just couldn't!

Gold glowed from her hand and within minutes, muscle, skin, and bone weaved back together until it looked as though he hadn't been touched by the demon. The scales on his wings came back together and strengthened, the cracks glowing before ceasing to exist.

He lay deathly still and when she reached for him, her hand trembling, he shushed her quietly, signaling to her that he was alright but not to move.

She stilled, feeling something hot on her neck and her breathing picked up, especially when a hiss echoed in her ear, making her jump. Everything in her told her to scream but panic paralyzed her, causing tears to spike her lashes.

The demon was leaning over her in outrage, his breathing heavy, as he slid closer, his intention clear.

He was going to kill them both.

Jasper kept his breathing even and whispered softly, "Do not move."

She felt dread move down her spine and from the corner of her eyes, she saw fangs dripping just next to her shoulder as it leaned in, ready to bite her.

Just as she felt her breath catch in her throat, Jasper shot to his feet and dove at it, taking it by surprise. He slammed it into the ground and started to beat it with his fists, his outrage taking over as he ripped at it.

She turned to watch in horror as Jasper tore at the demon's skin, claws elongating from his fingers to rip at the hard flesh. It screamed terribly as it writhed on the ground, then sank its long, black nails into Jasper's arm, trying to stop him. He didn't seem to notice as he finally snapped its neck, his chest heaving.

Once the demon turned to ashes on the ground, all fell silent. A soft, warm breeze brushed the tall grass around them, giving a false image of a calm, peaceful summer night, but the scent of blood and death lingered, ruining the image.

He sank to his knees, his hood falling back as he bowed his head and sat back on his haunches, clearly spent from the night's fights. She hurried toward him but stopped just behind him with her hand over her mouth, almost afraid to touch him for fear that he let loose his temper on her.

The way he had torn at that demon…like a man gone mad…

She shook her head. This was the same man who had saved her and defeated many demons who would have otherwise been let loose on the innocents of this realm. Tentatively, she reached a handout and touched his shoulder as she murmured, "Jasper?"

He didn't move except to raise his head slightly to look at the ashes.

She stepped closer as she whispered his name again, then finally circled him, ready to see the face of her savior. When she reached the front of him, she gasped in surprise, stepping backward with her hands over her mouth.

His eyes slowly lifted to meet hers, resigned in something she couldn't begin to guess.

Scars ran over him, glowing in the moonlight as though to highlight everything he must have endured to gain them. One ran through his eyebrow to his cheek while another small scar ran across the center of his crooked nose, as though it hadn't ever healed right. A cross scar marred his jawline, and a long scar ran on the other side of his face from brow to jaw. A single, thin scar ran vertically through his bottom lip and another trailed diagonally down his throat as though he had been cut and healed. Smaller scars ran down his chest and red scars wrapped around his arms as though from struggling to get free from a rope on fire.

Her lips parted as she focused on the one on his lip, her hands slowly falling away from her mouth. For reasons she couldn't understand, she wanted to know what it would be to kiss him, to feel that scar against her lip, her tongue. Something akin to desire ran through her, freezing her in place with her eyes wide in surprise.

He frowned and quickly pulled his hood up over his head.

Realizing he felt ashamed, she stepped forward almost involuntarily. "I'm sorry, I-"

He stood, fists clenched as he kept his face turned down, hiding beneath the hood, and tension thickened the air. "We need to leave before more demons come for you."

She swallowed hard and gave a nod, her heart aching for him. Though he was scarred, he had been breathtakingly handsome. Whatever had happened to him, he had never deserved any of it, but that he continued to fight made him all the more of a hero in her eyes.

She watched him stride away and barely registered her father as he ran to her, enveloping her in his arms. He murmured to her, but she couldn't hear him over the sound of her rapidly beating heart.

Oh, how it broke for Jasper!

She absently grabbed his arm around her shoulders and watched as Ana caught up to Jasper, muttering to him about something. Leaning back against her father, she frowned and watched as they began to disappear over the hill.

Navi circled his daughter and his brow was furrowed. "What is it, my dear?"

She finally met his gaze and shook her head slowly. There was no need to tell her father of her foolish fascination with the being who had rescued them.

"Nothing. Are you alright," she asked suddenly as she was brought out of the trance she seemed to be in. She looked over Navi with a skeptical eye, checking his burns and scrapes to ensure none of them had begun to become infected.

He gave a nod. "Ana says his name is Jasper Rogue."

"They want us to go with them," she said softly. "But how do we know we can trust them?"

Even as she said it, she felt ridiculous. There was no one aside from her father she felt she could trust more than Jasper.

Navi shifted from one foot to the other as he stood away from her, uncomfortable. "Do you remember the stories I used to tell you about the dragon shifters?"

"From the Afterlife legends?"

"Those very ones," he said with a chuckle.

She nodded absently. "I think so. Protectors of the innocents, stuck between Afterlife and Hell to do penance for their misdeeds in life?"

He looked over at Ana and Jasper, who had stopped to wait impatiently, then put his hands on Emeline's shoulders as though to brace her. "They are dragon shifters, Emeline. They will keep us safe, no harm will come to us now. But if we stay here, the demons will return and I dare not think of how many deaths would occur because of our ignorance."

She bit her lip and her heart hurt when Jasper's gaze met hers. Something akin to despair and sadness lingered there and she felt as though she had been stabbed in the chest when she remembered her horrible reaction to seeing his face.

But the scars there had frightened her at first. Not because of how captivating they were, but because of all the things she imagined he had been through to get them. What had he done to deserve such treatment?

"Emeline, please," Navi urged, mistaking her silence. "If we don't leave now, we will never be able to find them again."

She mentally shook herself, then gave a nod.

Navi approached Jasper with Emeline behind him and said firmly, "Take us where you may. You have our complete trust and faith in your noble hands."

Jasper eyed him suspiciously.

Ana seemed to understand the look, as she said in exasperation, "You know what we are."

"I do," Navi replied calmly.

Ana narrowed her eyes, suspicion in their depths. "How?"

"I will explain once we are in a safer place."

Jasper gave a curt shake of his head and looked skyward. "Then we will fly. The only way into our lands is through the fog and it is through the fog to Dragon City that you will be protected."

He pulled Navi to his side as though to keep Emeline from taking up the position and confusion hit her as she felt an odd sense of loss.

Ana rolled her eyes and offered her hand. "Don't let go."

Emeline took her hand and Ana thrust the elf onto her back before she opened her wings and looked unsteadily at Jasper. "Are you sure?"

He just stared at her.

Ana gave another roll of her eyes and shot off the ground unsteadily. Emeline wrapped her arms around Ana's neck and gasped as the wind rushed by her, their ascent much faster than she anticipated.

Ana gave a grunt, wobbling and struggling to get in the air. "I'm new at flying," she shouted to Emeline. "I don't know if I can handle your weight."

Emeline looked down to see the town growing smaller and swallowed hard. "You might have mentioned that beforehand."

"I did," Ana said with a wicked smile. "He ignored me. Which means he is chickening out again."

Before Emeline could ask what she meant, Ana spun and Emeline lost her grip.

She began to fall and she felt like she couldn't breathe as she struggled to find something, anything to hold onto. When nothing came in contact, she let out a scream that echoed through the skies. Wind whipped up through her hair and stole her breath as she watched the ground rushing up to keep her.

Jasper felt as though his heart stilled when Emeline began to fall toward him and cursed Ana under his breath for calling him out.

"Hang on, elf," he called to Navi.

Her father stiffened and gaped at his daughter as she fell. "Emeline!"

Jasper straightened until his feet were below him and held out his arms. With a hard slam, Emeline fell into his arms with a gasp. He stumbled under the weight but adjusted her into the cradle of his arms and waited for her scream of terror when she realized who caught her.

It never came.

Much to his surprise, she leaned her cheek against his chest and wrapped her arms around his neck, trembling. She tried to catch her breath, and he closed his eyes as her rosy scent wafted into his nose, only just slightly stifled by the smell of burn cloth. For just a moment, he allowed himself the luxury of feeling her in his arms, of being the one to save her.

"If it is all the same to you," Navi said with a nervous chuckle as he wiggled his feet, "I am just kind of hanging on back here and I would very much like to feel my feet on the ground. I'm sure my daughter would as well."

Jasper frowned and his wings propelled them forward.

Emeline finally caught her breath and muttered, "I think I hate that damnable dragon!"

He chuckled as he watched Ana fly in front of him without stumbling once. "She is getting used to flying, but her personality certainly leaves something to be desired."

He blinked at the sound and feel of the rumbled laugh in his throat. It had been decades since he had found something to laugh about. For too long, he was certain he would never know what it felt to laugh again, yet this remarkable woman had done it with a simple retort.

Before too long, the fog loomed above them and Jasper flew in front of Ana, intent on setting down the elves. Once they passed through into the night skies of the immortal realm, Jasper landed on a cloud and Navi dropped off with a grunt, shaking his arms free to regain feeling in them.

Ana stumbled unsteadily onto the cloud with her arms outstretched in front of her as though bracing for the fall.

Gently, Jasper set Emeline down, his hands sliding down the back of her thighs as she slowly gained her footing. When he was sure her feet had touched the cloud, he stepped away as he lifted his hood and turned away so as not to frighten her again.

Emeline crossed one arm over her middle as she watched Jasper's fists clench at his sides, his entire being tense. It was as though he thought she had condemned him or was too soft to look upon him again.

How many people had judged him wrongly for his appearance?

Navi twisted his torso from one side to the other to stretch himself out, then caught Emeline's stare at the dragon several feet away. "Emeline?"

She turned to face him with tears in her eyes. "I'm so sorry father. I didn't mean to disrespect him," she whispered sadly.

Navi shook his head, his voice low. "I will explain when we are a safer distance away."

A soft rustle above them made Emeline's gaze shoot upward. A large shadow soared behind a lightning cloud, its figure at least ten or twelve feet long and four feet wide. From the outline, its wingspan was almost fifteen feet from one end to the other.

She strained to watch it until she stumbled backward and onto her bottom. With a deafening thud, the huge dragon with icy blue eyes landed behind her father, giving him a start as well. Her eyes widened and she scrambled backward as her father hurried away from the beast, his own eyes round.

The dragon advanced, its eyes intent on her as it closed in.

She put her arms up with a whimper seconds before Jasper's deep voice rang out into the night.

"Enough."

A simple enough word, one that shouldn't have possibly stopped the large monster in front of her. Yet stop him it did, and before her eyes, the dragon shifted and contorted into a man who straightened the tie for his suit, his wings folded behind him.

Despite his hood hiding his features, Emeline thought she saw Jasper scowl as he strode in front of her. "Wynter, you need not enter that way."

"Oh, come on," Wynter said with a huff. "We disguise ourselves as dragons to the living for a reason." He leaned forward, leering with challenge. "Or maybe you have forgotten the rules set forth by Luke Rogue and Archangel Michael himself."

Jasper lifted his chin, his eyes lighting a brilliant yellow with outrage and she could have sworn she saw smoke wafting from his nose. For a long while, the two dragon shifters glared at one another, both tensed and waiting.

Ana put her hand on her hip and gave an exaggerated sigh. "This is fun and I know you both want a piece of this, but I think it's time we go. The demons won't be able to track them as easily here, but they will certainly find them just outside the fog leading to the world they have clearly infiltrated."

Jasper gave a frustrated huff. "Take the eldest elf and follow behind me. They will stay at the palace with," he hesitated, then lifted his chin proudly again, "With his highness, the king."

At the reminder, Wynter seemed to relent and moved over to Navi. "I am Wynter, the only ice dragon in existence. I pledge to you that your safety will be my top priority on your ride atop my back to the Realm of Dragons."

Navi gave a polite bow. "Navi Lilian of the Elven Isles." He held his hand out to Emeline and tugged her to his side. "This is my daughter, Emeline. We accept your pledge and in exchange, hereby swear not to share the location nor the knowledge of existence for the Realm of Dragons."

Wynter blinked his gaze to Jasper with a mixture of anger, confusion, and suspicion. Jasper bent his head lower and folded his hands in front of him but his eyes still glowed.

As though understanding what Jasper was thinking, Wynter gave a nod and opened his wings through his suit, the holes for their origins on his shoulders giving him the freedom to do so. Emeline watched Navi as he kissed her forehead and climbed on top of Wynter's back for the flight.

Jasper didn't say anything as he watched her intensely as though waiting for her to say something.

Toying with the new burn holes in her once favorite dress, she tilted her face up and said softly, "I feel it would be best if I were carried by you, Jasper. Please," she added politely, flickering her gaze toward Ana nervously.

He didn't move for so long that she was afraid he wouldn't accept her request. Guilt dug at her until she was twisting her hand into her skirt and shifting from one foot to the other uncomfortably.

Finally, he gave a nod. "Very well."

Ana threw her hands in the air with a scoff of annoyance. "Am I the only one thinking clearly? Let's move it!"

"You will fly beside Wynter and watch him to learn how to properly hold someone," he snapped at her without turning in her direction.

She scowled at him but did as he bade.

Once both dragons were gone, Jasper held his hand out to Emeline. "We will be quick. The palace is not far from here."

She bunched her hands into her skirts and opened her mouth to speak but no words would emerge. Finally, she managed to say softly, "I'm

sorry for my actions. I did not mean to upset or of-
fend you.”

“You didn’t,” he lied. “Many react as you
have. I am used to it.” Before she could say another
word, he stepped forward, his expression unreadable.
“Ana is right about one thing. The demons will not
be far behind us, we must leave now.”

Emeline gave a shaky nod and stepped close
enough to reach his wings as he turned away but hesitated.

He looked over his shoulder, his face invisible in the darkness of his hood as he asked, “What is
it?”

“I-I don’t feel comfortable on your back.”

Jasper took in a breath, then slowly, almost
hesitantly, turned to face her. Even in the dark, she
could see his displeasure at having to allow her to
look at him “You cannot move while in my arms or
I could lose my hold on you.”

She moved closer so he could pick her up and
he soared upward. The cold wind blew into her face,
making her shiver in her sleeveless dress and wrap
her arms around herself.

Without warning, his body heat increased,
warming her as though they were wrapped in a bubble in the air. She looked up at him as she nestled into
his arms and found his intense gaze was on her as
well.

Time seemed to stand still, the night around them fading into the background. Demons could have surrounded them right then and neither would have noticed.

Abruptly, he tore his attention away from her with a scowl and back to the sky ahead, leaving her to study what she could of him.

The scar across his throat was white against his golden skin, his chest bare beneath the hooded cape as she leaned against him. Every now and then, her exposed cleavage would touch his chest and send goosebumps over her skin. Her heartbeat faster in her chest as she breathed in his scent, a fiery, refined smell that made her want to wrap herself into him and never come out.

It was an odd sensation, one she had never had before and one she was becoming interested in exploring with every passing moment she spent in his company.

Chapter 5

Jasper tried not to notice her scrutinizing him as he flew, but it was as though her eyes were burning holes in him. Her gaze roved over each of his scars, her pupils dilating when she saw the one on his lip, and her tongue peeked out, flickering over her bottom lip as though doing so would make her feel it on her own lip.

Her observance of him was unnerving.

Yet for a reason he could not decipher, it did not feel as though she were judging him. It felt as though she were simply observing him, taking in what of him she could see. It didn't feel as it did when others stared at him with condemnation. Instead, this felt as though every mark that marred his body fascinated her.

He knew she had meant it when she had apologized, but that didn't change how hurt he felt when she had looked at him with fright.

But why?

For years, women and children had shied away from him, avoided him whenever possible and if the children didn't shy, they screamed. Men shielded their family's eyes from view and all Jasper had wanted to do was dig a hole to live in. After everything he had done to defend the city he loved most, his people condemned him because of the scars he bore to show for it. No woman wanted him, no man aside from Luke and Wynter would befriend him, and no child could look at him without terror in their eyes.

When Luke and his love, Fate, had handed Jasper the crown from their new-and hidden-home in Afterlife, he had initially rejected the very idea. But tradition dictated that the former king would be the one to choose his predecessor and with their little one on the way, Jasper couldn't say no.

So he had retired the staff and relocated the community members who had lived in the castle. Their homes were built in town, just as lavish and formal as the palace in the form of luxurious houses. He couldn't bear to have one more dragon gasp and jump out of his way when he moved down the hallway, even for something as simple as a drink of water. With everyone gone, it was never a problem.

Which just left him and Ana, who had refused to leave. Despite her insistence to stay, and as irritating as she was, Ana never criticized him for his scars, nor shied away from him. At the palace, neither of them bothered one another.

The way he preferred things, he told himself. No one around to judge him, no one to fear him or stare.

Just quiet and peace.

And the loneliness that seems to lurk constantly in the darkness of my heart, he added solemnly.

Emeline's cheek on his chest jerked him from his thoughts and he looked down to find her fast asleep in his arms. She had curled tighter to his chest and somehow, her hand had moved up to his on her arm, her smaller fingers between his on her shoulder. Her lashes cast hauntingly beautiful shadows against her cheeks, and her lips were parted, causing warm tendrils of her breath to brush against his skin.

The sight was unusual for him, yet something warmed inside of him and his arms tightened around her, his determination to protect her growing.

Maybe she wasn't as frightened of him as he had thought.

He frowned and shook his head as they approached his palace.

Nothing had changed. Once Lucifer and his band of demons were dealt with, Emeline and her father would return home, and his life could return to normal.

So why did the idea of being without her bother him so much?

Emeline rubbed at her eyes as she woke and snuggled deeper into her blankets, the satin and fleece brushing against her legs. Warmth met her and she gave a soft groan as she turned over, tugging the blankets over her head. Her side met with something solid and she smiled even as she kept her eyes shut.

"I know you're awake, bugger."

She chuckled behind her hand, her smile wide and airy. "Oh, father."

Navi laughed and whipped the blanket away from her grasp, teasing her. "I know it's early, but the dragons are awake and they wish to discuss some things with us."

She shot straight up as though pulled by an invisible force and looked around, disoriented, at the massive, formal bedroom. The bed was a four poster king-sized bed with warmed, midnight blue blankets atop it. To the side of the bed, there was a bay window seat with bookshelves on either side. The wispy blue curtains blew in the soft, warm breeze and brought with it the smell of saltwater. Across from the bed was a large dresser and a walk-in closet off to the right side of it. A bathroom sat opened invitingly next to the bathroom and a door large enough to fit a giant was to the left of the dresser, closed for privacy. Two tall, wooden nightstands sat to either side of the bed with lamps on each.

She gaped in amazement as her hands flew to her hands. "Oh my goodness! This is beautiful!"

Navi chuckled and patted her knee quickly. "You were so tired from the night's events, you fell right to sleep. I dressed you in a night gown Jasper found for you, but I feel you will want a shower and a more beautiful gown."

She blinked, lowering her hands. "Where is Jasper?"

He chuckled again and leaned his arm over to the other side of her. "Get dressed, pumpkin. We will need to discuss our next move with the dragons before they lose whatever patience they have left."

She gave a nod and watched as he left, before she slid from bed and sorted through the dresser and closet.

A pair of soft, gray pants and a white tank top caught her attention and her brow furrowed, but she made her way with them to the shower.

She didn't want to smell like smoke and fear when she saw Jasper again, and while it wasn't exactly her style, it *did* look comfortable.

The silence was deafening as Jasper sat, alone, eating in the dining room and he sank his teeth into his steak and eggs. The quiet was oppressive, making the air around him feel tense and uncomfortable, but the thought of a full table made him frown.

He knew where the attention would be.

Ana had yet to wake, and, likely, wouldn't for some time, which gave him plenty of time to eat and run. He planned to visit with Luke, Fate, and their newborn child, though the latter he wanted to see from a distance, not up close.

Truly.

The door opened and he nearly slumped his shoulders in annoyance but paused when Navi poked his head through and he hastily tugged his hood over his head.

"Am I catching you at a bad time?"

Jasper finished chewing his bite as he gestured to the chair at his left with his fork.

Navi took a seat after he shut the door behind him and straightened as he waited for Jasper to speak. When the dragon remained quiet, he took a breath and broke the silence as he said, "Thank you for rescuing us."

Jasper took another slow bite as though to keep himself from talking and turned away slightly, making it difficult for the elder man to see him.

Navi huffed out a breath. "I know who you are. My wife knew you as well, though I doubt you would have noticed her."

Jasper lifted his head slightly but remained quiet.

Navi leaned closer, his hands on the table in fists. "I know about the dragon wars, too. You needn't hide yourself from me. I admire you for your bravery, courage, and strength. I cannot imagine what you went through down there."

Jasper slammed his fist onto the table, his arms shaking.

"No, you can't," he ground out. "What is your point?"

Navi paused, staring at the new dent in the table under the fist of the mighty dragon as though fascinated. It reminded Jasper of Emeline and her gaze on him the night before but he pushed it to the back of his mind.

It would do neither of them any good to think of her like that.

"I do not wish to impose on your kindness and I certainly did not mean to upset you. I just wanted you to know that not everyone is as condemning as your people are."

"Why are you so knowledgeable about me and my people," he asked sharply.

Navi licked his lips and shifted uncomfortably in his seat. "Let's just say I have a personal investment in the dragon world. I never believed the legends were false, but long ago I was shown the confirmation I needed to believe in it fully. I studied your customs and made your rules, your standards, my own."

Jasper straightened slowly, his head still down as he contemplated what the man said. "I was scarred horribly enough to frighten anyone who looked upon me. If they didn't fear my appearance, they feared my wrath, which was just as bad."

"Is that why there is no one else in this palace?"

Jasper stood abruptly, dropping his fork loudly onto the plate before gathering it into his hands. "That is enough. The kitchen and its items are yours if you wish it. I must leave now, but I will return soon. Ana will protect you."

He strode to the doors but before he could open them, Navi said pointedly, "You should learn to trust in people again. They just might surprise you."

Jasper tightened his grip on the handle of the door, the plate cracking as he tightened his grip dangerously.

Navi continued, "Not all of us judge a book by its cover. Some of us just need a little time to get to know the man underneath the scars." He leaned forward in his chair, turning it so it fully faced Jasper's back. "And some of us have enough scars of our own that we won't judge yours."

Jasper thought on his words for a minute before he pushed the doors opened and made his way to the kitchen, his cracked plate in his hand.

Chapter 6

Fate Rogue bounced infant in her arms as she walked from one end of the house to the other, rocking her while she bounced gently. She smiled and cooed softly as she held the small pacifier in the baby girl's mouth, curling her fingers into the soft, pink blanket.

Luke had left for the market to pick up groceries just a few minutes earlier, and the second he had left, their daughter Anabelle started crying for him. Once Fate had lifted the baby up and began her bounces, she had calmed. Her eyes started to blink slower and stay closed for longer periods at a time until finally, she began to drift off to sleep.

A soft knock at the door made Fate start but she slowly approached the door. When she saw who was on the other side, she smiled and pulled the door open as she whispered, "Jasper! How are you, my friend?"

Jasper hurried by her and shoved his hood back. "Luke has made a mistake," he said at last as he faced away from her, fists clenched. His teeth ground together and he shut his eyes, willing away the headache that had begun.

Fate's brow furrowed. "What do you mean?"

He shook his head. "Where is he?"

She shushed him, scolding him with her expression, and gently placed Anabelle in her bassinet in the living room, then gestured with her chin to the kitchen. Jasper followed her and once they were clear, he crossed his arms over his chest. "Where is Luke?"

"He went to the market," she said, brow furrowed. "Why?"

"He needs to appoint the crown to someone else."

Fate's brow relaxed and she tilted her head at him as though he were being silly.

"Jasper-"

"No one can even look at me. No one will give me a second glance and if they do, it is only with terror in their eyes. I have even emptied the palace of citizens so that I may walk freely without judgment."

She watched him run his fingers through his too short hair and stare in agitation at her toaster on the counter. After a few moments, she said softly, "Something else is wrong. People have been wrongfully judging you for decades, so why all this hostility now?"

He gave a "humph" and leaned against the counter but refused to meet her gaze.

She raised an eyebrow and leaned on one foot with her hip against the counter, her arms crossed like his over her chest. "I'm not going to give up, so you might as well save yourself time and energy now."

He finally looked into her eyes and heaved a heavy sigh. "It is no concern of yours, Fate. You have enough to deal with here."

She jumped when Anabelle gave a small cry and waited, but no other sound emerged. Her attention moved to him again and she tucked her hands into the back pockets of her jeans. "It's a girl, isn't it?"

He rolled his eyes and straightened, pushing off the edge of the counter. "Tell Luke I stopped by."

"Jasper," she said with a hand on his arm.

He stilled, the warmth of her touch drawing his attention and he stared at her hand over the scars on his forearm. Yet somehow, it didn't bring the same thrill it once had. Whereas before, any touch of her hand brought him immense comfort, now, it felt almost too natural, as though he had grown used to the feeling.

Why was that?

She sighed sadly. "Jasper, not everyone is afraid of you. I wasn't," she added confidently. "I think they are badges of honor, of the battle you won when no one else could. Luke told me what happened and how he didn't even flinch while you recovered. You two are still best friends, are you not?"

Another cry made her shut her eyes as though in agony and she gave a groan as she moved by him back to the baby. "Lucky me, we got a daddy's girl."

He slowly followed, eager but nervous to meet the baby. As he stood just out of Annabelle's sight, Fate rocked and sang to the tiny, bundled infant and he leaned on the doorway as he watched.

How many times had he imagined this same picture? A woman who loved him enough to bear his children, to stay with him, and see who he was beneath the scars. One who would touch him and wish his touch on her?

Her gaze met his and he immediately dropped his gaze to the floor.

She sighed again and strode purposely toward him, the fussing child in her arms. "I am going to prove my point, once and for all."

He pushed off the wall as she adjusted Anabelle in her arms. "No. No, Fate," he protested as he put his hands up and stepped away from them. His hood slid from his head as he jerked back, but he barely noticed as Fate advanced, ignoring him.

Before he could bolt, she thrust the child into his arms as though to throw her at him, and, out of instinct, he just barely caught her, holding her against his chest as he cradled Anabelle in his arms awkwardly.

Fate stepped away and crossed her arms over her chest stubbornly.

Frozen with uncertainty, he looked down at Anabelle, panic rising within his chest, and waited for the screams, his breath caught in his throat.

Nothing happened.

Instead, his gaze caught two ruby red ones that blinked up at him. Her fussing ceased as she seemed to take him in, as though considering whether he was a friend or foe. Her tiny lips closed around her thumb, and her small, pink cap shifted on her head as she tried to look up at him, her eyes wide.

Unsure, he turned to Fate, who smiled and laced her hands in front of her.

He had to say something, didn't he? Try to assure the little one he was alright, before she panicked and squirmed?

"Hello, little one," he said gently.

Anabelle stared up at him and blinked her adorable eyes at him.

Suddenly, she reached her free hand up toward him, and he looked at it for a second before he placed his finger against her tiny palm. Instantly, her hand closed around it and a tiny smile curved her lips as her thumb brushed the scar on the top of his finger.

Fate's eyes watered and she smiled again. "Not everyone you encounter is going to hate and condemn you, Jase."

Anabelle let go of his finger and reached higher, touching his face when he cradled her more comfortably in his arm, and the scars along it. He stiffened at first, unsure, before he shut his eyes and let her touch him, the feel of her tiny fingers almost like heaven as she traced the raised skin.

Fate sniffled when he kissed the baby's fingers as Annabelle toyed with the scar on his lip. "She loves you."

He smiled despite himself and unconsciously started rocking from side to side. "She is beautiful, Fate." His eyes lifted to meet Fate's and he struggled to keep his own tears of joy from shedding. "Just like her mother."

"Watch it," Luke said with a growl as he came through the door with bags of groceries in his hands. "She's still mine."

Fate wiped at her eyes and Luke dropped the bags to cross to her side. His arm wrapped around her and he asked urgently, "What is it?"

She gestured to Jasper, who had taken to speaking softly to their daughter.

Luke smiled, his stance relaxing, and moved his arm around Fate's shoulders as he watched. "Good thing you are her godfather, then."

Jasper's head snapped up in surprise and he gaped for a few seconds before sputtering, "Me? You chose me?"

"Should anything else happen to us, I trust you will protect her more fiercely than anyone else. You are also the only one aside from us that she has allowed to hold her."

"Him, being your best friend, didn't help that decision at all," she quipped sarcastically.

Luke shrugged with a grin.

Anabelle giggled and laughed at Jasper's silly faces and sounds. He took in a deep breath and huffed through his nose, causing smoke to encircle just above her, his eyes glowing as he allowed the dragon within him to play, if only for a moment.

The infant squealed with delight.

Fate reluctantly stepped forward, regret in her eyes. "She is going to need her nap soon but promise me that you will visit her again very soon."

He held her a minute longer, unwilling to let her go, before he settled Anabelle into her mother's arms with one final kiss on her downy soft forehead. "I swear it."

Fate took the babe upstairs, bouncing and rocking as she moved and sang, her voice beautiful as it echoed upstairs.

Luke put his hands on his hips and looked at his best friend, his expression one of bliss. "What is it that brings you here, Jase?"

Jasper frowned and crossed his arms over his chest, his own haze popped like a bubble at the reminder of why he was truly there. "You need to name someone else king. I am not suitable for the task and no one wants me as their king. Surely there are plenty of dragons-"

"None as good as you," Luke insisted. "My choice will not be undone."

"Luke," Jasper reasoned. "No one in the village will disobey me out of fear. They loved and respected you as their king enough to listen to you. That is what they should have, not someone they fear like a dictator."

Luke paced slowly to Jasper. "You are no dictator," he said firmly. "It took a long time to get the respect and love from our people when I began too, Jasper. Nobody wanted an outsider as their king, either." He paused in front of his friend and raised an eyebrow. "I have heard rumors that you have made the staff find new jobs and took the residents from their homes into new ones that you had built."

Jasper looked away, shame flooding him. "They would not stop gawking at me. I do not require staff to run the palace and I do not wish to be stared at as though I belong in chains for the masses to pay to see. I am no king."

"Not with that attitude," Luke grumbled. "Where is my headstrong best friend? The one who came back from that war with dignity and love for his people?"

"He was condemned and shunned by them."

"Then show them that they have nothing to fear from you," Luke urged. "Show them how much you love them and how much you want to help them."

Jasper shook his head and stepped back. "It is time to go. Give Fate my best."

"Jasper-"

His friend shut the door behind him and Luke sighed, dropping his arm.

If only Jasper and the dragons could see him as Luke saw him. A fierce and loyal warrior, one who had once been loved and respected, who now hid in the palace in shame of how he appeared.

Fate rounded the corner and looked at the front door. "Was that Jasper leaving?"

Luke blew out a sigh and gave a curt nod. "Yes. Yes it was."

Chapter 7

Emeline tucked her wet locks behind her ear as she strolled down the palace hallways. Paintings of waterfalls from the clouds and dragons in all forms of shifting, playing together, and laughing in happiness. Even a painting of the palace she stood in on a warm, sunny day was displayed in the main hall, and the city surrounding it ran over the length of the wall.

Yet more art followed of kings and queens from before her time sat regally along another hall, each more extravagant than the last. She paused at the end when she reached the most recent king, one who, according to the inscription, had died protecting the ones that he loved most.

The dragons.

She looked at the gray stone walls and touched it, feeling the life within them. So many lives had run their course here and she could feel it ebb and flow through the very bones of the castle. Dropping her hand, she stopped at one particular painting and tilted her head as she studied it. In it, the background was red and the sky was blacked out by smoke, the ground covered in blood, bodies, and ashes. Demons converged on one dragon in the center, the poor warrior falling before their masses, and a bright light shone above them like a star, but this one had more menace to it, something powerful and dangerous all at once.

She leaned in closer and the scene began to play out before her eyes as though by magic. Warriors clashed their swords while dragons dove and attacked what appeared to be demons with their claws and teeth. One dragon in particular stuck out to her and she leaned even closer to take a look.

The warrior moved in slow motion, slicing through first one, then another demon, never breaking a stride as he fought. As she watched, she realized that she knew the moves, knew the fighting style the warrior had, but she couldn't be sure, as his face was turned away from her, his red hair dark in the dim light.

Suddenly, Jasper's face in the picture turned toward her, and she gasped hard in surprise, stumbling backward and into a tall, warm body behind her.

"Are you alright," came a deep, murmured voice behind her as his arms came up to catch her.

She stiffened, eyes wide and looked down at the hand holding her up by her arm. A scar ran from the back of his hand up his arm, and she turned quickly, stepping back in embarrassment. It wasn't enough that she had insulted him upon seeing him for the first time, she had to be a jinx too?

She could only imagine what he could be thinking of her just then.

"I'm sorry. It's just," she turned back to look at the artwork, but it was once again still as though a normal piece of artwork, the warriors back in their places.

"The painting. It was just…"

She trailed off as she turned back to him, and Jasper tilted his head curiously, his hood up over his head as always.

She shook her head, realizing she must have been seeing things. "Um, never mind. Must have just been my imagination."

He blinked, then looked at his feet but she could have sworn she saw a smile.

She stepped closer to him, trying to peer under his hood but he turned away as though studying a painting full of fairies behind him.

She licked her lip and hesitated as she looked at his cloaked back. Reacting as she had, she knew she had hurt him, but she had wanted so badly to see him again, to make up for how she had gasped before.

To see that scar across his bottom lip that had so haunted her dreams so erotically the night before. It had been almost a torturous bliss, dreaming of his fingers tracing her curves, touching her skin, making her writhe and call out in pleasure.

And that damnable scar as it traced every inch of her…

Nervously, she shook the images from her mind, and played with her fingers, as she asked softly, "Jasper, can I see you? Without the hood, I mean?"

He stiffened, his shoulders straightening as his muscles tensed beneath his hooded cape, and the unmistakable shift of his wings moved his cape, making her flinch. He had every right to be angry with her, perhaps angry enough to strike her with his wings, if he wished it.

She couldn't blame him if he did.

She stepped close enough to gingerly touch his scaled wings and they twitched beneath her touch, quivering as though no one else had touched them before. Scars bumped up against her fingers and she traced each one, fascinated by them.

He lifted his head and his fists clenched at his sides. "You do not know of what you ask, Emeline."

Her name on his lips made shivers move up and down her back and a warmth to pool in her stomach, making her more determined than ever to get her way.

"Yes I do," she said softly. "Please, Jasper."

He was silent as he stood stock still, his fists clenching harder at his sides. Finally, as though he had made his decision, he slowly turned and faced her, his chest only inches from her own and took in air as he awaited her move.

She licked her lips and hesitated, then lifted her hands and paused once more before pulling the hood gently back, careful not to shock him with the light that encompassed the darkness beneath his hood.

He had his eyes closed as she dropped the hood behind his head, but fear wasn't what tingled down her spine. The same scars that had glowed in the moonlight now seemed more faded and less terrifying. His eyes seemed to harden as he looked at her and he started to turn away, but she moved her hand to his cheek and stopped him.

"Please don't," she said softly as he shut his eyes. "You don't frighten me, I swear it."

He turned back to her hesitantly, as he seemed to look for the deception in her eyes, his gaze intense on her own. Uncertainty lit his golden eyes, and his lips tightened into a thin line as he seemed to brace for her condemnation.

Her lips parted and for a reason she didn't know, her attention was caught on the white of his scar over his lip as it seemed to tempt her into kissing him. To run her tongue along it and feel his sharp intake of breath against her mouth.

Her mind seemed to fall into a cavern as she contemplated what it would feel like to have his lips against hers. Would he be gentle and hesitant? Or would the warrior in him devour her and sweep her away into the sky where no one but them existed?

He seemed to be thinking the same as he lifted his hand up to meet hers on his cheek tenderly and he held it there. His eyes closed as though he were savoring her touch on his skin, and she found herself moving closer, brushing her chest against his.

"Well it's about time you damn time you got back," Ana snapped from around the corner.

Emeline gave a start and Jasper stepped back as though he had been slapped, quickly pulling his hood over his head once more. "Go," he muttered. "You won't want to be around when she is on a tirade."

Ana turned the corner and stopped as though she had run into a wall. She smiled and leaned on the wall. "Well, what do we have here?"

Emeline narrowed her eyes at the girl, irritated to have been interrupted. "What do you want?"

Ana blinked in surprise, then laughed. "Ballsy. I like it."

"You tried to drop me out of the sky," Emeline said in disbelief.

Ana studied her nails as though she felt nonchalant. "That was an accident."

"Accident, my aunt fanny!" Emeline retorted.

"Isn't Daddy dearest waiting for you some-where?"

Emeline snapped her lips shut and glared at Ana as she stormed by her like she was nothing more than an ant beneath her boot and disappeared down the hall.

Before Ana could turn her attention back, Jasper had her against the wall with his hand around her throat. "Keep bullying her and you can live out the rest of your days without a vocal cord."

She coughed but sputtered, "Sounds kinky, when can we start?"

He dropped her with a dragon's growl of warning.

She smiled up at him. "Aww, the dragon king has a crush on the new girl he met five minutes ago."

His chest heaved as his pupils narrowed and heat radiated from his skin as he struggled to control himself. Smoke began to blow in tendrils out of his nose and he felt his dragon roaring inside of him to protect what was his, to rip Ana apart, to teach her a lesson in manners. He fisted his hands at his sides and glowered at her, wondering if she knew how close she was to death.

Ana rolled her eyes as she looked up at him and sighed. "So handsome but can't take a joke. Definitely not my type," she grumbled. With another bratty sigh, she met his angry gaze with sincerity.

"Honestly Jase, I think it is cute. She had a thing for you," she added with a smile. "I say go for it."

His breathing eased slowly as he forced himself to calm, to think of anything but tearing his charge apart, and his eyes returned to normal. The temperature in the hallway seemed to drop back to normal and he put a hand on the wall to steady himself.

She raised an eyebrow with her hand around her bruising throat. "Do all dragons have tempers like yours? Or is that something specifically catered to you?"

He blinked a hard glare to her and she pushed herself up to her feet, her throat already beginning to heal. "Anyway, I was coming up to tell you that Navi and Wynter are in the dining room, awaiting your presence to address your concerns, and tensions seem to be just a little high between them."

Jasper's eyes widened and he pushed away from the wall to stride down the hallway.

"Elves are tricksters, at least in my experience," Wynter scoffed, stuffing his hands in his pockets with a wary glare toward the elder elf.

"How so," Navi said, measuring his words.

"You claim you can heal all," he said harshly. "Yet you cannot. Some die on your watch because your magic is so miniscule. How is that a claim to heal all?"

Emeline opened the door and looked between the two, brow furrowed, as they stood glaring at one another. "What is going on?"

Navi sat at the table, one leg bent up so his ankle rested on his knee and his hand on his ankle, the picture of calm, but Emeline knew better.

"I was just hearing the *delightful* opinions dragons have of elves." He leveled a glare at Wynter. "It is apparently a very dark view."

Wynter leaned his arm up on the wall and rubbed the scruff on his jaw. "Not dark, just truthful. Elves cannot heal anyone, they simple prolong the effects of injury and illness before it takes the victim." He shrugged. "It isn't my fault you all false advertise and create a false image for yourselves."

"If I could save everyone," Navi said as he leaned forward, his eyes full of menace. "My wife would still be alive and she would be here."

"Enough," Jasper's voice rang through the room.

All attention shifted to the doorway where Jasper stood calmly, his arms crossed over his large, muscular chest. Smoke puffed from his nose every time he breathed and his eyes glowed as his temper sparked.

Emeline couldn't take her eyes off him.

Ana stepped up behind him and smiled over at Wynter with a finger wave. "Hello, Wynter, darling. Tell me you are not angering our guests or Jasper here, because from what I've seen, he may look pretty but Jase has quite a temper, and it appears to be particularly active today."

Jase, Emeline thought with intrigue. The nickname suited him, making her wonder if he actually like the name, or if Ana only used it to tease him. Was it a term of endearment? Something they shared?

She heard Wynter's response but it was faint, as though he were speaking through a tube and she was on the other end. Jasper looked angrily at his friend, his eyes glowing fiercely in the sunlight that spilled through the window.

Even on edge, he drew her in. She wanted to run her hands over his face, to be the one to calm his anger, and to remind him that someone cared about him.

It was too bad she had botched it with her initial reaction.

"Emeline?"

Jasper's golden gaze met hers and she took a step back at the intensity she saw there. For a moment, his eyes were full of a rage and sadness that broke her heart into pieces for him. In the next instant, they seemed to focus on her, seeing through her and into her far more than anyone else ever had before. Warmth pooled in her belly and it was all she could do not to throw herself across the room at him.

"Emeline, are you alright?"

She nearly jumped out of her skin at the sound of her father's voice and the way he caught her wrist to check on her. "Yes, I'm fine."

Jasper turned away and the warmth that had spread through her vanished, leaving her cold and empty. She sank into the chair beside her father absently as Jasper moved behind her into his elegant high-backed chair. This was much more than desire, more than a longing for him, it was something deeper and more intense than anything she had ever felt before.

Ana hurried over and put her bottom on the chair Wynter had pulled out for himself, folding her hands in her lap. "Such a gentlemen!"

Wynter rolled his eyes in annoyance but said nothing as he took the seat beside her.

Was this how she was with everyone?

Jasper leaned forward and folded his hands on the table as though to give himself strength for the coming conversation.

"Navi," he said softly.

Her father straightened and looked formally at Jasper. "Yes?"

"Why has the elven people not sought help for the destruction of their race?"

Emeline turned her chair and looked at the table as she spoke, careful to avoid his gaze lest her mind should run away with her. "We are a proud people. We thought we could divide ourselves and the demons would leave us alone."

"Divide yourselves where?"

Navi gave a shrug before she could answer. "We don't know. Nobody told any other where they took their families so no one could out one another."

Ana's brow furrowed and she leaned forward in disbelief. "That isn't possible. Elves are close knit, they cannot survive without one another. Your villages are created to protect one another, how is it possible for a village to just split?"

"Ana is right," Jasper said softly. "Elves draw off one another for power, why would separating be the smarter move?"

"Because great power is easier to find," Emeline said, finally lifting her lashes to see him. Their gazes caught and held, nearly making it impossible to speak past the hitch in her throat. "Our primary power is to heal, but if the demons won then so did Lucifer."

"Why would Lucifer want a bunch of elves," Wynter retorted. "You are a peaceful people, you wouldn't have put up a fight."

"No," Navi said roughly as he sat up straighter and put his own hands on the table. "But we can heal and we do have warriors who protect us."

"I'm afraid I don't understand," Wynter said dryly.

Ana's eyes lightened in recognition as she put her hand on her chin in thought. "Lucifer wants your souls."

Jasper snapped his attention to Emeline, sending shivers down her spine. "So he can heal his demons on the battlefield?"

"If they can bend us to his will, yes," she said softly.

"Oh, he can," Ana said gravely, dropping against the back of the chair as though in defeat. "Anyone you have lost has by now given up their loyalty to Lucifer to stop the pain and torment, I can assure you of that."

"That's enough, Ana," Jasper said deeply. His eyes turned dark, conveying his grave thoughts. "It goes much deeper than that."

Navi stiffened and leaned forward, his brow furrowed in concern. "How much deeper?"

The dragons looked at one another as though debating on what secrets to tell.

Emeline watched for a second before she said hurriedly, "We already know about your home and your existence, as well as your customs, to some extent. Surely the stature of limitation has been lifted by now."

Jasper heaved a heavy breath and leaned his chin on his hand as he stroked his chin. "Lucifer can channel the power of the other side. Every ability, every memory, even every breath."

Navi closed his eyes in acute pain. "He can heal himself."

"And it will only get stronger with every elf he kills," Ana said stiffly.

Jasper dropped his hands to the arms of the chair, lifting his chin in thought. "The elves will come here then."

Emeline blinked as though she hadn't heard him correctly. "As we have just told you, we will not be able to find them."

"But we can," Wynter supplied, leaning to one side. "Dragons are telepathic. We can follow the link in you to them. If there are any left," he added grimly.

Jasper gave a nod and frowned as though considering what Wynter was implying. "We will put them in a safe house."

"Why not here," Emeline blurted. Her cheeks colored when every pair of eyes moved to her and she sank back into the chair.

Jasper's lips twitched and a slight smile curved her mouth.

He was laughing at her.

Instead of being annoyed, the warmth she was becoming familiar with when she was near him returned, and she fought a smile of her own.

Ana patted Emeline's hands as though she were a child. "It's alright dear. Jasper enjoys his privacy. I'm surprised he allows you both to stay here."

"They will be moved to the safe house as well."

"No," Navi said quickly. "We need to be where she…we," he corrected himself, "are safest."

Jasper flicked his gaze to the older elf and raised an eyebrow as he stared hard at Navi. It was as though he could see right through her father and to her surprise, Navi shifted uncomfortably. "Anything you want to share with the class?"

Navi squirmed in his seat as he seemed to ponder his next words. Finally, he heaved a sigh and shut his eyes, rubbing them. "Emeline comes from two very powerful elven families. Of the elves, the demons will want her most of all."

Her brow furrowed as she looked at how oddly her father was acting. The dragons may not have known it, but she could tell he was hiding something.

Then she frowned. She thought her mother was a fairy, so why had he suddenly changed it to two 'elven families'?

Ana must've noticed too because she said slowly, "Then I guess they should stay here."

With how fast Navi's neck turned, Emeline was surprised she didn't hear a pop. "What?"

"If she is as powerful as you say, it would be a terrible idea to put her where Lucifer will look first."

"What about our people," Navi asked, indignant. "You would leave them where if demons find one, they find them all?"

"No demon has dared to breach these walls in centuries," Jasper said. "They would not be willingly do so now."

Emeline bit her lip, then turned to her father. "May we speak in private?"

He gave a nod and together, they left the room out into the hallway. Navi caught her arm before she could go farther and turned her around. "Emeline-"

"You have never kept secrets from me," she snapped. "Why are you hiding things now? What didn't you tell Jasper and the dragons?"

He snapped his lips shut.

She glared at him and crossed her arms over her chest indignantly. "Tell me or I will leave right now without you."

He slumped like a deflated balloon and scrubbed a hand down his face as he put a hand on her arm. "It's better that you don't know, Emeline."

She pulled her arm from his grasp and strode passed him. He hurried to circle in front of her. "Emeline, please."

"Just tell me," she said, exasperated.

He was silent for several minutes before he finally blew out a sigh through his nose in defeat. "Emeline, do you remember the legends of the dragon stories your mother and I told you as a child?"

She nodded slowly, her eyes intense on his.

"They weren't stories," he said softly. He paused and blew out air as he paced behind her, toying with his fingers. When he seemed to get courage, he turned back to face her again. "Your mother wasn't a fairy like I told you she was, Emeline."

She stepped closer cautiously, her attention now wholly on her father, and her eyes widened, as a lump formed in her throat. "Then what was she?"

He toyed with the wedding ring on his finger and smile fondly. "I promised her that I would protect her and her kind by not telling you or anyone else. It was easier to let you believe you were simply an elf. Like me," he added quickly.

She waited, unable to form any words passed the fear coursing through her.

Navi blew a sigh. "Emeline, you are half dragon."

Chapter 8

Wynter and Ana went back and forth, throwing insults from one side to the other like children.

Jasper sat with his head bowed, his forehead against his raised hands, and his fingers laced together as he unabashedly used his dragon hearing to listen to Navi and Emeline.

"Emeline, you are half dragon."

His head lifted slowly and he stared at the door with something of anger and shock.

A half dragon? A *hidden* half dragon?

That, he could not stand for. Secrets were forbidden when it came to the whereabouts of his dragons. Dragons lived in this realm for their protection and to have Emeline taken to the elves…

His knuckles turned white and his eyes glowed against the shine of the table.

Ana noticed and her teasing stopped instantly. "What is it, Jasper?"

He glared at the door as he continued to listen.

Emeline gaped at her father and it felt like a vise had grabbed her heart in shock. "Half-dragon?

That isn't possible. If all those stories are true, dragons and elves were forbidden to be together! It's impossible!"

He dropped his hands and his eyes pleaded with her to understand. "It is. When Sarafine and I met, I didn't know that she was a dragon. She saved me from demons the first time they attacked the elves and there was just this…" He paused, searching for the right word before he continued, "Spark. A warmth in my chest. She was everything to me, and when she continued to come back to my cottage outside of our village, I knew she felt the same." He paced away from her, then back, staring at the floor. "A few months later, she told me she was with child. She had hidden her wings much as the other dragons do, I guess. I didn't know. I just knew it was a joyous time, one I was overjoyed to share with her." He smiled fondly at the memory. "Before she could stop me, I ran from the house with her hand in mine and told everyone. A party was thrown, and everyone but Sara was happy."

He paused and took in a breath as though to calm himself as he tugged a necklace with a small, golden dragon charm on it from his shirt pocket. Absently, he toyed with it in his hands, rubbing his thumb over the ruby eye, and frowned, troubled. "I confronted her about it afterwards, and she told me about her origins."

Emeline sank into the wall, sitting on the floor as she tried to take it in.

She was a dragon.

That's why the demons had been so harsh to her back in the mortal world.

She buried her fingers in her hair as her head spun and she fought for breath. "She left her family, her life here for you."

He nodded. "It broke her heart, but once she was with child, we had to hide her and you. Dragons are not allowed to be with elves, or anyone in the world of the living for that matter. That is as much to protect us as it is to protect them."

Emeline shut her eyes and stumbled to her feet. "I can't do this right now." She took off down the hallway on a run. She had to get away from him, away from everything, and get her bearings.

Who was she? Who had she been without the half of herself she hadn't known existed?

"Emeline," Navi called out.

She ignored him and ran for the front door, determined to go back to the Elven Isles, where everything was normal again.

Where none of this existed.

She pushed through the doors and out into the sunlight, uncaring where she may end up.

Navi pushed through the doors of the dining room, his eyes wide in panic as he immediately sought Jasper. "Emeline…she's gone! Please, you have to find her!"

Jasper slowly stood, resting his fingertips on the table as he glowered at Navi, outraged. "She is a dragon, and you didn't tell anyone. You risked her safety, and the safety of our kingdom, had she been exposed before now. She may come and go as she pleases in a kingdom that claims her as one of their own."

Navi looked over to the other two dragons but they glowered at him in silence. Ana had her arms crossed over her chest as she leaned on one foot and Wynter's fists clenched at his sides.

He looked pleadingly over at Jasper. "I did what I had to do to protect my daughter and my wife. Do you know what the heavenly council would have done to my baby girl? They would have treated her as an abomination," he supplied. "They would have taken her away from us, perhaps killed her."

Jasper shook his head. "It is not up to me to decide your punishment. Sarafine," he said sourly. "I remember her, but only from when I was a boy. We thought she was killed by demons some decades ago. Many of our people mourned her loss, and some never fully recovered because of your selfishness."

"How ironic that she was killed by them some years later," Wynter retorted coldly.

Navi dove for the dragon but Ana jumped in the middle and pushed him back. "You did this," she reminded harshly.

"Please," Navi said after an angry pause. His eyes promised vengeance on Wynter before he reluctantly turned back to Jasper pleadingly, "She does not know this city, she is lost and confused. You cannot be so cold hearted that you would leave her out there on her own, where anyone can get their hands on her."

Jasper stared for several minutes before he turned his attention to Ana. "He stays here. Do not let him leave, even if you must knock him unconscious to do so."

Ana leaned forward with her hands on the table, her eyes flashing red, as she offered an unsympathetic and demonic smile. "With pleasure."

Navi's eyes widened and he stepped back as though to bolt. "A demon? You have let a demon into this realm!"

Jasper moved so quickly that Navi didn't have time to react before Jasper was face to face with him, looking down on the smaller man. "You will respect Ana. She has earned her right to be here, unlike the likes of you."

Navi flinched as Jasper strode passed him.

He looked incredulously at Ana, who popped a bubble with the gum she had stolen from Wynter and sat down in her chair. She twirled a strand of hair around her finger and chewed obnoxiously with a smile. "Please try to leave," she dared as she cracked her fingers. "I could go for a good rump right about now."

Navi seemed to debate before he finally just flopped into his chair with a defeated sigh.

Emeline walked and walked, unsure of where she was going or how to go back, but she was sure she didn't want to be at the palace anymore. Her father had lied to her for her entire life about who she was and she just couldn't risk being near him right now.

She just wanted to go home.

The sound of shattering glass made her stop, flatten herself against an alley wall, and look around the corner cautiously.

A brick building sat in between two closed businesses, music and laughter echoing out from its dark windows and open front door. Blinds covered a few windows but one with an "open" sign on it was left bare, showing people dancing and moving to the beat like shadows. Smoke wafted from the doorway, clouding the sunlight over the building until it faded, as though shadowing the building in the night darkness.

She sniffed and wiped at her tears as she watched in fascination. Nothing like this had ever been done on Elven Isles. Elegance and peace were always the theme for most of the elves there, but the people standing outside the building danced and talked animatedly, laughing as they had a good time with drinks in their hands.

A place for parties was a great idea, one she would have to make when she came home. But if she was going to create a party building for the elves, she needed to know what was going on in the inside.

She flinched as her bare foot hit a particularly sharp rock but inched her way across the cobblestone walkway to the building, smiling as people laughed and stumbled out.

No, not people. Dragons.

She stopped in surprise, ready to turn back and forget she had even considered going inside, but it was too late. The crowd pulled her inside and out of the doorway, tugging her down the steps to the dance floor. Startled, she tried to find her way through the dancing bodies to get back out, but it was packed. There was barely any room for her to move, let alone escape the floor. Lights danced on and in the floor, and music blared from large speakers around the room so loudly that it felt as though

Emeline's eardrums might burst. Other than the dance floor lights and the lights lighting the shelves of the bar on the backside of the place, no other lights lit the interior.

She squeezed between two dancing couples with a polite, "Excuse me" and tried to make her way to the door but every time she did, someone bumped her further back until she was almost to the bar. She turned and made her way to a free stool with an exasperated huff, leaning over to get the attention of the handsome bartender. Maybe he could help her, or at least point her to another exit.

He smiled and leaned over toward her, causing her to lean back. "What can I do for you, beautiful?"

She smiled at the compliment. "I'm trying to find my way out of here."

"Well, you'll have to wait until rush hour is over. People are piling in."

She gave a hesitant nod. "An hour. I can do an hour."

He gave a knowing nod and leaned his arms on the other side of the bar, raising his eyebrows. "Want something to drink while you wait?"

Emeline bit her lip as she eyed the liquids on the shelves uncertainly. "What do you have?"

"How about some dragon's juice? Goes down smooth and soft."

She smiled again. "That sounds heavenly, thank you."

With a nod of confirmation, he turned to mix the drink and she looked to the dance floor. People were grinding and moving on the dance floor to the heavy beat, some moving further to kissing one another and letting their hands roam. One couple were just about to strip their clothes off when a bouncer stopped them and pointed to the door, obviously telling them to go have at it elsewhere.

Her mind drifted to Jasper and she shut her eyes with a sigh. It was hard to imagine him in a place like this, with his guard down and dancing like he hadn't a care in the world. Yet somehow, she could imagine a slower pace dance, to more romantic music, with him, his arms around her as they swayed.

Elves and dragons were forbidden, she reminded herself. She couldn't imagine what would become of her if anyone found out she was here, let alone interested in Jasper. An elven dragon, interested in one of the most powerful dragons in this realm?

Chaos would erupt, she was sure.

And she knew that Jasper and Navi would be the ones to pay for it.

Emeline let her mind drift for a long while.

Their moment in the hallway floated to the forefront of her mind and she let herself imagine what would have happened if Ana hadn't interrupted them. If she had given in to her desires to press her lips to his. To feel the ridge of that tantalizing line against her tongue, and to wash away the anger and sorrow that seemed to cling to him like a second skin.

She opened her eyes and sighed.

Perhaps she really was losing her mind.

A dragon sank into the seat beside her, his breath smelling of something sour as he looked at her. "Fun party, right?"

She gave a start and turned her attention to him. He was tall, but not as tall as Jasper had been with brown, long hair that hung loose around his shoulders. Muscles bulged from his muscle shirt and ran down to his sweatpants. His wings were bouncing on his back as he moved, his orange eyes drowsy and fogged at once.

She smiled slightly. "I guess so."

He chuckled drunkenly. "What's your name, pretty lady?"

"Emeline," she yelled over the music.

He nodded to the beat. "Cool! I'm Tucker."

He held his hand out and she shook it with a nervous smile. He stood and leaned over her shoulder to whisper next to her hair-covered ear, "Want to go have some fun?"

She rubbed her thighs, her hands sweating from the warmth of the place, as she looked nervously out at the crowd. "Oh, I don't think so. I got lost in it last time and I am just waiting for rush hour to be over with so I can go home."

He waved a hand in front of him, shaking his head. "Rush hour could be hours away." He took her hands and pulled her to her feet. "Might as well have some fun while we're waiting, right?" He grabbed a beer from the counter and started dancing as he led her onto the dance floor, his beer held over his head to avoid spilling its contents.

She reluctantly followed, gasping when one dragon stepped on her foot. Tucker put his hands up and moved his hips, dancing and laughing in fun. Giving him a once over, she giggled, then started to dance with him, shyly at first until she finally threw caution to the wind. It truly was going to be a long wait, and Tucker seemed nice enough.

Why not have fun, indeed?

He took a swig of his beer, then leaned close enough for her to hear him. "You're a really good dancer!"

She smiled shyly and absently brushed her hair behind her ear. "Thank you!"

He stilled and his smile widened as though he had found his amusement for the night. "An elf! I didn't think your kind was welcome here!"

She stopped dancing as just about every eye around them looked at her, drawn by Tucker's outburst, and the music paused as the DJ stopped to listen.

The silence was deafening, and she rubbed the back of her opposite arm awkwardly. "I-I am not an elf, I was just born with these."

He snorted, his smile fading as menace covered what amusement had been in his eyes just moments before. "Yeah, right. Do I look stupid to you now?"

He advanced toward her and she stepped away, eyes wide in fright as the monster of a man advanced toward her. "No, of course not! I-I am just-"

"Too good for the likes of us dragons, eh," he taunted "You elves, always thinking you are high and mighty, when in reality, you are cowards when you are up close and personal with the real gods."

The crowd murmured their agreements.

She shook her head as she continued to step back until her back hit the bar, and she gasped. "I don't think that, honest! I'm just trying to get home, but I got stuck in here and-"

"Stuck," Tucker bellowed, turning to address the room, and drawing laughter from the crowd. "Now our parties aren't fun enough for you?"

The crowd roared with shouts and laughter.

He leaned forward, pinning her to the bar with his body, as he leered, "Let me show you how much fun a real party can be."

She leaned back over the bar as he slammed his beer beside her and she jumped against him in fright, eyes wide. Terrifying images ran through her mind, causing her to tremble and her breath to catch in her throat.

What is he going to do to me?

He laughed, amused at her terror of him, and it made her stomach churn. "She wants me already, boys!"

She put her hands up to block him when he tried to kiss her, but he caught them in his and held them above her head. "I wonder how powerful an elf really is against a dragon as strong as me."

He leaned in closer and a protest cried out from her lips as tears spiked her eyelashes.

Chapter 9

Suddenly, the door to the bar slammed open, the sound echoing through the silence surrounding Tucker and Emeline. Sunlight from outside spilled inside, and grunts and groans from the sudden exposure erupted from the darkness.

Slowly, a large figure began moving down the stairs, causing people to part ways instantly at his presence with gasps and shoves. It was as though the air had been sucked out of the room, and whoever had entered had made everyone less worried about breathing and more concerned about what he might do next.

Tucker straightened, his back stiff, and held her hands in front of her to ensure she didn't leave, but she was more enthralled with the mysterious stranger who had entered. Something about the way he moved, the power he exuded, struck her as familiar, and her heart raced faster in recognition.

"Who the hell are you to interrupt the party right when it's about to get good," Tucker demanded, a growl underlying his words as he spoke.

The man continued, the crowd moving far out of the way even at the expense of the people behind them to make room for his dominating presence. When he finally stopped in front of Tucker, he threw the hood of his cloak back to reveal himself and the crowd gasped. As a whole, the group seemed to step backward and cries of alarm echoed throughout the bar as murmurs filled the otherwise quiet bar.

Tucker swallowed hard as his eyes met Jasper's, the anger and outrage clear in the elder man's eyes, as Jasper stepped closer, his nose nearly touching Tucker's. "You would do well to release her right now, lest you should risk condemnation to Hell for the rest of your miserable death."

Tucker dropped her hands like she was on fire, but in his haste, he pulled on her, causing her to stumble off the stool and onto the floor with a gasp. Her hands slammed into the wood floors and she flinched, rubbing her sore palms.

Jasper glanced from her to the young dragon, who seemed to shrink beneath his rage filled gaze. Jasper's eyes began to glow, a threatening golden ring around his iris, and Tucker backed into the crowd, hiding behind two other dragons, as though he could escape Jasper's intimidating glare.

Elated, Emeline stood, tears in her eyes, and rushed into Jasper's arms, the only place she felt the safest in the hostile environment. How foolish she had been to run from him! This city was much worse than she thought it was, and Jasper seemed to be the only trustworthy man left in it.

At first, Jasper didn't move, too surprised at her action to budge, and stiffened. When he did move, his arms embraced her protectively. The shock wore off quickly though, and his anger rose higher to dangerous levels. Even from her position in his arms, she could feel him tampering down his dragon, willing himself to remain calm.

He glowered at Tucker over her head as he enveloped her into his embrace, silently assuring her that he was there, he would keep her safe.

"Enjoy your final hours in this realm," he told Tucker in a low voice, his dragon underneath his words. "Your redemption has been revoked."

He turned and the crowd jumped, too terrified of him to do much else, and even a couple of loud gasps sounded. "Anyone seem harming an elf, especially this one, will be condemned in the same manner. Any protests?"

No one dared to utter a sound.

Despite the drama, Emeline's heart wept for Jasper as she caught glimpses of the revulsion in his people's eyes as Jasper led her outside. No one was compassionate or admiring of him, instead acting hateful and frightened of him.

No wonder he lived alone in that big castle.

Fools, she thought angrily, glaring at each one as they made eye contact with her. Everyone there should have felt ashamed of themselves!

Jasper made his way back out of the bar with Emeline at his side and tugged his hood back over his face, the rage there faded into one of almost embarrassment. Once they had cleared the bar, the music started up again and faded with every step they took, everyone inside pleased to see them gone.

They walked in silence for a long while, each lost in their thoughts.

Finally, he stopped a couple blocks away and turned into an alleyway and gently placed her against the wall as he checked for any threats. Satisfied at last, he started looking at her from head to toe, a faint glow showing in the shadows. Emeline was certain that Jasper was fighting his anger at Tucker, instead choosing to see to her wellbeing instead.

"Did he hurt you?"

She shook her head. "No, he didn't get that far before you showed up to save me."

He met her gaze and stepped back, clenching his hands at his sides as though to keep himself from touching her.

"Navi was worried about you."

She licked her suddenly dry lips as she stared at him, but he kept his gaze downcast. Still, she straightened her back and reached for the confidence that she didn't feel as she said softly, "It wasn't right of them to look at you like that, Jasper. Or react that way to seeing you."

He turned his head away and pretended to scan the empty street, but not before Emeline caught a hint of hurt in his gaze. "Everyone does." His gaze met hers and for a moment, the sadness that lived inside of him seemed to filter from him into her, even as he said cruelly, "You did."

"I did out of surprise," she insisted quickly. "Not because I thought you looked frightening." She tucked her hair behind her ear nervously, as she murmured, "I don't find you unattractive at all, actually."

"Stop that," he snapped suddenly between clenched teeth.

She gave a start in surprise, eyes wide as she tried to think of what she must have done wrong. Her brow furrowed in confusion as she asked with a shrug, "Stop what?"

"Stop trying to make this better," he said gruffly. "Lies are not going to change anything. Elves used to be honest and noble, the best of us from the days of the living. It must be that times have changed without me."

"I am *not* lying," she said stubbornly, her own anger rising. "I do not feel the same way about you as those people back in the bar, and I can't stand the idea that you think I do!"

Smoke wafted from beneath the hood and his knuckles turned white at his sides as he fisted them. "Stop."

"No," she said indignantly. Without thinking, she lurched forward and pulled the hood back from his face, determined to see his face. "I am *not* afraid of you!"

He turned away fast, looking at the brick wall as he tried to control his breathing, his temper getting the better of him. His arms slowly lowered to the sides, but with how tight he had his hands clenched, she was surprised she didn't hear bones popping out of place.

She licked her lips again and stepped closer, a dull ache beginning in her chest. Pulling his hood back, revealing him against his wishes, had gone too far, but she craved it. She wanted to see his beautiful golden eyes, the intriguing scar in his lips.

"Why will you not let me see you?"

He was silent for a long while, his chest heaving as though he struggled to contain himself against his emotions.

"Because I do not wish to see your pity," he said finally.

"What if it wasn't pity you saw," she murmured, tracing the scar as it trailed down his bicep, ending in its center. "What if there was something else instead?"

He didn't move, stiffening as though he had turned to stone, but his breathing began to ease as she stilled her motions.

She let her fingertips touch his cape-covered shoulder and encountered a ridge along the rounded edge of his arm. The scar ran over his shoulder, wide in the beginning and thinning at the edges, and nearly pulled away when the skin there twitched. Her fingers continued over the soft cloth until she felt his skin peeking out from beneath the edge and traced another scar on his forearm.

She started to circle to the front of him slowly, as though approaching a frightened animal, and her hand moved down his powerful arms, the muscles jumping under her touch, as though begging for her to continue.

Nervous, she stood before him, but his gaze remained on the ground, his refusal to look at her like a knife to the chest.

"I know we just met, but I feel something about you, Jasper. A warmth I have never felt, and a desire that I have never known for anyone."

He remained silent for so long, she began to wonder if he would answer her. Still, she had to know, the need burning through her like a torch, if he felt the same about her, or she had imagined their connection.

After a few moments of silence, she hesitantly whispered, "How is that for honesty?"

Chapter 10

Jasper felt something soften within him and before he realized what he was doing, his hand raised toward her, the need to touch her almost overpowering, only to let it fall back to his side with a frown.

She wasn't his to touch, let alone half of the things he was imagining doing to her. He had no business even considering touching Emeline. She deserved more than a man who hid away in his palace, ashamed to be out amongst his people.

Emeline needed someone she could dance in the sunshine with, someone who would be more understanding about her than he was. Yet, even the thought of another man in her life made a tendril of smoke to waft from his nose, his fire burning within him as it hovered on the brink of explosion.

If she was with someone else, he would have to walk away. Otherwise, no one would be able to stop him from tearing the man apart.

Her lashes fell to half-mast and he could feel her gaze on his lips again, making him feel the scar there acutely. She ran the tip of her tongue along her lips as she lifted her gaze to meet his again, waiting for his response, and shifted from one foot to the other nervously.

How adorable, he thought before he could stop himself.

He stiffened more, doing everything in his power to keep himself from pushing her into the wall and taking her right there. He could already feel that tongue against his lips, imagine her taste as she writhed against him, crying his name. Everything in his being called out to take her, to tell her how he was feeling, but he resisted, barely.

Her fear could not have been faked when she had seen him beneath his hood. She was afraid, and horrified, yet she stood before him, her gaze determined, as she allowed him time to consider her words.

If she was lying to gain his favor, she certainly had him fooled.

He stared down at her, watched as a fine sheen covered her lip when she released it, and yearned to take her mouth in a kiss. To taste her and feel the warmth of her against him as he had not felt in decades, but he forced himself to remain still, and tried to control his breathing as well as his arousal.

If she didn't stop looking at him like that, he knew wouldn't be able to stop himself either.

"Emeline," he groaned, scrubbing a hand down his face. "You just found out you what you are and one of the worst dragons in the realm just assaulted you. You cannot know what you are doing right now, and rest might help you to think clearer.

Her gaze fell and disappointment clouded her face as she toyed with her fingers and mumbled, "If you do not feel the same for me, I wish you would simply say it and get it over with so I can go home. There is no need to insult the clarity of my mind to get me away from you. Perhaps I am inadequate because of what I am, but-"

The hurt in her tone broke something inside of him. *Get her away from him?* He could hardly bear the mere inches between them, and she thought that he wanted to be rid of her?

With a groan he charged forward, making her step backward until her back touched against the alley wall, ending her retreat. Her gaze jumped to his in surprise as he leaned his arm on the wall above her head and, at long last, gave in to his desires, pressing his lips to hers in a desperate, hard kiss.

Emeline gasped in surprise, her eyes at first wide, then drifting shut as she moved her hands to his face, cradling his ears between her thumbs and first fingers as she threw herself into the kiss. Had she been thinking, she would have reminded herself not to throw herself at him as she was, but the second he had kissed her, all rational thought flew from her mind, leaving behind only desire.

She gave in to what she wanted and ran her tongue along his bottom lip, feeling the scar there, and he growled low. Pleasure moved down her spine, and the desire to run her tongue against it, to feel the ridge pressing heatedly into her lip, grew stronger. As though a taste of what she desired was never going to be enough.

His hands slid down her arms to her hips and pulled her off her feet, wrapping her legs around his waist. He settled his body against hers, holding her up with his strength, as he moved his hand to her knee, sliding its way up toward her center.

She threw her head back and moaned, hugging around his shoulders to keep herself from sliding down the wall, but he had her pinned. With her throat exposed to him, he trailed kisses down to her collarbone, lost in her taste and scent as his hands moved to her bottom and squeezed. She writhed against him, pulling him tighter against her with her feet in the small of his back, desperate to feel him against her even more, to ease the tension building up inside of her.

She ran her hands along his arms, feeling the ridges there, as she bared him from beneath the cape, and kissed along the scars of his face as he came back up to take her mouth once more. His tongue slid inside and groaned, moving his hips against her as though he were ready to release with her right then.

She pulled at his cape to loosen it, desperate to see more of him, as he continued to kiss her, his hands roving over her, driving her mad.

Voices sounded down the walkway, and at first, they ignored it, continuing their exploration of one another. One of the voices laughing jerked Emeline from her desire-fogged mind and Jasper's eyes shot open as he froze, his lips against hers. Suddenly, she felt her feet on the ground and Jasper was faced away from her, his breathing ragged. His wings moved with his shoulders, up and down, as though he had run a marathon, but she knew he was trying to control himself. He pulled his hood back up and fixed his cape as he waited, his gaze on the walkway to see who had interrupted.

Behind him, Emeline leaned on the wall, her own breathing heavy as she looked at his back, her mind clearing slowly.

Why did he stop?

Seconds later, a couple with their baby strolled by, the stroller crunching on the stones of the sidewalk as they spoke happily about their planned dinner for the evening, while their baby slept peacefully.

Emeline watched Jasper even as they passed, uncaring who saw her raw feelings for him, and when she caught her breath, she straightened and said softly, "Jasper?"

He lifted his head and looked to the sky, then put his hands on his hips.

Finally, he turned to face her, his expression soft. "Emeline."

She slowly closed her mouth and stood, her feet brushing on the stones of the ground as she moved and put a hand to her stomach to still the butterflies fluttering there.

Jasper shut his eyes, unable to stop his heart from thundering in his chest just from the sight of her. Perhaps, if he didn't see her, he wouldn't want her as much, he thought to himself, but to his dismay, it only intensified the desire coursing through him and he opened his eyes again.

"We need to go back to the palace," he said angrily, more so than he intended. "You are not safe out here in the open and more dragons will discover you are here."

She flinched, making him wish he could steal the words back, but it was too late. His tone was condemning and cold, but it couldn't helped. This couldn't happen, he couldn't allow it, and one day, she would understand.

Still, he frowned.

It's for the best, he told himself.

Emeline felt as though she had been stabbed in the heart with the emotionless look in his eyes, the frosty tone in his voice, and his stiff stance. Just minutes ago, she had thought she had seen such heat and desire in his eyes with an intensity that matched her own. Yet as he looked at her, his gaze was hard and cold, almost as though he were putting a distance between them, and it stung.

Perhaps now he is rejecting me, she thought sadly. Had she done something wrong, or something to upset him?

She raised her chin defiantly. No dragon was going to bring her down, not even Jasper himself, even if it did hurt.

"Very well," she said coolly. "But only so I can tell my father that I will return home. I do not wish to stay here any longer."

Something dangerous flickered across his gaze, but it was gone as quickly as it had come and back was the emotionless shield he seemed to constantly keep up.

He shook his head. "You will not be permitted to leave."

She put her hands on her hips, raising an eyebrow in challenge. "You can't stop me. Free will is still a thing, even here."

"Not when you are a dragon in danger."

"*Half*-dragon," she snapped. "And I was uninformed until now. Maybe I will reject my dragon heritage, be solely an elf for the rest of my life." Her eyes watered but she refused to shed a single tear, especially in front of the most infuriating man she had ever met. If he could shut off his emotions so easily when it came to her, than she would try to do it too, even if it was out of spite. "If I live a quiet existence like my mother, maybe no one will find out about what I am. I won't be the misfit abomination that will likely be killed for existing by the angels. If angels exist."

"No harm will come to you," he said firmly, his eyes glowing as though to challenge anyone who would say anything to the contrary. "I will not allow it."

"What power do you have," she snapped, her hurt making her mouth run without her. "What could you possibly think you could do that would stop them?"

He blinked in what seemed to be astonishment, the harshness fading if only for a short time, as he seemed to consider her.

"Do you not know?"

Her brow furrowed and she leaned her head back on the wall as she braced herself for whatever bit of news she was about to receive.

"Know what?"

He crossed his arms over his chest stubbornly as though lost in thought. Finally, he shook his head again. "Never mind. It is not important. What is important is that you know you are safe with me."

She shrugged, her heart softening toward him once more. *Dammit!* "That's great, really, and I appreciate it, but I just need some space right now. I do not wish to see my father, not after finding out that he's lied to me my entire life about who I am."

"He was trying to protect you," Jasper said gently.

She snorted and looked skyward as she raised her hands, then let them slap to her sides. "How ironic, that in his attempt to protect me, he actually put me in more danger." She sighed. "What powers do dragons even have, anyway? I don't have wings, so I cannot fly. The demons want me for my power, but I don't even know what that power is." She closed her eyes and sighed, her shoulders drooping in defeat. "I don't know who I am anymore."

Jasper fisted his hands as his arms remained crossed to keep himself from stepping forward to steal her mouth in a kiss again, to hold her to him and promise her that he would fix everything. But no matter what she meant to him, no matter his desires, he knew beyond a shadow of a doubt that he would help her, even if it meant keeping his distance.

Absently, he was glowering at her, angry at himself, and his knuckles turned white as he clenched his fists. He couldn't even help himself, how could he ever hope to help her?

She lifted her foot and flattened it to the wall behind her as she worried her bottom lip. "I'm sure I will be fine on my own."

"Like you were with Tucker," he snapped before he could stop himself, his frustration reaching its end.

She glared at him, but her cheeks flushed in embarrassment. "I appreciate your concern but I will not wander into a bar full of dragons ever again." Her glare faded into regret and she shut her eyes, leaning her head back so she could look up into the sky. "I was just confused, alright? Elves party to celebrate love, happiness, and peace. Parties are open to all, and we take great pride in them." She scowled in disgust, her fingernails scratching at the wall behind her as she fisted her hands behind her. "Those dragons were making a farce of tradition. Why would I ever want to be a part of this world, when it goes against everything that I am?"

The knots forming in his shoulders relaxed, and, before he could stop himself, he inquired, "If I can prove to you that this world is not defined by its raunchy bars, will you promise to stay here for your safety?"

At her uneasy gaze, he wanted to kick himself for how cold he had been just moments before, but to his surprise, she smiled slightly at him in appreciation.

"I guess I could spare a few hours before I leave to give you a chance. You obviously love your home," she added softly.

He gave a curt nod and gestured for her to follow him. She stepped up beside him and together, they began to walk down the street in silence. The sun was beginning to fall toward the horizon, its rays casting shadows on the buildings as they passed. Dinner time was approaching, and the once thick crowd thinned, each dragon going home for a good night's rest. Families laughed and smiled, leading their children toward their homes for a well-cooked meal.

After a few quiet blocks, she hesitantly asked, "W-Where are we going?"

He tugged at his hood uncomfortably until he was sure it was in place, hiding him from sight as they drew closer to one of the more popular spots in town. "You will see."

As they rounded a corner sometime later, Emeline stopped in her tracks with a gasp, surprise and delight shivering down her spine. The waterfall that she had seen flowing just behind the palace crashed down into a beautiful, crystal clear pond, the water glistening and gleaming in the sunlight. Clouds surrounded the water, holding it together for the children and their parents to enjoy the day as they enjoyed the last of the sunlight pouring in from above. Trees provided shade off to the side, and some of the dragons were spread on towels, soaking in the sunlight as though the warmth would wash away the stresses of the day.

Emeline laughed despite herself, as children jumped into the water and squealed with fun as they splashed one another, the scene completely contrasting the one from the bar. Here, there was love, there was laughter, and there was true happiness.

A haven, she realized.

Jasper stepped back into the shadows of a nearby tree, watching cautiously from several feet behind her, his gaze warm.

"Not all dragons are like Tucker," he said softly. "These dragons were once humans, supernaturals, even some a mix of both, and when they arrived here, they just wanted a place to go home to. Somewhere that was safe and warm, just like their lives had been, and here, they can find their peace." He frowned when a toddler started toward them before being gathered into the arms of his mother. "Just when they were sure they were ready to go to Afterlife, they met someone special, and created families. They found jobs in the field of their choice, they saw the beauty of this city, and even when the time for redemption presented itself, many chose to stay here, instead of moving on into Afterlife."

Her lips parted at his moving words, as she turned her attention back to him, her mind full of questions.

"What do you mean by 'redemption'?"

He was quiet for a few minutes, as he seemed to gather his thoughts, before he finally answered her. "The realm of the dragons is a place between heaven and hell for those whose souls were not wholly good, nor were they wholly evil. The previous king was almost a pure man before he came here, but he committed a great act of violence against a demon and reveled in it, which darkened his soul." He leaned his shoulder on the wall of the building beside him and crossed his arms over his chest, his gaze locked on a family, laughing as they swam and played in the water. "When he died, he was granted entry into Afterlife because for centuries, he was a great ruler who cared for his people. He had finally paid his dues, and the woman he loved was in Afterlife, waiting for him."

"Centuries? People live here for centuries?"

He nodded, amusement flickering over his gaze. "Some millennia, before they decide to move on."

Suddenly, he frowned, and turned his attention away from her. "Some never do."

Chapter 11

Emeline pondered his words, wondering what it must be like to be so sure of where she wanted to be, before nodding, and her brow furrowed as she stepped closer to him. He seemed to be hiding in the shadows, his gaze wary on anyone who ventured too close, and she felt that familiar ache in her heart for him that she had begun to grow used to around him.

"Why do you hide from your own people?"

"You saw the people at the bar," he grumbled, his voice harsh. "You know why."

"But they shouldn't judge you based on your looks, or alienate you because of them," she insisted, gesturing to the people before them. "You must have been through something truly terrible, and been very brave in the face of it, to come out as you have."

His nostrils flared in anger and his gaze started to glow. "So they should pity me?"

She narrowed her eyes, cautious of her next words. "Why not? At least then they wouldn't act afraid of you. Perhaps they would see you as the warrior that you are, the hero that you have become for them. Pity-"

His gaze was pure menace and his eyes glowed fiercely. "I do not want their pity."

"Then what do you want?"

"To be left alone," he snarled, his voice rising. "To be allowed to live my death the way I wish, without fear of judgement. I wish to roam my hallways alone, without anyone to stare at me. Where I can feel normal, and at peace, while the rest of the world lives in the same way."

Her lips snapped shut and she frowned, scolding, "Well that is a truly terrible way to live, then."

"It is of no concern of yours," he muttered.

She sighed, shaking her head, as she muttered, "You are right about that."

With that, she stormed away from him, fists clenched at her sides, but to her chagrin, she could hear his footfalls behind her as he followed. She tried to take a fast turn, taking off at a run down the alley and around the corner where he wouldn't see her. The time had come for him to leave her alone, and she was going to take it whether he liked it or not. If all he wanted was to be left alone, so be it.

She hit into what could only be a wall and fell backward onto the street with a grunt. When the stars faded from her eyes, she looked up to see Jasper glaring down at her, his arms crossed arrogantly over his chest, and she let herself fall back onto the pavement with a groan, laying there in exasperation with her hand over her eyes.

"Just let me go already!"

His glare softened and he heaved a sigh before he knelt, his hand out to her. "I am sorry."

She blinked, lifting her hand from her eyes to peek out at him.

Did she just hear him right?

The corner of his lip twitched and she felt something in her heart warm, causing her to scowl at herself. He was a jerk, she shouldn't be thrilled that she had created something for him to laugh at, yet her heartbeat faster at the amusement in his eyes.

She sighed and took his hand. With one mighty tug, she was on her feet and brushing her sweatpants off. "Thanks."

He shrugged.

He suddenly looked up, his pupils narrowing, as he listened to the wind. Everything inside her went on alert and she instinctively stepped behind him, tucking herself between his wings. His back was ramrod straight and tensed, as though waiting for something to attack them at any moment, and he crouched, his hand hovering over his sword.

"What is it," she whispered, looking around.

A low, inhuman growl rumbled from deep inside of him, but it wasn't the beast within him that frightened her so much as the scratching sound that grew in volume as it came closer. Soon, heavy breathing and growls echoed down the empty street, sending terror into Emeline's heart, making her wish she didn't know what awaited them on the other side of the alleyway, but she did.

Demons.

Jasper's eyes roamed the street, looking for the source of the noise but nothing seemed out of place. The sun continued to shine, the wind was warm and pleasurable as it brushed dirt and dust across the empty street, yet still, the beast taunted them. Jasper could hear his claws tearing at the stone somewhere close, its breath quickening as it grew excited.

"Show yourself," he demanded, his gaze narrowing as his dragon began to rise higher, ever on alert.

From behind an abandoned, half-torn down building, a red-skinned demon emerged, his black teeth shining as he bared them menacingly. He was at least eight feet tall, his long, black claws scrapping on the stone of the building beside him as he walked, a silent threat, as pebbles broke off and fell to the street. His eyes were black and his body was skinny, almost as though its muscles had long faded away, but Jasper knew better.

Wynter, Ana, he called telepathically, *we have at least one demon in the city, but where there is one-*

There are more, Wynter finished for him. *I'll get civilians out of harm's way on my way to you. Ana is staying here to guard the palace and Navi but will be on standby if we need her. We don't know how big this is yet.*

Jasper drew his sword, moving Emeline to his back for safety. No demon had dared to set foot in the realm of dragons in centuries, aside from Fate's evil stepmother the year before, and even she had kept her distance, recognizing the city's power for what it was. And Ana, though she was less demon and more witch these days.

This demon would learn his mistake soon enough.

Emeline went on tiptoe to look over his shoulder and her eyes went wide as she saw it, a gasp echoing near his ear. "How will we get away from that thing?"

He put his arm out to steady her behind him and drew his sword. "We won't. You will stay behind me," he added firmly.

"But my father-"

"Is with Ana," he said firmly. "No demon will be near him, but if you want to get through this one, you must do as I say."

She seemed to take a deep breath of relief and gave a nod of understanding.

He watched as the demon stopped directly across the street, his chest heaving in outraged breaths, as he ripped his claws from the stone, making pieces of it ricochet off the walls around Jasper and Emeline.

He reared back, his blackened eyes glaring at Jasper, before he thrust the top half of his body forward, and roared, his voice bellowing off the buildings surrounding them, and causing every dragon within hearing distance to scatter. Emeline's arms brushed his back as she covered her ears with a gasp and flinched, her face against the skin between his wings.

A challenge, then.

He stepped back, embracing Emeline between his wings and the wall of the building behind them. "Stay here."

She shook her head, fingers curled into his cape. "You can't, he'll kill you!"

"I've fought worse than him before," he said absently touching the scar over his brow. He remembered a demon similar to this one, and the scar was all the demon had left behind when Jasper had finished with it.

Her lips parted in realization when he turned, his hand dropping to his side. "You got those fighting demons."

He didn't answer her.

Emeline held tighter to the base of his wings, her fear evident in her wide eyes. "Please, Jasper. Please don't go!"

He eased from her grasp and he felt himself soften toward her again as he focused on the demon, who had begun to stomp his hooved feet, ready to charge. "Stay here, Emeline. I will return to you."

Emeline reluctantly released him, watching in fright as he charged for the beast.

The demon gave a roar, and lunged for Jasper, its fangs dripping onto the pavement and melting the stone beneath him.

Emeline put her hands up to hide what happened from view, but at the sound of a shriek, couldn't stop herself from checking to ensure Jasper wasn't injured.

Jasper approached the demon, his every step measured, as though he were planning his attack in his mind.

Emeline's heart jumped into her throat as he drew closer, fearful for him. Suddenly, as he lunged for the monster, something began to burn through her veins, making her gasp and lean hard on the wall. Only moments passed before white magic glowed on her hands, making her eyes widen, and pure power raced through her veins, crackling and buzzing like nothing she had ever felt before.

She looked up to see if Jasper had taken notice, but found the demon was then thrown against the empty building, the wall cracking behind it. With one mighty shake of its head, it stood back up but Jasper was on him, swinging his sword with a threatening growl of his own. The demon grabbed the blade with its huge fingers and threw it aside, but Jasper didn't let go, instead using the momentum to roundhouse kick the demon in the face. It screamed in pain, its nose bleeding and crooked. Jasper followed it up with a punch to the gut, then to the jaw and the demon went onto the ground.

Emeline watched in fright, alternating between her glowing hands and the ensuing battle as the demon flipped back onto its feet, striking faster than she could see. Jasper was grabbed by the throat, the demon's claws digging into his skin, and she gasped in horror. She stumbled forward, the need to help stronger than ever, and the power coursing through her strengthened, intensifying the glow of her hands.

Something wet hit her shoulder and she stiffened, eyes wide as heat followed, skittering down her spine along with a shiver of fear as whatever was above her drew closer.

Please be water, please be water, she repeated in her head, but she knew better.

A low growl echoed behind her and she turned slowly, fear clogging her throat as she tried desperately to swallow back tears of fright.

"Jasper," she finally screamed.

A demon, much like the one Jasper was fighting, swung its mighty hand, sending her flying into the middle of the street with one blow. She gave a cry as pain radiated through her as her body slammed into the ground and tried to catch the wind that was blown from her lungs. His heavy footfalls caught her attention and she whipped around. The demon roared at her and she looked down at her hands as blood began to flow from several cuts.

She shut her eyes as the demon began to thunder toward her, his fangs bared, and willed her hands to glow again.

Surely that much power could save her now!

"Glow, glow, glow, come on," she whispered, panic settling into her chest.

To her surprise, within seconds, a white light glowed around her hands, and she put her palms up in front of her defensively, causing the demon to pause. The demon dismissed the glow and lunged for her with a terrible roar, his jaw wide open for the bite that would surely kill her. She shut her eyes as she braced for the impact, but seconds later, the demon screamed horribly as it flew into the air and dust fell against her face. Her eyes went wide again when she dared to take a look and she watched in astonishment as it struggled in the air, its limbs grasping for anything to hold onto, but found no purchase as it disintegrated slowly.

Determination surged through her, and she stood, keeping one hand up to hold the demon in the air. She lifted her other hand to join the first and clenched her fingers as she pulled them apart, ripping its head, arms, and legs off before she knew what she was doing. Within seconds, the screams finally stopped and nothing but ashes hung in the air.

She dropped her hands as she gaped in shock at herself, then turned to find Jasper with his sword deep in the heart of the demon he'd been fighting. He ripped it free as the demon ashed and ran toward her. "Go!"

She took off down the alley with his feet pounding behind her and came out on another empty street. Her hands rose to her lips in fright as she saw Wynter in the street just to the other side of the alley, barely holding the arms of five demons above his head to keep from being crushed beneath their weight.

Jasper shot past her and jumped, his sword raised above his head as he cut into one, then another demon to free his friend, his speed causing his motions to blur. It was like watching a dance, only much more terrifying.

She squelched her fears as best she could and raced forward, holding her hand out to grab hold of one of the demons with her magic. Calling for her new powers, she threw him so high into the air that he disappeared before he fell back to the ground, turning into ashes on impact.

Wynter, now only fighting one, grabbed the hilt of a sword in his hand from the holder on his belt and her brow furrowed. It was only a dull gray hilt with a blue gem in the handle, but nothing protruded from it like a normal sword.

What good was a hilt with no blade?

To her astonishment, within seconds, a blade made of pure ice formed, its blade covered in frost as mist came off it in waves. It grew to a full blade and he pushed it deep into the chest of the monster he fought. With one final scream, the demon turned black as the frost spread through him and then disappeared.

Wynter scoffed and scrapped his ash-covered boots on the street with a grunt, his chest heaving with his breathing. "Damnable demons, always leaving behind a mess."

She would have laughed at his joke if it wasn't for the circumstances.

Jasper turned his attention to Wynter, his sword still in his hand, as his gaze scanned over the street. "Anymore?"

"I stopped about five more on their way to the palace," he reported. "But I don't think it's Navi that the demons want."

Both men looked to her and she gave a start as she stepped back, eyes wide. "I had no idea about the magic. I swear it!"

Wynter dismissed her and looked to Jasper, his expression serious as he shifted his sword in his hand. "She would be an excellent asset, if she were trained correctly. Being a dragon, she will pick up on the moves quickly and-"

"No," Jasper said gruffly. At her stunned expression, he added in a softer voice, "We need more time to figure out what you can do before we even consider training you to fight, Emeline."

Overwhelmed, she took another step back, her head spinning in confusion, and shut her eyes. "I can't do this right now. I-I can't…"

Wynter growled as mist came off his wings, and his eyes glowed an angry dark blue, as though he wanted to freeze her on the spot. "Yes, you can and you will," he said firmly. "Our people suffered today because of you. I helped to load three women, two men, and four children into the intensive care unit before I came here." He stepped toward her, his sword tapping on the street as he fisted his hand. "This is because of you; you will fix this."

Jasper grabbed Wynter's shoulder, jerking him backward, his eyes glowing, and his tone was firm, angry even, as he said, "I command you to seek out more demons, and to protect our people while I take Emeline to the palace. The demons will sense her magic and follow us, but you can lessen their numbers as they chase us."

Wynter stormed up to Jasper, baring his teeth, as he stopped with his face inches from Jasper's and he snared, "I don't know who you think you are, but you are no king to me. Not if you would take the side of an elf over your own people!"

With that, he stormed off, disappearing between two buildings.

Chapter 12

The sun faded behind dark clouds, a soft wind picking up, and brushing leaves across the street with crinkles and cracks. His cape picked up in the wind and it waved in the new breeze, his fist clenched around his sword, and to her, he almost looked like a haunted angel.

Emeline stood rooted to the spot, Wynter's statement making her stomach sink to the ground. She rubbed her thumbs over her clenched fingers and licked her lips, before she managed to say, "What does he mean?"

Jasper stayed still, his hood hiding his face as he stared out at the city, ever on alert, but from the tension in his wings, she knew he had heard her.

She stepped closer, her anger rising, as she demanded, "What did he mean, Jasper?"

Still, he remained quiet.

She stomped closer, her fists starting to glow, and she fisted her hands at her sides. This was not something she was going to let him keep from her!

"Tell me!"

"I am the king of this realm," he muttered, a soft growl underlying his words. "Though if I can help it, not for much longer."

She froze, eyes wide, as she tried to process this new bit of information, and repeated dumbly, "King?"

He sheathed his sword, his eyes ever watchful. "Let's go."

That explains it, she realized. Why Ana and Wynter had listen to his every command, why his presence in any room was met with silence, his voice a decree regardless of what was being said.

He moved to walk away and she shook her head, tears in her eyes. "No. Not until you tell me exactly why you didn't tell my father or I who you really are."

He shifted from one foot to the other and sighed, rubbing his eyes as though in exasperation.

Or defeat.

"Emeline, I did not wish to be king. Luke, the previous king I told you about, made it so. I have begged him to choose someone else, but he refuses, determined to prove himself right. He never will," he added softly. "I am not meant to be king, and it is made more obvious to me by the day."

She was speechless.

He threw his free arm up, then let them fall to his side with a soft slap. "We must go, Emeline."

"No," she said softly. "*You* must go to save your people." He opened his mouth to protest but she cut him short with her hand up. "Wynter is right, this is my doing by being here. If I leave, the demons will follow me, and your people will be safe."

He stepped up to her, grabbing the sides of her shoulders with a hard squeeze, and his eyes were intense on hers. "They will not have you. I will not allow it, Emeline."

She gasped in surprise, raising her hands up to touch his forearms, and tried to steady herself as she trembled. "They must."

He rested his forehead on hers. "You cannot go, Emeline. They will kill you. I cannot protect you if I do not know where you are."

"They also will have no use for you if you don't," she pointed out. "I'll get word back to you when I am safe." She put her hands on his face, holding him still as she looked up to meet his gaze. "I promise you."

He grit his teeth, his muscles twitching beneath her fingertips. "You will not do this."

"I'm sorry," she whispered before she gave him a soft, lingering kiss. "But I have no choice."

It became clear that he had no intention of letting her go, and she felt a deep sadness at what she was about to do.

Without warning, her hands glowed, and he shot backward with a shout of surprise, knocking his head on a nearby building. His eyes shut and he fell haphazardly onto the ground with a thud, unconscious, his body slumped on the street.

She hurried over to him, checking his pulse, before she used her elven magic to heal the wound on his head that had begun to bleed. She stood, ready to take her chance to run, but paused long enough to kiss his forehead. Once she was determined he would be alright, she took off at a run for the edge of the cloud.

Before she could reconsider, she jumped onto a nearby one and waved her arms to steady herself when her heels encountered nothing but air. When she was secure, she looked at her hands, then willed herself into the air, hands down to push magic on the cloud. The puffs below her began to glow like a beacon, bright enough for any demon below to find her.

With her loudest voice, she shouted, "Come and get me, if you dare, demons!"

Silence reigned through the city and she scoured what she could see of it, looking for any sign of the monsters within.

Within minutes, she watched as over a dozen demons began spilling through the streets, each intent on seeking her out as they made a jump for her, clawing and kicking at one another to be the one to capture her.

She shut her eyes and waited for them to reach her, certain that no demon was left, as tears ran down her cheeks.

The dragons were finally safe. Her father was safe. That was all that mattered.

Navi used his magic once more to heal the child who was covered in bruises and cuts and blinked away his fatigue. He had healed dozens of dragons in the last hour, and the amount of magic it took to heal an afterlife being was taking a toll on the elder elf. The last victim of their demonic invasion, and his heart broke when the boy moaned in what could only be pain as bone restored itself and cuts began to seal together, healing without a scar.

Healing was an incredible power, but it didn't always mean it was painless.

Jasper slammed the front doors of the palace open, his eyes wild as he looked around the foyer, and Navi felt a pit in his stomach. Something was very wrong, if the calm king himself was in a frantic state.

He frowned and looked around for his daughter trailing behind Jasper, but no one stood around him, and Navi began to understand Jasper's panic.

"Emeline?"

Navi was on his feet in seconds when no one answered him and rushed angrily to Jasper with his eyes wide, as he demanded, "Where is she? Where is my daughter?"

Jasper wouldn't look at the elf as his gaze ran over the room as though he might find her hiding behind a pillar or coming down the stairs. "She knocked me out with her magic, and when I came to, she was gone. I had hopes she was here, but it appears they were for nothing."

"The demons are leaving," Wynter announced behind Jasper as he entered, his expression grim. "We must have scared them off, the beasts."

Navi's eyes widened impossibly more and he felt his heart stop in his chest in terror. "No, you didn't."

Recognition lit Jasper's golden gaze before he sharply turned and took off out the door, his wings open wide, and in seconds, he was gone.

Emeline groaned as she came to, her head and muscles sore. She tried to pull on her arms, but they were bound above her, holding her hostage. Her lips felt dry and held open from the cloth gag placed there. Her legs were chained shoulder width apart to the floor and she looked up to find the chain holding her hands locked onto the ceiling. She pulled at the chain again, trying to use her magic but she couldn't access it.

What had happened?

She remembered the demons jumping for her, then the moment one of their hands grabbed her ankle, and nothing after.

She pulled hard with a cry of frustration but the chain held.

Stuck, she took in her surroundings as she fought to remain calm. The walls were black stone, the ceiling made from the same stone, and the two windows of the place were barred, but she could smell sulfur, blood, and tears filtering in from outside. Cries, screams, and moans of pain echoed just outside the window, the sounds bringing terror into her very soul, and tears spiked her lashes.

The demons had brought her to hell.

She struggled anew, then froze when the door creaked open, eyes wide.

A man with blackened wings strode in purposely, his black suit and red tie pressed and proper, as though he were going to a board meeting. His eyes were red and rimmed with black, his black hair contrasting with his pale complexion.

The hairs on the back of her neck stood on end and her eyes widened when she recognized him from books and scriptures she had seen. The man was known by reputation primarily, but everyone knew the devil when he appeared, and very few lived to tell about it. The ones who did chose to forget the man of their worst nightmares, bound to live their lives in abject fear and pain.

Lucifer himself.

She pulled at the chains as panic tightened her chest, her breath heaving as he approached, and she tried to plea through the gag for mercy, for her friends to be spared, but it came out muffled by the gag.

He smiled and put his hand on her cheek. "I do love a good struggle," he said with a chuckle, "but you won't be escaping from here anytime soon, my dear."

She glared at him even as tears welled in her eyes, her stomach twisting into knots at what he would do to her.

He trailed a finger down her face and she flinched away. He ignored her action, continuing to trace down to her jaw line. "You really are as beautiful as they said. I have seen many women in my long existence," he said as his pupils flared. "Not a single one of them has captured my attention quite like you have."

She jerked on the chains once more, her muffled grunt echoing through the room.

He scowled, whipping his hand away. "You needn't do that. Those chains will not break, I forged them myself. You have no magic here, no way out."

She pulled again with a muffled cry of frustration.

He stared at her, his hateful gaze roaming down her body, and she felt as though a thousand ants crawled over her. "I could do things to make you calm down. I could control your every move, your every thought, but free will is so much more fun to watch. This illusion of escaping this place, this *Hell*, is one everyone assumes they have but in reality, you have no chance for it."

He circled her, his finger trailing down her back to the base of her spine. "When we are finished here, maybe I will sample you as I have all others. The most beautiful elf, and you can be mine." He chuckled. "It's almost anticlimactic." He watched her backside tighten as she tried to pull away from him and lifted his hand from her to rest at his side. "And you would have no choice but to take me."

He sighed as he came back to her front. "Unfortunately, I need your compliance more. You see, I cannot take possession of a soul without them choosing to give it to me. The rules of this horrid magic game we play."

His blackened fingers grabbed her jaw sharply as he pulled the gag from her mouth, drawing a gasp from her. "Give yourself to me, and you will not suffer as those outside these walls suffered."

She trembled, but her gaze was fierce as she reminded herself of whom she had given herself up for. Her mind fluttered to Jasper and a new kind of tightness caused her to calm herself. If he was anywhere near as fierce as he had been at the bar with the thug who tried to take her, she could only imagine what he would do to the king of hell for taking her.

"When I am found, it will not be me who is forced to suffer."

He snorted. "Do you really believe that hideous dragon king will find you? Beyond my wards, my magic, my demons? He is nothing."

She jerked on her chains, her glare intensifying, as her face came into his, but he didn't flinch. "He is more of a man than you ever will be. Envy does not shine a pretty light on you," she taunted, giving him a disgusted once over. "If you feel the need to force girls to take you, then you really have no confidence at all."

"On the contrary," he said with a wave of his hand. Pure power raced through her veins, taking hold of her body, and she started bouncing on her toes against her will, unable to stop despite her attempts. "This kind of power is intoxicating. I have all the confidence in the world, and women will flock to me to join me by my side simply for the chance to be the queen of Hell." He grabbed the chain holding her up and grinned maliciously as the power surging through her began to fade. "And when I am finished with them or bored, I will kill them slowly, adding them to my list as I rule overall."

She stopped bouncing, out of breath and he watched her chest rise and fall before he spoke again. "Your soul will go a long way towards achieving my goal. I didn't get Fate's soul, but that is no matter. There are others who will assist me in fulfilling my plans."

"You are insane if you think for one minute that I would ever choose you, no matter the torture you put on me!"

"Many of your elven brethren said the same," he said in an almost bored tone, with a shrug. "I now have almost a three dozen elven souls who are mine. The same souls you have heard screaming just outside of these walls."

She jerked at her chains again, anger rising within her at what this horrible man must have done to her people. "Let them go."

"For a price, maybe," he added as he folded his hands behind his back, looking every inch the businessman, but she could now see the cruelty that lived within him, the darkness that reflected back at her in the black of his eyes.

She licked her suddenly dry lips, her hair sticking to her face as the heat of hell bore down on her and jumped when a scream shuddered into the space around her. "What is the price?"

"Your allegiance, of course."

She heard another terrible scream and started to panic. She could free almost three dozen innocent elves, help them to find peace after all that had been done to them.

Thirty-six for the price of one.

She had promised to let Jasper know she was safe, but she had lied. She would never be safe so long as Lucifer wanted her, she knew that as well as she knew what her choice was going to be.

"Will you hurt Jasper?"

He snorted and rolled his eyes. "I will kill all who get in my way. Dragons and angels protect every pure living being, they will be the first to go."

She nibbled her lip as she imagined Jasper, the strongest dragon in existence, writhing in pain as demons remade the scars on his body, tortured him and brought him to his knees. A proud king, and one of the kindest men she had ever met, torn down because of her.

If she didn't give in, if she let those souls suffer, then they would be lost to the darkness here. Yet if she gave Lucifer her soul, he would use her to destroy dragons, angels, and anyone else who would stop his evil from manifesting in the world above.

She shut her eyes and dropped her head. The right decision was there, and it was going to be a difficult one to make, but she knew in her heart that it was the right one.

"I cannot put the fate of the worlds over the souls of the ones here."

"Then you condemn your brethren to a fate worse than death."

Jasper stood atop the palace, overlooking the city as he reached his mind out, looking for any sign of Emeline. There had to be a sign, a flicker, anything to indicate that she was alright, and that none of the demons had gotten to her.

Anger, red hot as it burned through his veins, rose and he felt his dragon roar inside of him, clawing for his way out, to seek revenge over whoever would dare to harm Emeline. Jasper reached for calm but settled for assuring the dragon that they would get their revenge, and it would taste delicious.

His heart thundered in his chest and he shut his eyes, folding his hands in front of him as he attempted to calm himself, but he knew where she was, and he knew what it would take to bring her back. There could be no doubt in his mind that he would do exactly that, long before anyone laid a hand on her.

But would it be too late?

She could have already pledged her soul to Lucifer, in too much pain to say no or given a bargain she couldn't refuse.

Or worse.

He felt a small link lock into his mind as he reached for a connection below ground to the layers of hell, the strain causing his knuckles to turn white, and his eyes shot open, his eyes glowing gold as he reached further, as far as his mind would allow. He allowed himself to fall behind the castle and off the cloud before opening his wings and soaring toward where he felt it the strongest.

He felt her determination as he drew closer to the ground, felt her anger, her fear, and his dragon began to take over, opening his mouth to release a rage-filled roar the likes of which he was sure no dragon had ever heard before.

Emeline, he whispered toward her in hopes that her dragon half would hear him. *Emeline, I am coming for you.*

Chapter 13

"It's very simple, Emeline," Lucifer said coyly. "Make the choice to save your people. Either way, you are going to die; but if you surrender, your people go free and you will not endure the pain and suffering that they did before your demise."

She stared at the floor, then shut her eyes. Condemn the dragons to death, or save the elves who never belonged in hell to begin with? The dragons could fend for themselves, but she knew that the people beyond the walls couldn't.

Emeline.

She stiffened, feeling warmth seep into her consciousness, and nearly moaned in relief as tears rose again. Just the sound of his voice, so fierce, so confident, with just a hint of desperation, broke her heart, and it was all she could do not to cry out for him, to beg him to come rescue her.

Jasper.

Emeline, I'm coming for you.

She glanced up at her chains as she felt the connection between them strengthen. But could he hear her?

Lucifer is here, she tried to warn him, *and he is trying to give me a deal. My soul for the elven people. I'm sorry, but I have to save them. I can't take hearing their screams anymore, they are innocents!*

No, he said firmly, and her knees nearly gave out in relief that he had heard her, that he was truly coming for her.

If their souls have been tortured enough to submit to him, then they are already lost to us, he continued. *Good beings turning to the dark side only turns them into demons and once released, they could seek out the other elves, not just from your village but from others as well. He would bring Hell to Earth anyway with his tainted souls released.*

Her eyes opened to glare at Lucifer, who was still waiting to hear her response. "Those souls are tainted, aren't they?"

Fire lit his gaze and he stepped closer even as he stiffened, staring so intensely into her eyes that she was sure he could see the bottom of her soul.

"How do you know that?"

She narrowed her eyes, anger rising, as she realized it had been a ploy, an attempt to trick her into giving him her powers so he could take over everything.

"So it's true, then? You've already turned them into demons!"

Before she could flinch, his hand shot out, hitting her hard in the face and she cried out as pain exploded in her cheek. "No living being knows how the Afterlife works, not even you! How do you know such things? Tell me," he demanded, grabbing her by the throat and forcing her to look at him.

She gasped for breath, choking as his grip tightened, and somehow, she knew Jasper's rage was growing, that his dragon was clawing at the confines of his body to rip Lucifer apart. Seconds later, she heard an angry roar chase through her mind, an anger she didn't recognize growing from their connection.

Jasper was dangerously enraged.

He looked down at her with a look of satisfaction, as though he had found what he was looking for and jerked her away from him.

"I see you have chosen the dragon," he said as his pupils grew in size. "The new dragon king is stronger than I thought. He can see passed my barriers, push his magic passed mine, to connect with you. How interesting," he mused. "And how unfortunate for him that he should be so foolish."

Suddenly, the door slammed open, and Jasper strode inside, his golden gaze glowing as his wings remained stiffly open. His arms were outstretched on either side of him, a struggling demon's throat in each hand. He glowered at Lucifer from beneath his hood, his pupils narrowed as though his dragon simmered just below the surface, waiting for any sign that he could come out and play.

"Let her go," he said in a voice so low and menacing, that even Emeline shivered nervously.

Lucifer released her throat slowly, and she gasped in air, tugging at her chains weakly for freedom.

"Jasper," she whimpered, wishing nothing more than to feel him around her. Just seeing him there, a protector of the innocent, as frightening and angered as he was, brought joy to her heart.

With one mighty, almost effortless strength, he threw the demons to either side of the room hard enough to crack the stone walls, marring the otherwise perfect black walls, and neither moved.

Lucifer snorted, turning away from Emeline and folded his hands behind him, but she could see the tension through his shoulders. One move from Jasper and there would be bloodshed, of that she was certain.

"I see my demons had some fun at your expense. I would apologize, but you stood in my way. How you didn't die during that war is beyond anything I have ever seen."

Jasper slowly withdrew his sword, twisting it in his hand. "Wait until you see what I will do to you." He raised his sword in challenge, smoke heaving from his nose with every heavy breath he took. "I will not ask again."

Lucifer shrugged, unbothered by Jasper's threats. "I will find her again and when I do, she will be the first to die."

The chains holding Emeline up vanished, leaving her to fall limply to the floor with a grunt of surprise as blood began circulating back into her arms.

Jasper didn't move, his eyes never straying from Lucifer as though he were anticipating on the devil to make a move. "Are you alright?"

She rubbed her sore wrists and managed to sit up gingerly. "I think so."

Lucifer raised a hand and she rose with it into the air with a gasp, waving her hands to catch hold of something, but met only air. She tried to reach her foot to the floor, but it was no use as Lucifer held her up.

Jasper smiled, his fangs peeking over his bottom lip, as though relishing the thought of a fight. "I had hoped you would challenge me. It is a shame you are not Lucifer himself, or I would have enjoyed this much more, Imenda."

Lucifer smiled, raising an eyebrow. "How did you know it was me?"

"The way you spoke," Jasper said stiffly. "I recognized that sickening tone from when you helped to torture me."

Emeline shook her hands, quietly urging them to glow. If ever there was time for her to use her magic, it was right then.

"Come on, come on," she whispered like a mantra, as she rubbed her hands together, but nothing happened, and panic began to rise into her chest.

Do not be afraid, his voice echoed in her head, sending warmth and comfort with it. *Fear will hold back your abilities. Embrace it, use it to strengthen your magic, not hinder it.*

She risked a glance at him, but he was still glaring at Imenda-as-Lucifer with no sign that he had spoken to her.

Emeline bit her lip, and forced her fear onto her magic, staring hard at her hand. At first, nothing happened and she scowled. Suddenly, her hands began to glow, and she shot it out toward the demon, the magic soaring through the air like lightning. It shrieked as it shot into the air, and, in its shock, dropped Emeline. She fell with a cry, shutting her eyes as she waited for the impact to the floor.

Instead, she felt her body land squarely into Jasper's waiting arms, his sword sheathed, and he took off at a sprint out the door.

She squirmed uncomfortably. As nice as it felt to have him holding her, she knew her weight would slow him down, and Imenda would catch up to them faster.

"I can run."

"I can run faster," he snapped, his pupils narrowed a sure hint of the beast within.

She wisely closed her mouth as she realized that part of his anger was toward her, and simply held on tight. The last thing she wanted to do was turn his dragon on her for what she had done, not when they were escaping for their lives.

He came to a sudden stop once he was outside the gates, and slowly set her down, as though afraid to make any sudden moves. When her bare feet touched the dry, burnt ground, she could only gasp at the angry crowd of demons surrounding them outside the dark, gothic palace in the courtyards. Wilted trees and a redden sky with dark clouds only aided in giving the monsters their horrific appearances, as each heaved and snarled. The stench of death hung heavy in the air, and the demons' growls and hisses banished the silence, leaving only menace and dark intentions.

Emeline stepped back instinctively, slipping behind Jasper, with her eyes wide. There had to be hundreds of demons, all looking at them as though they were a delicious meal, handed to them by the gods. There was no way they could defeat that many demons, not by themselves, perhaps not even with an army of dragons at their side.

There would be no surviving this, and it struck Emeline to her core as the crowd of demons took a collective step forward.

Death suddenly didn't seem quite as far away as she had hoped.

Jasper glowered at all of them from beneath his hood, his eyes glowing gold with a hint of red around the rim of his iris. He was rigid, his fists clenched at his sides as his chest heaved, fighting to keep his dragon leashed until he needed it.

Ana, Wynter, he reached out. *If you can hear me, Imenda took Emeline, and in my foolish attempt to get her out of hell, I was not expecting to be ambushed. Seek us out in the seventieth level near some gothic ruins.*

"Ah, how the mighty have fallen," came a distinctly feminine voice from the doorway behind them, echoing through the halls of the entrance he had left open.

Jasper stiffened as he slowly turned, not wishing to provoke the demons before he was ready to battle them.

What they needed was time to stall so Ana and Wynter would have time to reach them before they were eaten alive.

Imenda strolled forward from the shadows of the tower behind them as though she were out for a walk instead of leading a band of demons on a dragon hunt with her arms swaying at her sides, one delicate, barefoot in front of the other. Reverted to her original form, her red scaled scars shined against the dim light of the sky. Long, lush black hair flowed down to the center of her back, enveloping the sides of her face. Her eyes were black and her smile, though perfect and white, contained fangs that dripped with menace. Her half-shirt was torn just above her bosom and her black jeans were torn as well, leading down to delicately small feet. Black toenails adorned her feet and her fingernails were long, matching the dark shade of her toenails.

If she wasn't the leader of the demons set on killing them and their sordid past, Jasper might have thought she was beautiful. Luckily, he knew a snake when he saw one, and this was the worst of the worst. He knew that beneath all her beauty, she had an ugly soul, and a dark heart, one that had burned him several times over.

Jasper stiffened with Emeline behind him, peeking around him to see what had caused his distress, and Imenda toyed with her hair. "Hello, handsome. I was hoping you would come for your new little wallflower." She smiled coyly, a baring of teeth, as she continued to approach him, her hips swaying. "We hadn't finished our little game from so many years ago."

"Shut up," he snapped. "Or I will cut you where you stand."

She laughed, the sound echoing off the walls. "You will do no such thing. These demons would rip you apart before you had taken up your blade." She boldly stepped forward and moved inches from him, tracing a dark fingernail down his lips, her tone sickeningly sweet. "Besides, you don't want to kill me in front of your little wench, do you?"

"How can you imitate Lucifer's powers," he demanded, seemingly unbothered by the monsters who stood staring at them. Let them try to hurt Emeline, let them see what beast he held within him, struggling and writhing for the blood of those demons in his claws.

Not one of them would survive.

Emeline gasped behind him, leaning against his back with her own when the demons inched yet closer. It was as though they were waiting for an order, an indication that they could finally sate their desires, and finally get a taste of dragon and elven souls.

Imenda giggled, the sound like nails on a chalk board, and he grit his teeth. "Every girl has her secrets, my love."

He pushed her away from him, bumping Emeline back, as his anger rose to dangerous levels. "Does Lucifer know about these tricks?"

She snorted, her shoulders shaking in barely repressed laughter, as she rolled her eyes. "Do you think I would be alive if he did? Not that he could stop me now," she retorted. "Not with the amount of elven souls we have turned."

Emeline looked around in fright, her head brushing against his shoulder, as the demons stepped closer and said on an alarmed whisper, "Jasper!"

His wings twitched around her but her trembling didn't ease as the demons started to lick their lips, eyeing her up. They were planning on doing much worse than killing them, that much Jasper knew.

He narrowed his eyes as he taunted her, "Suppose someone told him?"

"Do you see these walls," she asked nonchalantly, circling him as though viewing her crumbled walls for the first time, and waved a hand toward them. "We are seventy levels down. He doesn't care about us. We've given our time, we can live here without a care in the world because he sees this world as several levels below him. Not worth his time, or his energy, to upkeep. Why would he be interested in us, when he has other things to do up there?"

Jasper wrapped his hand around the hilt of his sword uneasily, frowning. *Ana, answer me.*

Shut up, Ana snapped at him. *I have a plan. Keep your demonic ex busy!*

Emeline came a familiar, feminine voice in Emeline's mind.

Surrounded as they were, Emeline jumped and her eyes widened before she realized Ana had reached her telepathically. *A-Ana?* She couldn't decide which demon to watch as they all seemed to close in on them. *Help! Help us, please!*

Ana snorted. *When you get back to the palace, you and I are going to work on that fearfulness. Also, I'm teaching you to fight no matter what the big guy thinks, because honestly, this damsel in distress nonsense is so-*

Ana!

Right. Well, we are coming, but you both must be too far down because we can't reach him. We need a distraction, a way to stall, but from what I've gathered, Jasper has that one covered.

Her brows unclenched as recognition hit her.

He was stalling!

Now Emeline, Ana said urgently, *we need you to use your magic.*

Attempting to slow her heartbeat, she looked down at her hands and willed them to glow with magic but nothing happened.

I-I can't!

Silence met her claim at first, then Ana said firmly, *You have to. There is no choice, Emeline. We are too far away, we won't make it in time to save you both, and your deaths will be something worse than nightmares. You have to fight, you must be fearless! You are a dragon shifter, one of the most powerful creatures of their kind, and I refuse to believe that you don't have a spine!*

Emeline straightened as though to demonstrate that she had a spine but it did her no good. The sneers and glares from the monsters chilled her to the bone, no matter how much she tried to squelch it.

Imenda circled Jasper and smiled wide when she saw Emeline, tucked between Jasper's wings for protection. "Well, well, well, if it isn't the beautiful little elven girl. Is she the replacement for me in your heart, dear Jasper?"

Jasper's wings opened enough to release her and he turned, the heat of his back pushing its way into hers as he leaned over her head slightly. "You will not touch her."

"Oh, won't I," Imenda sneered and gave Emeline a onceover with a shrug. "Obviously she means something to you, or you wouldn't care one way or another." She leaned in close, getting her face into his. "Your soul is tainted, just like mine. The sooner you realize that, oh mighty king, the better."

Chapter 14

Jasper glowered at her. "I am nothing like you."

"You are everything like me," she said with a sadistic smile. "And now, you even look every inch the broken warrior, unstable, monstrous. Why, this little tuft of nothing here," she picked up Emeline's brunette locks from her face and let them fall, causing the elf to shudder, "I bet even *she* is afraid of you. And look at her! A beautiful girl like this wouldn't be able to handle a terrifying monster like you, let alone stomach you in bed with her."

Emeline felt anger begin to replace her fear, and she slowly straightened enough to glare at the demon, her eyes beginning to glow white in her hatred of her. "He is not a monster, you hateful bitch."

Before Imenda could respond, Emeline ducked beneath Jasper's open wings as she pulled her hands to her chest with her palms out, then thrust them forward into Imenda's chest. White magic burst between them, making every demon shriek and back away, and Imenda flew back with a scream of anguish far into the crowd, disappearing behind them.

Emeline watched, her power surging through her like lightning. Her gaze wandered around the enclosing crowd, more anger bursting through her that they would dare to threaten her and the man her heart cried out for. Rage that these horrible monsters would steal her people away to torture and confuse them into becoming demons filled her and she grit her teeth, ready to fight.

Jasper stared at her in astonishment. "Emeline, that wasn't a wise-"

"Attack," Imenda shrieked, rising from behind the army of demons and hovering in the air as her hair flew around her. "Kill the witch, capture the king!"

Chaos erupted as the demons screamed and cried out their battle cries. Claws dragged on the ground, rising the dirt into the air like a thick fog, and roars echoed high into the sky for all to hear.

Seconds after they began to converge on Jasper and Emeline, screams of pain and the whoosh of ashes falling made the crowd turn toward the other side of them. Blood stained the ground, and more demons began to vanish as swords and arrows flew directly into their intended targets. From above the fog, Ana and Wynter soared through the sky, throwing blades as they moved seamlessly, their bodies blurring with their actions. They finally landed on either side of Jasper and Emeline, blades raised, and formed a circle with their backs to one another.

Ana grinned at Emeline, who had no weapon but her hands glowed as though a white flame had engulfed them, ready to strike. "I knew you had it in you."

Emeline's glowing eyes shifted to Ana, then back, her fear and anger fueling her on. "I want these monsters gone."

Imenda stepped to the front of the crowd, shoving demons to the side as she glared hatefully at Jasper, her eyes a deadly black in fury. "You think it is that simple to be rid of me?" She raised her to the sky hand and red flames burned around them as she cried out, a demonic growl beneath her words, "Kill them all!"

That was all the permission the demons needed.

Emeline grabbed one by the throat with her magic as it dove on her, roaring in outrage, and used her other hand to rip off its head, turning it into ashes in an instant. Another reached for her outstretched arm and she threw it into the air until it disappeared, letting it fall with a scream toward the ground. Somewhere deep down, she knew she should be repulsed by the scent of blood and ash, as the dragons beside her took hits and landed blows. She should have abhorred the idea of killing these demons, souls who had been damned by the devil and tortured to within an inch of their lives.

Yet she didn't.

Beneath the revulsion, under the disgust, was a fury she hadn't known she had possessed. Not because of the secrets that flew around her like wildfire, not because of how Imenda had tortured her.

This was something else. Something dark, and fierce that threatened to consume her and she knew in an instant what had caused it.

No one was going to be taking Jasper away from her, and she would be damned before she allowed anyone to torture him for thrills ever again.

She would die first.

As she tore her hand through the chest of yet another demon and dodged a blow from the next, she felt her magic surge through her and both demons screamed horribly when she grabbed them, obliterating them in a flash.

It didn't matter how dark her soul would get from her new power.

They would be safe, no matter what it cost her, and she fought harder, determination taking the place of fear.

It was time to fight.

Imenda had encircled a group of demons toward Jasper, glaring up at him with her hands raised, and her fingers playing with the fire that heated his skin as she drew closer. "You would be considered beautiful here now, Jasper. You should bring your dragons down here, help me take over Hell, and finally get the respect that you deserve."

He raised his blade, easily slicing to the side into one of her minions, effectively cutting it in half to cause ashes to fall around him like a fog. Another dove from his side and without breaking eye contact with Imenda, Jasper cut his blade to his side, the blade a mere flash of movement, as it decapitated the monster. His sword flashed over his head, landing hilt up in the head of another one of her demons as it tried to sneak up behind him, who could only get out a short cry before it finally died.

She smiled, her deceitful gaze roaming over him as his chest heaved and sweat began to bead on his body, but he barely noticed. "Simply a work of art."

He yanked the sword from the demon before it turned to dust and leveled it at her throat, the demon's acidic blood still dripping from its blade. His teeth ground together and he saw his gaze narrow in what he was sure was his dragon fighting to be free. He could already taste her blood on his tongue, feel her helpless screams as she begged for mercy.

And he would give her none.

"I will kill every last demon under your command and I don't care if it is before or after you die. But your death will be the one I savor," he growled,

"I will enjoy watching you suffer and beg for a mercy that I will never grant you."

Imenda tsked under her breath, studying her flamed fingernail as though she were bored, but he knew better. Rage, pure and unadulterated, was seething below the surface, betrayed only by how hot the flames around her grew.

"You will see." She looked to see Emeline tearing into the demons around them, focused on surviving. "That little elf may mean something to you, but you will never be anything to her. Soon enough, you will see what I already do. We were meant to be from the moment we met, an epic romance that never really died. And because of that, you will never get up the guts to kill me, slow or otherwise."

He cut his sword through the air, narrowly missing her cheek before she ducked to the side and turned, landing a punch to his cheek. His head jerked to the side, her fire burning into his skin to form an open wound there, and he could feel the skin sizzling and bubbling.

Imenda stepped back, swinging her arms as though she had already won.

"We will meet again and you will see," she taunted, her voice grating on him like nothing else ever had.

With a wave of her hand, the demons left disappeared, leaving Ana and Wynter to stumble forward from their blows, unprepared for the retreat. Imenda winked at him with a smile and rose into the air before she disappeared from view.

Emeline's glow dimmed until it was gone, and she looked at her hands in shock, the color fading from her cheeks.

"How did I do that?"

Ana clasped her hand on the elf's shoulder, with a triumphant smile. "Seems your trigger is anger, my dear."

Jasper turned sharply, his cape swinging behind him, as leftover anger colored his words red. "We will leave. Now."

Without waiting, he swung Emeline into his arms to cradle her there, wanting, needing to feel her, safe and unharmed, against him, then took off into the sky.

Ana and Wynter exchanged a confused look and a shrug before they followed.

Jasper dropped to the front of the palace and set Emeline down gently before storming ahead of her into the grand hall, his intentions clear as he left her there.

She struggled to keep up with him, confused on what she had done to make him so angry. Of course, she had knocked him unconscious and gone against his wishes, but surely that couldn't be the only thing troubling him. He had saved her, everything was alright now, wasn't it?

"Jasper-"

"Go find your father."

She blinked in surprise at his harsh tone and stopped to stand in the center of the room, watching helplessly as he didn't break his stride.

"Jasper," she whispered, her heart breaking.

He continued to storm into the dark, empty hallway like he was on a mission, and nothing was going to stop him.

Ana snorted as she landed behind Emeline with Wynter just behind her, her arms crossed over her chest. "He's got such a temper, that one."

Emeline watched Ana follow Jasper before turning to Wynter with a scowl. Both stood in silence for a long time before she finally crossed her arms over her chest and heaved a sigh. The ice dragon was obviously not a fan of her or her father, and it would be hard to say what she wanted to without some kind of retort, she knew. Still, she managed to mumble a soft, "Thank you for coming to save us."

"I wasn't coming to *your* rescue," he said sharply, nodding his head toward where Jasper had disappeared to. "I was coming to his." He shifted his attention to her from the corner of his eyes, amusement flickering over the icy blue depths. "But you are welcome."

She almost smiled at his reluctant acceptance of her gratitude but refrained.

Wynter blew out a sigh after several awkward minutes had passed in silence and shifted from one foot to the other. "You are probably curious about what just happened, and to stem any interrogation you might give him when he doesn't need it, I guess I should probably tell you the grueling tale." He paused as though considering his words, or, knowing him, perhaps his actions.

"Imenda and Jasper used to be a couple," he said softly. "She betrayed him by turning her allegiance to Lucifer during the Dragon Wars." He gave a shrug when Emeline looked at him in shock and continued, "He thought they were going to fight together, to rid the world of demons forever, but she was working for the devil the entire time, right under his nose. When a band of her demons came for Jasper, they pretended to capture her, too. According to him, she put on quite a show, screaming and hollering, like she was truly frightened for her life. It wasn't until after his captivity that he discovered her lies."

Emeline stared into the dark hallway once more, sadness for him making her wrap her arms around herself. How dreadful, how painful, it must have been to love someone so deeply, only for them to betray him.

It was no wonder he was reluctant to have anything to do with her, romantically.

Realization hit hard, and her lips parted as she put a hand to her stomach. "Imenda tortured him, didn't she?"

"She claimed that she had no choice," he said with disgust, his eyes distanced as he glared at nothing in particular. "But she did. Lucifer promised her everything she could have ever wanted in exchange for the information that only Jasper could give them about the dragons."

Emeline licked her suddenly dry bottom lip and swallowed back tears. "Did he break?"

"No," he said grimly. "And he is a hero for it."

"Then why do you give him such a hard time about being king?"

Wynter gave her a hard stare, his arms crossed over his chest, and she shivered as a cold frost began to waft from his wings. "Because he is not mentally stable enough for the job. Even if he loves his people, even if he is the bravest of us all, why would the people want someone who wants nothing to do with them?"

She glowered at him and copied his stance, unyielding. "Well maybe if they weren't so busy condemning him for his heroism, they would discover exactly why he chooses to hide in his palace instead of living amongst them."

Wynter narrowed his gaze on her as though he had found himself a new enemy. "They fear what they do not understand, Emeline. Just as you did when you discovered your dragon side. You tried to run from it, too afraid to find out more about it, because it is dangerous, frightening, and unpredictable." He shrugged again, but more frost began to dust the floor beneath him with snow. "Jasper never told anyone but me and Luke about what happened, though I imagine Fate knows now too."

"Fate?"

He snickered, but no humor emerged with it. "Right. You are a newbie, I must have forgotten. Fate is a person, one of the only purely good souls in existence, who was chosen to make the choice between life and death when no one else could. She could see the past, future, and present of whomever she wants, so long as she could touch their timeline. A warrior to the end, even if she did find peace in her own way." He rolled his eyes and then shut them as though pained. "Though I only just recently learned of their secret from him, so I am afraid you may not be privy to that information just yet."

Emeline gave a nod, dismissing the story. "Not something I need to know right now."

He gave a corporal nod, back to business, as his gaze hardened. "Good. Because anything else you need to know will have to be earned."

Her brow furrowed. "What?"

His arm shot out and she gasped, ducking on instinct, as his blow waved above her.

He smiled, pride in his eyes. "Nice move."

"I'm not completely helpless," she retorted as she stood.

"Could've fooled me."

She scoffed. "My father taught me *some* things to defend myself. Elves may be peaceful by nature, but we aren't stupid."

"Speaking of," he said with a sigh as he began to stride away, "you need to go find your father."

"Wait," she protested. "I should have earned one answer!"

He wiped his palms on his pants and grinned, his perfect white teeth gleaming in the waning sunlight as he paused. "Shoot."

"Why do you have such disdain for elves?"

His grin faded into a frown and he stepped back again, the amusement gone as though it had never been. "Because elves were supposed to heal Jasper," he said sourly. He leaned in closer, his eyes holding a soft blue glow to them, and ice began to build on her arms from the frost emerging from his wings. "Look what good that did him."

Her brow furrowed and she rubbed her arms. "But even the deepest cuts should have been healed with elven magic."

He snorted, leaning back so the harsh wintry magic was replaced with the natural warmth of the palace, and strode to the steps off to the side of the main room to disappear upstairs, leaving her alone with more questions than answers.

Chapter 15

Ana caught up with Jasper as he strode angrily down the hall, just about jogging to keep up, and sighed from beside him as she matched his steps. After catching her breath, she finally said with sarcasm, "*So*, that was dramatic."

"Not now, Ana," he growled, fists clenched as he found his way to the training arena, taking the steps two at a time. If he didn't work out his frustration on something soon, his dragon would cause more damage and chaos than he ever could, and he couldn't allow that.

"But Imenda is a worthless bitch," she insisted. "You can't listen to everything she says as though she speaks the truth. She's insane, remember?"

He grit his teeth, his mind flashing to Imenda once again. Even as a demon, she had caused his heart to clench painfully, as though she held it in a vise. His love had long since diminished for her, but she had been the only woman he had imagined having a normal life with, the only one who loved him, even as tormented as he was. Often, they had spoken of creating a family, building a house on one of the outlying clouds, and finally finding peace where they had found happiness.

Until, that is, she had chosen to side with Lucifer.

The weight of her betrayal always stabbed him worse when he had seen her, and this time had been no different. That she seemed sincere had changed nothing, and her mind, having, no doubt, been warped in her time in Hell, showed just how far away she had gone.

He felt strongly for what they used to have, for the fierce and witty, beautiful woman he had once loved so dearly, but it had been a long time ago. The dull ache may still ebb, but he knew her better than she thought he did. The lie that she had fed him until she could get what she really wanted wasn't going to dissuade him from realizing who she truly was.

Ana looked at his face with raised eyebrows, and then rolled her eyes. "I heard what she was saying through our link, even though you were trying to keep me out, you know." She stepped in front of him, nearly causing him to topple over her before he could stop himself. "She isn't right about Emeline, Jasper. That elf really cares about you; she doesn't fear you like the others, no matter what you've done to prove otherwise."

He narrowed his eyes to glare down at her, his nostrils flaring in his rising anger. The last thing he needed was more anger, but if she kept her mouth running, he wasn't sure how much longer he could keep his beast in check.

"Ana, I'm warning you. Get out of my way and leave this alone."

She pushed at his chest to make him stumble back as he tried to sidestep her, her strength surprising him enough for him to fall back a step. She glowered at him, fisting her hands at her sides, and preparing for whatever fight awaited her.

"No. No way," she snapped. "You are a coward, Jasper Rogue." Ana gave him a disgusted once over, then wrinkled her nose as though he were the most pathetic man she had ever seen. "This isn't the hero I have heard so much about. This is a cowardly man who is too afraid to take what he wants for fear of rejection." She leaned in closer to snarl, "Absolutely pathetic!"

He whipped his arm up faster than he could think, but Ana grabbed his arm, flipping him over so that he landed on his back with a grunt, his wings caught beneath him.

Hands on her hips, she placed the toes of her boots near his temples and glowered down at him, eyebrows raised with disappointment. "You taught me to fight starting with that temperamental move, did you really think I wouldn't anticipate it?"

He curled his middle and his feet met her abdomen, propelling her backward with the motion and she grunted as she hit the wall.

He stood, fists clenched, and smoke wafted like a cloud around him, showing the glow of his eyes against the dim interior of the training area. "I taught you what you needed to know to survive," he grit out between clenched teeth. "You will remember who your superiors are, and respect my boundaries, or the consequences will not be in your favor."

Ana shook the stars from her gaze and stared, wide-eyed, at him in surprise. "I've never seen you like this. Temper tantrums, anger, on the verge of losing all the carefully erected control you always seem to have. It's all because of her, I know it, and it's time you admit that to yourself before you lose everything."

He closed his eyes and rubbed the bridge of his nose with one hand to stay the migraine growing. Even if he did admit to wanting her, even if he allowed himself to feel for her, it wouldn't be wise. Emeline was beautiful and soft, a true angel in his world, whereas he was rough, damaged, and dangerous. She was pure and sweet, without being weak and helpless, something so tantalizing that it drove him mad.

The memories of their kiss flooded him and a sigh blew from his mouth. That kiss would forever haunt him, leave him craving something more in a way that not even Imenda could. The softness of her lips, the taste of her, it was like a drug, one that he knew he would be wise to avoid, but one that he craved every second of every day that he was around her.

Ana stood and studied him, tilting her head. "Something happened?"

He dropped his hand from his eyes and dropped it with a soft clap on his leg. "You really aren't going to leave me alone unless I knock you out, are you?"

Ana smiled, a hand on her hip. "As if you could get that far."

He swung his arm but she held her hand up and magic shot him into the wall, pinning him with his arms and wings out to his sides. "Nice try. But I want to know now, more than ever, what is making you act so crazy. Admit it to me, Jasper."

He jerked at his arms but they didn't budge, her magic stronger than he had given her credit for.

She leaned to one side, her hand on her hip, and raised an eyebrow in disbelief. "There is only one way out of my magic. Answer me," she added firmly. "Tell me what has gotten you so twisted in knots, and why you just went from seething and foaming at the mouth to daydreaming."

"I kissed her, alright," he snapped, giving a jerk on his arms. "Now, release me!"

Her hands flew to her mouth in surprise. His arms dropped suddenly as he pulled them free and he stood, dusting himself off, and avoiding her gaze.

"Oh! Didn't she like it?"

"Yes," he snapped, agitated. He ran his fingers through his short hair and inwardly cursed himself for being so awkward. "No?" He shook his head and rubbed his face with his hands with a groan. "I don't know."

A laugh escaped her but she sobered when he looked at her over his hands, murder in his eyes.

"So go kiss her again!"

"When she's no doubt figured out my tarnished past? No," he said firmly. "Besides, it is safer for her if I keep my distance. She deserves more than I can give her, and one day, she will understand that."

"But-"

"I am finished," he snapped. "You got your answers. Allow me to train my soldiers in peace, or I will lock you in that cage down below, as Luke did, for a century, and I will even find a way to bind your voice so I don't have to hear you."

She snapped her mouth shut and watched as he strode away, her glare practically burning a hole through his shoulders.

Navi paced Emeline's room with his hands clenched behind his back, nervously awaiting the arrival of his daughter. How angry she must be at him, how hurt, but surely she would give him a chance to explain. But would she accept his apologies or his explanations?

The door creaked open before he could find an answer, and he froze, eyes wide, as he anticipated whoever was on the other side.

Emeline peeked in around the door and he let out the breath he didn't know he had been holding.

It seemed as though everyone was on the side against him, hating him for one reason or another, and knowing it wasn't one of them coming to threaten him seemed to make breathing easier than he had ever known it to be.

"Emeline," he breathed in relief as he pulled her into his arms, stroking her hair. "Thank heaven you're alright!"

She eased away from him, giving him an uneasy look, as she backed a couple of heartbreaking steps backward.

He dropped his arms and licked his lip with a nervous sigh. "Emeline-"

"I had a right to know," she said sharply. "I should have known about this world, about where I had come from. I should have been trained like Ana to fight and to defend myself, and the people I cared about."

He shook his head. "You deserved a normal childhood, Emeline, and that was what we fought so hard to give you. If you had known, you might have told someone, and you and your mother would have been in terrible danger, can't you see that now?"

She gave a nod. "I do, but I am old enough now to understand that I should have known."

"We had to protect you," he said firmly. "You are our daughter. We couldn't allow the angels or dragons to steal you away from us and do heaven only knew what to you. As it was, the demons know of your presence now, and somehow knew how to track you. We had to cast wards over you everywhere we went or they would have found you."

Her jaw dropped and she stepped backward. It felt as though a huge weight had landed squarely on her chest, making it difficult to breathe. "That's why we moved to that wretched place in the mortal realm, isn't it? The demons never wanted the elves, they only wanted me," she said in disbelief. "They found out about me and attacked our people for try-ing to protect me. Imenda found out about me," she added gravely, her voice thin as she balled a fist to her mouth, bile rising in her throat.

He gave a sad, regretful nod. "Demons fight for the throne all the time, even if it is only for their level of hell, but only the most powerful dare try to take it from Lucifer. I guess Imenda is the first demon brave enough to venture above the surface to challenge Lucifer."

She shut her eyes as the sounds of her people's pain, of their suffering, echoed through her mind, and tears hovered at the edge of her lashes, struggling not to fall. Such good people turned demons for relief, all for protecting one of their own.

"Those elves-"

"Were willing to sacrifice their lives to protect you," he finished for her as he held her to him. "It was known that demons could not get their hands on you, or there would be dire consequences, even if they didn't know why."

Her brow furrowed and she stiffened. "I thought they didn't know about me."

"They didn't," he replied. "But they knew you were special. We could all feel your strength from birth, and we knew that the elves would cherish it."

"Did you know about Imenda?"

"I only knew a demon knew about you, because your mother felt it. If a demon knows about someone as special as you, Lucifer usually knows it, too. Doesn't he?"

She shook her head. "I don't think so. Not from the way she spoke."

He looked down at her trembling hands and urged her to sit on the bed, concern dotting his brow. "What happened, Emeline? Did they hurt you?"

She took a breath and told him about the bar, hell, and, finally, Imenda. When she had finished, he watched her as she stared at her hands inside of his.

"I'm glad you are safe." He tilted her chin up to meet his gaze and studied her carefully, squinting his eyes. "What else is troubling you?"

She looked startled, and the trembling in her hands grew. "What do you mean?"

He smiled. "I know that look, darling. Your mother and I shared one similar when we were sure we wouldn't be able to make it."

She shook her head with a scoff. "Nonsense. Aside from a demonic ex of Jasper's seeking my death, nothing is wrong."

"Emeline," he said firmly in a no-nonsense tone.

She sighed, shifting on the bed uncomfortably. "Father, I," she paused, hesitating. "I kissed Jasper last night."

He gasped, delight in his eyes. "Oh?"

She moved her saddened gaze to the window as gray clouds began to gather, further darkening the skies around the realm of the dragons. "He doesn't want me. He is avoiding me; he won't even look me in the eye, and when we returned, he was so very angry. I thought sure fire was going to come up from his feet when he left me in the front hall."

He chuckled. "That may have very little to do with you and more to do with him, dearest heart. Perhaps it is *he* who is afraid of *your* rejection."

Confusion furrowed her brow and she turned back to him. "My rejection?"

"You are a powerful, beautiful elf," he said with a smile. "Maybe he believes he is not worthy enough for you or that you will forever fear him as a beast."

Her eyes glowed white as her gaze hardened, and his smile widened.

"Oh my stars," he said in wonder. "You are your mother's daughter. Anger and the white light."

"He is not a beast," she said angrily.

He chuckled, patting her hands. "I know. I never said that was what I thought, but it seems to be what he thinks."

She licked her lips, then gave a nod as the glow faded. "You're right."

"I usually am," he said with a soft snicker.

She sighed. "So what do I do?"

"Do you care for him?"

Her attention moved to the door, as though she expected the man in question to stride through them any moment, then back. "Yes."

"Then chase him," he whispered conspiratorially.

She hesitated, her mind somewhere far away, as she thought it over. Finally, she smiled, kissed Navi's cheek, and raced through the door.

Navi looked to the ceiling with a saddened smile. "That's our girl."

Chapter 16

Emeline hurried down the hallway, getting more and more lost as she went. She knew how large the palace was, had seen its grand towers during her time in the city, but she had thought that she had already figured her way around.

Apparently, she had been mistaken.

Finally she stopped and looked around the hall for a window, just for a glimpse of where she was, but there were none. Turning back, she tried to make her way back to where she had started, but she didn't remember that, either.

An entire, extraordinary palace without a single soul roaming the hallways, no one to find her when she had foolishly gotten herself lost.

She sighed and leaned on the wall.

There had to be a way out.

Emeline rested the back of her head on the wall as her thoughts traveled back to the way Ana and Jasper had spoken in her mind while down in Hell. It stood to reason that dragons must have been linked, somehow.

Maybe if she could just reach her mind out, use her dragon's mind to touch theirs, someone could find her.

She closed her eyes and tried to push her mind out to someone's, anyone's, but nothing was forthcoming. All she heard were her own thoughts as she scolded herself for thinking she would pick up such a skill in so short a time.

"Lost?"

Emeline's body jolted in surprise, and then again when Ana leaned on the wall across the hallway, her eyebrows raised. The witch pulled out her dagger, the golden hilt shimmering in the lights from above, and studied the blade.

Emeline put a hand to her chest and asked breathlessly, "How did you know?"

"You kissed the king," Ana said sharply, pointedly ignoring Emeline's question. She began twisting the tip of her dagger against her finger, then tracing the sharp edges as though it was the most interesting thing she had ever seen.

Emeline watched, both fascinated and nervous, as Ana played with her dagger, and it struck her, how innocent it seemed, and yet so threatening at the same time.

"I didn't know he was the king at the time."

Ana snorted, her amusement as plain as the darkness in her eyes. "What difference would that make? A man is a man, no matter his title or form."

Emeline give a slight incline of her head to agree, darting her gaze between Ana and that wretched dagger in her hands, wondering what the woman was getting at.

Ana pushed off the wall, sheathing her dagger at her hip, and instead toyed with her fingers. That, and the menace in her eyes, made Emeline wonder if magic would begin to twirl intricately between Ana's fingers.

"You have him all kinds of twisted up inside, you know."

Her eyebrows rose in surprise and butterflies took flight in her stomach as a slight smile curved her lips. "I do?"

The ex-demon rolled her eyes and snorted. "You can't tell?"

Just like that, the butterflies dropped heavy into the pit of her stomach, and she frowned. "How do you know that isn't for Imenda's reappearance?"

Ana rolled her eyes again with a sigh, as though she were dealing with an unruly toddler. "I'm going to punish that boy for talking the next time I see him, temperament or not." She raised an eyebrow and gave Emeline a onceover. "Jasper has no interest in rekindling a relationship with that she-devil, I can promise you that. I mean, did you even see her? Do you know *why* she might be a little crazy and dangerous?"

Emeline shrugged nimbly. "Not really. She betrayed him, not the other way around, so why would she come after either of us?"

Ana snorted. "Well yes, she certainly was the one in the wrong, but he gave her a punishment that I know only too well." She paused, frowning as though lost in her thoughts, then said sharply, "He personally put her in Hell to suffer for her sins."

Emeline thought on that, then shrugged. So what if he had put the demon in Hell? Imenda was horrible for betraying her love for power. Only the worst villains would do that, and Jasper, with his kindness and strength, had never deserved the horrible things she had done to him. And how he hid himself because of it…

His scars were nothing to be ashamed of. He should have been proud to stride through town, his honor and integrity in place as his people praised him.

"From where I am standing, she deserved it," she muttered.

"Ah," Ana said on a sigh of pride, finally giving in to something other than her protective attitude. "There is that spark."

"Spark?"

Ana smiled wide. "That little dragon in you that is just waiting to come out and play."

"How do you know so much about dragons," Emeline challenged. "I thought you were a demon or a witch not too long ago. Based on your flying skills, I would guess you haven't been a dragon long enough to know all of this."

"I *was* a witch," Ana said, her smile faltering. "So I am your best chance at understanding what is happening to you."

Emeline remained quiet.

Ana shrugged, tugging her dagger free to play with it again absently. "When I became a dragon, I felt the fierceness that dragons often feel, the strength and the bravery. At first it scared the hell out of me." She smiled, beginning to pace away and back. "Well, not literally. You can take the girl out of hell, but not the hell out of the girl and blah, blah, blah." She landed the sharp tip of her blade over Emeline's heart. "You have fight and bravery within you, you just need to learn how to trigger it."

Emeline shook her head. As fun as the conversation was growing to be, she had other things she had to do first.

"I don't have time for this, Ana. I am looking for Jasper. I need to talk to him."

"So you can play damsel again," Ana snapped. "So he has to save your sorry hide again from demons?"

"I saved myself last time," Emeline snapped. "I didn't need his help."

"Yes, you did," Ana continued. "If he hadn't burst in when he had, you would be demon bait or something much worse."

Emeline swallowed hard, remembering the terrible sounds of screams as souls were tortured. Had Jasper not come to save her when he had, she would likely belong to Imenda, hers to torture for all eternity.

"Alright, so maybe I needed him."

"And you shouldn't have," Ana scoffed. "You are half elf, half dragon. You are stronger than you realize, even if you do hide it behind a cowardly façade. It's in there somewhere, waiting to emerge, so buck up."

Emeline pushed off the wall, glaring at Ana, as her patience grew thin. "I do not understand anything about this world or its people. Dragons are far different from the elven people I was raised around, and I only just found out that I am one of them. I wasn't born into it, I wasn't trained like you were."

"So let's train," Ana said, dangling her dagger as placed her arms out at her sides. "Hit me."

"I don't think-"

"Good, don't," Ana interrupted with a wicked smile. "Hit me or I will hit you."

Emeline hesitated.

Before she could react, Ana swung her arm out and hit her hard, the blow slamming into Emeline's cheekbone hard enough to crack bone.

Emeline fell backward to the floor in shock, gasping with a hand to her cheek as she gaped at the woman. Had she just…?

Ana nudged her with her foot. "Get up already, I'm bored."

Emeline pulled her hand from her cheek and backed away from Ana when the ex-demon put her dagger against her nose.

"I said get up."

Emeline stood, hands up, as the dagger grazed down her cheek, then her throat before she backed away. "Ana, please stop this."

"I'm a demon," she said smartly with an arrogant shrugged. "I'm not going to be reasoned with. So get a spine and make me stop."

Emeline looked at her hands, then shook her head, defeated. What kind of dragon was she, if she couldn't defend her own fears?

"No. I don't know how to fight outside of what my father taught me."

"But you do," Ana said fiercely. "You were ferocious with your ability to destroy the demons in Hell, I saw you. It is in your mind, if you just trust the dragon within you to show it to you."

"Dragon within me?"

"It is as much a part of you as you are of it," she said with a curt nod. "Trust it to rise up to protect you, to give you the strength to be brave."

Emeline reached deep, looking for the dragon that hid within the depths of her soul. After several seconds, something began to stir within her, something dark and fierce that rose as she called to it as though it yawned, awakening. When her eyes opened, her hands were lit with white, and the mirror across the hall revealed the white glow around her eyes.

Battles, both won and lost, flashed through her mind, and she suddenly wanted to fight, wanted to find the demons responsible for hurting her people, and rip them apart. She wanted to feel them struggle once her white fire slammed through them, disintegrating them from the inside out.

Without warning, Ana struck, and her dagger cutting through the air for Emeline's throat, To her surprise, Emeline grabbed Ana's hand that held the blade without looking away from the mirror, her movements a blur, and twisted, spinning Ana through the air to the floor. Ana shrieked and slammed to the floor with a grunt, her dagger skittering down the hallway.

She looked down at Ana with a raise eyebrow, confidence and pride shining through her as she smiled. "I see what you mean about trusting the dragon within me."

Ana laughed, dropping the back of her head to the floor as she caught the wind Emeline had knocked out of her. "I'm going to like you."

Emeline held her hand out to help Ana up, the glow still strong, and smiled. "I think I'm going to like you too, once I get over how annoying you are."

Ana shrugged delicately. "One of my many wonderful attributes, really."

The glow faded until it disappeared but Emeline felt the courageous beast within her thrumming through her like wildfire, the power simmering beneath the surface as though waiting for the next chance to strike.

"I can still feel it."

Ana chuckled, picking up her dagger. "It is simply you, Emeline. A part of you that was dormant until you felt that anger for anyone who had hurt someone you loved. Your dragon half simply rose to protect you, as it has likely always done."

"I want to learn more," she said eagerly, intrigued.

Ana crossed her arms over her chest and raised her eyebrow, reminding her a little of Wynter when he was at his most arrogant. Finally, she said, "I *could* teach you to fight, but I think you know where you can learn the best techniques. And maybe get closer to a certain *hot*-tempered dragon," she hinted none-too-subtly, with a wag of her eyebrows.

Emeline's eyes widened, reminded of her objective before Ana had interrupted. This was her in!

"You're right! Thanks, Ana!"

She took off down the hallway, her dragon now ready to track down her destination, as she hurried to find Jasper.

Before the massive wooden doors, Emeline hesitated, toying with her fingers as they fisted. The last time Jasper had seen her, he had strode away, angry with her, and clearly in no rush to see her, since he hadn't sought her out. Perhaps he didn't feel the same way about her anymore. He could have decided that what she had done was a betrayal and changed his mind about her.

And what if he was still in love with Imenda?

She shook her head to rid herself of the questions that plagued her and called on any of the confidence she had felt before as she pushed the doors open.

Low below the palace, the training room was at least the size of a football field, with pillars on other side of the room and gray stone on the others. Clouds blocked the view from the city like a wall and the dome ceiling was decorated with gold and diamonds. The floor was dirt with scorch marks outlining the arena and weightlifting areas along the outskirts. A boxing ring was at the other end with gloves hanging off the corners, and punching bags were placed in the corners of the room, waiting for the first strike from one of the dragons who trained there.

Across the room, she saw a lone figure beating the largest punching bag she had ever seen, and her heart clenched in her chest. No one else occupied the large space, no voices filled the air, just the sound of his labored breathing and his powerful blows as he struck. If he hit any harder, she wondered how far the punching bag would fly.

She moved across the room slowly, careful to keep her feet quiet on the floor as she moved, so as not to disturb him. As she drew closer, she heard his grunts and heavy breaths and could smell the sweat as it poured off him. A hooded men's shirt sat on a bench with a water bottle beside it, and she realized as she drew close that only his wings hid his bare torso from her hungry gaze. He hit the bag with black, fingerless gloves protecting his knuckles, but many more hits and even those gloves wouldn't stop a finger from breaking.

She stood behind him for a moment to appreciate his muscular back and traced the scars with her eyes that danced up onto his wings, shining in the sun that shone through the clouds into the otherwise dark interior.

He stiffened and stood straighter, then turned slowly to face her, and for a split second, panic moved across his eyes, but was quickly replaced with something hotter, something darker that touched her in places she hadn't known existed.

"Emeline," he said deeply.

Her lips parted as she looked down his powerful chest to the light dusting of red hair that traced down to the waistband of his pants and swallowed hard. For a reason she couldn't name, images came, unbidden, of her lips against the scars that danced down his torso. She would take her time, tracing the fine line of hair to its origins with her tongue, and taking him in her mouth for a taste, as he groaned and tangled his hands in her hair.

Jasper shifted from one foot to the other, uncomfortable, and she took in the scars dancing over his skin, glaringly white against gold. Though others feared them, she couldn't stop seeing them for what they were. Symbols of his strength, a reminder of everything he had been through, and it made her want him even more.

"Emeline," he said with strain, his pupils dilated. "If you don't stop looking at me like that, I cannot be held responsible for my actions."

Her tongue flicked out to lick her lips and he turned away sharply, grabbing the towel at his feet to soak up some of the sweat on his face. His motions were stiff and she frowned, studying him curiously.

What had she done this time?

Chapter 17

"What is it, Emeline," he barked out impatiently, keeping his back to her.

If she continued to look at him that way, he wasn't sure how much longer he was going to last. Her gaze, hot and filled with desire, for *him,* was enough for him to forget the world around him. All he wanted was to feel her beneath him, writhing and crying out his name as he brought her to orgasm, again and again.

He scowled. There would be no touching of any kind, he would make sure of it. Among those who hadn't seen him since the war, he was admire for his restraint and resolve, yet this one woman was tearing it to shreds inside. It took every ounce of his strength not to turn to her, not to take her mouth in a kiss full of promises he wasn't sure he would be able to keep.

From the corner of his eye, he caught Emeline as she toyed with a lock of her hair that had fallen from her braid, the shorter strand easily winding around her finger. How he wanted to feel the silken strands around his own, to tangle his fingers there as he kissed her, tasted her, *devoured* her.

"Ana suggested you might be able to help me understand being a dragon better. I…"

She trailed off, leaving him to reassemble his thoughts once more. So that was it, then. He should have felt relieved, should have jumped for joy that she understood the dangers of being with a man like him, yet disappointment buried itself deep in his heart.

It's better this way.

He let go of the breath he was holding and forced himself to roll his stiff shoulders to ease the tension there. If she wanted to learn more about her dragon side, then Ana had been right, for once. There was no better teacher than Jasper, and she had sought him out to learn, just as she always had.

Finally, he turned to face her, gripping the towel in his hand, and braced himself.

"What do you want to know?"

She nervously rubbed the back of her arm, and even the motion made him watch her fingers trail up and down, heating him. Desire beat through him and he imagined those fingers on him again, as they had been before. He could still feel her finger tracing the scar on his lip, see the fascination she had, even right then, in it.

The way her tongue rolled against it, like a delicious treat she couldn't get enough of.

"Why doesn't anyone know about dragon shifters?"

He shrugged, pushing the thoughts from his head as he frowned. "It is against the rules set forth by demons, dragons, and angels long ago. The living cannot grasp the concepts of the Afterlife, and free will is big up here. Knowing what is on the death side of the world tampers with free will, and everyone must be held accountable for their actions."

She shifted her attention to the cloudy walls and, after a long pause, she moved over to touch one, her delicate fingers wafting through the warm air. When she turned back, her smile was brilliant against the sun as it shone through, sending warmth through his heart. Even that smile was making his heart skip a beat, and it made him want to smile with her, but he resisted.

Barely.

"Why can we stand on the clouds?"

"The clouds are simply a part of us," he said, tossing his towel back on the bench. "We become part of the world once again, which means the clouds accept us onto them. Dragons discovered this long ago, and, to keep us safe, we built our home here, in the lower level of the clouds, where the angels rarely travel."

"Do angels really exist?"

He chuckled, tugging his hooded shirt over his head. "Yes."

She intertwined her fingers into the mist as though fascinated, but sadness swam in the depths of her eyes, despite her neutral tone.

"How did you become a dragon shifter?"

He stiffened again, his heated thoughts brought to an abrupt halt, and he frowned. "Why do you wish to know that?"

She gave a start at his harsh tone and looked up at him apologetically. "Oh, I didn't mean to pry. I just wondered, since you said the others died to become shifters."

A few minutes passed in silence as he watched her stare into the clouds, uncertain of what to say. Should he tell her of his origins? Perhaps it would be better to keep his personal life to himself as much as possible. She had made it very clear from the start that she had no intention of staying in the city and building on the connection they already had wasn't going to change that.

Still, he had agreed to help her learn more about the dragons, and given his origins, it would lend credit to what he told her.

He started toward her slowly, tugging the hood on his tank over his head, as he watched her damnable fingers toy with the mists that seemed to cling to her, urging her to never stop stroking them.

"I didn't die," he said finally. "I was the first born dragon shifter to ever exist, many centuries ago."

Her golden gaze met his, surprise and intrigue in the depths. "Really?"

He gave a sharp nod.

"Kind of like me," she murmured, a smile playing on her lips. Her eyes became downcast, as though she thought she had spoken out of turn. "Well, not exactly."

He stepped in front of her, gazing down at her as she avoided his gaze.

After a pause, he finally asked gently, "May I ask you something?"

She gave a gentle nod, her gaze meeting his, and he felt like a truck had slammed into his chest, making his heart stop and restart once more.

He licked his lips and rubbed at his nose as he shifted from one foot to the other. "Why are you not repulsed by me?"

Her eyes widened as though he had surprised her with the blunt question, and her smile turned into a frown. "Why would I be repulsed by you?"

His eyebrows rose as if to say, 'Really?'

She blushed, her heated gaze locked onto the scar over his bottom lip. "Because I see who you are underneath the scars." She turned to fully face him finally, abandoning the clouded walls to give him her full attention, and reached her hand up to trace the scar that ran from his eyebrow to his jaw. His hands trembled with the urge to pull her into his embrace, to kiss her as though there were no consequences, no dangers, no barriers keeping them apart.

"I can see the bravery, the courage," she murmured, watching as he let her touch him, reveling in the feel of her fingers on him. She smiled sadly as she watched her fingers follow the ridges of the scar, tantalizingly slow. "I can see your pain, your anger over what happened to you, over what is happening now. Yet somehow, underneath it, you are kind and just to everyone around you, regardless of how they treat you. It's beautiful to me. *You* are beautiful to be," she added in a soft murmur.

He closed his eyes and leaned into her touch, craving more of her. When her hand settled on his cheek, he couldn't stop himself from pressing his lips to the base of her hand, nipping at the skin there. His tone was ragged as he breathed her name, "Emeline…"

Her lashes fell to half-mast and she bit her full bottom lip, making him ache to take her mouth in a kiss. He wanted to feel their surrender together, giving in to their desires, and finally let himself feel passion and affection for a woman who cared for him as a man despite his beastly appearance.

He gently took her hand off his cheek, his hand trembling, and held it in both of his, his voice soft and pleading, but firm as he told her, "You cannot do this, Emeline. You cannot keep tempting me. There are dangers, restrictions, to being with a man like me, ones that you don't yet understand."

Her golden eyes were like molten honey, breathing yet more desire into his body, and his raging arousal was driving him mad. All common sense and reason was hanging on by a thin thread, one that was very close to snapping, if he didn't convince her to stop now.

Instead of shying away, she stepped closer still to him, her flowery scent making his blood heat in his veins, as her toes nudged against his.

"I can't help it," she whispered.

Her gaze rose to his once more and he was lost. His hand tightened around hers and a soft growl rumbled through his chest. His dragon called out for hers as though it, too, could sense her desire, could feel how much she wanted him, and fought against Jasper's wishes.

He frowned, cursing the dragon within him, and he forced himself to step away from her. Everything in him protested and rebelled, demanding that he take what she so clearly wanted, yet he managed to drop her hand, and immediately missed the contact of her soft fingers wrapped within his own.

With every ounce of energy he could muster, he stepped back again, trying to shake his need of her from him, yet still, he trembled. He wanted to go to her, to stop himself from rejecting her, and let the consequences be damned.

Dammit, this was only getting harder!

"Please go," he grit out sharply.

"But-"

"Go, Emeline," he said firmly, his dragon raging inside of him for freedom. "This…we can't do this. I'm not a safe choice for you, and I cannot bear putting you in danger like this."

She quickly caught up with him, grasping his face in her hands even when his own hands rose to grasp her forearms. Whether to push her away or pull her closer, he couldn't be sure, but the contact frayed whatever remained of his reasons for not taking what he wanted.

"I am safe with you," she insisted, her breathing beginning to grow heavy. She bit her bottom lip and, with her forehead on his, she looked up at him. Every desire, every feeling she had for him was written there, in her eyes, begging him to see it, to want her as badly as she wanted him.

"I want you," she whispered, nuzzling his nose with hers. "Only you, Jasper."

His carefully and revered control snapped at her proclamation, her tone too hot, and, before he could stop himself, he let out a growl, his dragon roaring inside his mind in triumph. He caught her jaw in his rough grasp, his thumb on her chin as he tugged her mouth open, and slammed his mouth onto hers, tasting, devouring, demanding everything from her.

In that moment, he knew he had never had any control over his desires. He had only been putting off the inevitable, staving off his hunger for her. And now that he had her, he knew he would never be able to let her go.

Fire raced down Emeline's spine as he took over her mouth, his desire infectious as he took control of the kiss, making her feel needy, desperate for him. His arms came around her, pulling her into the line of his body, and she gasped, the sound short between one breath and the next. The moment their bodies touched, she let out a moan and settled her arms around his neck as she rubbed against him, unable to stay still with the tension that strum through her.

Jasper tangled his fingers in her hair, holding her against him with his free arm as though to keep her from running away, and she felt her stomach clench, as another rush of passion ran through her. She clung to him as he did to her, just as determined that she wouldn't let him stop, wouldn't let him think long enough to pull away.

His leg slid passed hers, urging her back a step, and the cool surface of the pillar behind her touched her back, drawing another excited breath from her. His thigh nudged between hers, pressing against the swollen, damp spot that she needed touched most, and she groaned, long and loud. Unable to remain still, she wiggled her hips, rubbing against him and tugged at his shirt, already impatient to lose it.

Her lips pulled from his to trail down his throat and her tongue flickered out at the hollow there, the salty taste of his skin addictive. His fingers sank deeper into her hair, pushing her gently but firmly to him, and moaned when she licked the long scar that ran the length of his throat. Silken strands from her newly-loosened braid tickled her face, but she ignored it as she continued to lick and nibble at him.

She pushed his hood back and he groaned as she nibbled on his collarbone, all rational thought long gone. He buried his face into her hair as he murmured her name over and over again, the sound warm and soothing, like a caress that pleasured her senses every time she heard it.

He pulled her back so she looked at him, breathing heavily with loose strands of hair waving with every exhale. Her lips were no doubt red and puffy from his harsh kisses, the same heated desire lit his eyes as she was sure was in her own, and it felt as though the heat of him was going to set her aflame.

He moved in to kiss her throat, his hands on either side of her head, as he trailed down to the swell of her breasts, then his tongue traced beneath her bra to touch her nipple.

Like electric, her back arched and she released a cry, her hands bunching on either side of the pillar for support, as she rocked against him. He pulled on the thin material of her shirt and it easily split to her ribs, the sound echoing through the room, and he groaned before he took her mouth in a sharp, hungry kiss.

Yet, it wasn't enough. Jasper wanted more from her, he wanted to feel her around him, hear her cry out his name and beg him for more. There was too much between them, too many clothes that needed to be taken off and thrown away so he could feel her skin on his own. So she was bared for his hands, his lips, his tongue on every inch of her.

Bad news, boss, Ana said into his mind suddenly, jarring him.

He growled in denial, sinking his tongue into her mouth for another taste, and bunched his fist in her hair again. Ana was not going to steal another moment with Emeline away from him. He wasn't about to let go of what was his, not now, not ever. Lucifer could be standing in his front hall, and still, he wouldn't be able to stop himself.

Not now. Handle it, whatever it is.

Emeline drew in air in surprise when he suddenly lifted her, his hands on her thighs to hold her around him, and he laid her on the mat behind the punching bag, out of sight from the main door. Settling between her thighs, he rubbed against her center with a muffled growl into her shoulder, and a moan dragged from her lips as she arched to meet him.

He kissed down her throat again, unhooking the front of her bra so her breasts spilled out into his hands. His thumb rubbed over her hardened nipple, and she whimpered, squirming anxiously. A groan rumbled through his chest and he ducked his head when she gave a mew of encouragement, suckling first one nipple, then the other into his mouth. Her back arched and her fingers threaded through his hair as her breathing grew ragged, her need as great as his own.

Jasper, I wouldn't interrupt if it wasn't important. Or time sensitive.

His gaze narrowed and his wings stiffened as he ignored Ana, pushing her out of his mind with a sharp mental shove. Satisfied that Ana was locked out, he continued his exploration down Emeline's stomach, relishing in the way her muscles quivered beneath his lips, then tugged her pants down to her knees, baring her most intimate part to him. His blood heated in his veins and he nibbled on the sensitive skin of her abdomen, drawing more desperate moans from her. Her fingernails dug into his shoulders, urging him on and he hissed in a breath as he twitched against her thigh. His arousal demanded he take her now, that he stop the exploration and teasing, and finally take what he wanted.

Don't make me come in there, Ana snapped, pushing back into his mind.

Jasper stiffened, his lips just a couple of inches from her, and grit his teeth, his dragon roaring with frustration.

If you do, I will rip out your throat, he warned.

Well, what if Imenda has come here seeking the very elf you are kissing?

His eyes snapped open and he shot to his feet as though Emeline was aflame, his glare narrowed on the doorway as though Ana and Imenda stood before him.

"Dammit," he muttered.

Chapter 18

Emeline lay still, dazed with desire and tried to catch her breath as she processed what had happened. One moment, he was kissing her senseless, driving her to the edge of her control, the next, nothing. Just a minute more, and she knew she would have given him anything, would have promised him her heart and more if it meant he would finally give her what she craved.

When she caught her breath, she hurriedly pulled up her sweats and tugged at the torn edges of her shirt, confused.

One look at his grim face and she sat up, putting her arms on her knees with a frown. "Jasper?"

"We need to go," he said gruffly.

Her brow furrowed. "Jasper, I didn't mean-"

He was by her side in an instant, the anger in his golden eyes melted, and held her face in his hand as he knelt beside her. His tone was firm when he locked his gaze with hers, keeping her hypnotized there. "You did nothing wrong, Emeline. Nothing at all."

She opened her mouth to protest, but he dove in for another earth shattering kiss, clearing her mind in an instant of what she had wanted to say. Her hand raised to grasp his wrist and he broke off to take one last look, then stood and strode from the room, his gait sure.

"Stay here," he demanded as he paused by the stairs. "There are matters I have to attend to, but I will return to you when I am done."

She gave a nod, but he was already gone.

Jasper stormed into the throne room, his gaze murderous, as it landed on Ana, who silently smiled behind her hand as though he wouldn't see. He grit his teeth together so hard that he was sure he would crack bone and made a note to strangle the witch-demon once he was through with Imenda.

Imenda stood in the center of the room, studying her nails as she waited for him to approach her, leaning on the conference table as though she hadn't a care in the world.

He stormed to her until his face was inches from hers, but it was anything except inviting, as smoke billowed from his nose.

His voice was more growl and rage than ever, his control long gone. "How did you escape hell?"

"Why, the same way I imagine the Grey brats did," she said simply with a shrug. "I have my ways."

Wynter stiffened beside Ana, but the demon-witch merely glared at Imenda, her eyes glowing a deep shade of red. Had Jasper been calmer, he might have been shocked at her lack of comment, but the witch remained silent. Still, her gaze promised a world of pain for the demon before him, and somewhere in his mind, he hoped she got to deliver exactly that.

Imenda smiled and arched her back as though inviting him in as she looked to Jasper's mouth, then back to his eyes, lust in her eyes. "So, she fell for your bad boy looks anyway, did she?" She paced away, one arm crossed over the other, then turned back with a frown. "I wonder if she knows what happened to your last great love."

"Shut up," he muttered, a silent warning, as his dragon clawed at his insides.

"Does she know that you would leave her in Hell if she angered you," she sneered. "That you have the ability to grant shifters entry into heaven or hell? Or perhaps, you decided to keep that bit of information to yourself to keep her in the dark?"

Jasper stepped forward closer, and his pupils narrowing he warned louder, "I said shut up!"

She gave a low giggle, and shook her head as though addressing a child instead of a powerful dragon king. "If only it were that simple, huh? Just demanding what you want and getting it? I wonder what it is you would wish for," she added, tapping her chin with one long, blackened fingernail. "Perhaps it would be for your little whore to finally put out for you? To not fear you because of your scars, hmm?"

Jasper's eyes glowed gold and Wynter lunged forward, catching his arm before he could tear into the demon.

"Why are you here," the ice dragon demanded, his blue eyes glowing as frost came from his wings, chilling the room.

Imenda winked at him with a smile, giving Wynter a once-over. "You are cute, and you would make an excellent side dish, but I'm looking for the main course."

Jasper growled.

Ana stepped forward, her hips swaying as her heeled boots clicked one in front of the other and raised an eyebrow as she stilled beside Jasper. She raised her chin and narrowed her eyes, every inch the confident witch, as she stared Imenda down. "Maybe you don't remember Juliet and I," Ana said quietly. "But we have a reputation in hell."

"As a demon's whore, I know," Imenda chuckled, waving her off.

Ana smiled, her fangs showing just over her bottom lip. "At first, maybe. But our powers grew during our time in captivity, but as we turned from witches to demons, our magic mixed with the power of hell. The torturers became the tortured, and we were unable to be defeated by those who had wronged us."

Imenda snorted and rolled her eyes, bored. "Oh, boo hoo."

Ana strode by the boys just as Jasper jerked free and walked her red fingernails down Imenda's chest to tweak her nose. "We have connections down there that you don't even know about, people who hadn't fully changed into demons yet that escaped, thanks to us. So let me warn you now," she leaned close into Imenda's face, her pupils narrowing as her cocky smile turned into a sneer of menace, "Back off, and go seek leadership and insanity in another level of Afterlife. You won't be getting this one."

Imenda giggled and clutched Ana's nose long enough to shake her head from side to side. "Oh, how foolish you are. I do not fear a demon's whore, and I'm not planning to take over his realm. Yet," she added with a wink to Jasper. "Right now, I have much more planned, but I will only talk to the king about those little tidbits."

Wynter stepped forward but Jasper put his hand up to stop him. "Leave us."

Ana whipped her attention to him with incredulity and she gaped at him. "What?"

"I said leave," he said low. *Check on Emeline,* he added mentally. Despite Imenda's presence, he had to know that Emeline was safe and looked after. His abrupt departure no doubt left her confused, perhaps hurt, and Ana would be the right woman to explain things to her until he was able to.

Ana scoffed with a roll of her eyes but stomped out of the room. *Fine, but I am not going far. You call me if the bitch does anything stupid, or I will be really pissed off and you wouldn't want to see it!*

Wynter looked first to Jasper, then to Imenda, ice dancing around his eyes before he reluctantly followed Ana, his frost leaving ice on the floor of the room behind him.

Once the door shut, Imenda smiled with glee. "Alone at last."

Jasper fisted his hands, the muscles in his arms twitching and tightening, as he barely restrained the urge to grab Imenda to throw her out of the palace.

"What do you want, Imenda?"

"You," she said simply.

He snorted in disbelief. "What do you take me for?"

She strolled forward, her short, tight skirt following her every movement, but unlike when Emeline had been near him only minutes before, he felt nothing. Only hatred and anger, one that Imenda wasn't taking into consideration as she approached him like a seductress.

"A handsome," she paused to run her hand up his arm, her gaze softening as she traced a few of his scars, "fierce man in need of some true darkness to match his own."

He didn't move, glaring down at her.

She smiled again, removing her hand. "You still love me. I know you do, otherwise I would be dead by now. You want me," she taunted. "Look at how uptight you are around me. Are you imagining me in the throes of passion as you used to?"

"I have never, nor will I ever, love you," he ground out.

She giggled, the sound echoing off the ceiling and walls. "If you think that little trollop will fulfill whatever it is you think you need, then we can always keep her. Maybe I could even enjoy myself with her," she added coyly. "She is very beautiful, even for an abomination." She leaned her back on his chest, tracing his scars over his chest with a long fingernail. "When your obsession has finally faded, we can kill her together."

Magic moved from Imenda's finger to him and images, unbidden, rose in front of his eyes, showing him and Imenda ripping Emeline apart as she screamed horribly, begging for mercy as Imenda laughed with glee.

He blinked it away and his hand whipped up in a blur, grabbing her by the throat tightly enough for her to gasp. "You ever touch her, and I will make sure your death is slow and torturous!"

Imenda laughed despite her struggles to get free, her feet dangling below her, and she rasped in a singsong voice, "I know how to fix your scars."

Jasper froze, his hand tight enough around her throat to nearly break her windpipe in half, as he considered her words.

She choked and he dropped her in a heap on the floor as he stepped away, only for her to begin laughing. "You are so predictable. One mention of getting rid of what makes you beautiful, and you are willing to lay down and play dead." She stood and dusted herself off, then began to walk in a circle around Jasper. "Just think of it. No more worrying about how fearful your people are of you. Respect and admiration on their faces for their handsome, dashing king."

She touched the back of his head, bringing images again only this time, he saw his people applauding him as he walked down the street, smiles abound. Pride swelled in his chest as he received the praise he had always wished for, but the vision continued. At the end of the street stood Emeline, all in white, a brilliant smile on her face as he approached. Her pride matched his own, and she looked eager to see him, as she laughed with unrestrained joy.

"Emeline won't have to hide her beauty from the world with you," Imenda's voice resonated through her vision. "She can proudly stand by your side, and everyone will know you have claimed her as your own, the true queen of Dragon City. Imagine it," she added on an awed whisper.

He shook his head to dislodge her vision from his mind and his eyes narrowed at her. "Enough with your games. What do you want, Imenda?"

"If you come with me," she murmured, "I will rid you of your scars. Come rule by my side, and we can take over hell, take Lucifer's powers, and you can keep your people here safe from anything that can come out of Hell. I forgive you for throwing me in Hell, by the way," she added, dipping a finger between her generous breasts as lust returned to her blackened gaze, "I was a bad girl and I needed to be punished for my actions, but we can overcome our past for a much more brilliant future."

"If you think I will fall for your tricks again, then you truly are insane," he snapped.

"Insanely crazy about you," she sneered. "Emeline will never love you as I do, Jasper."

A sharp pang ran through his chest and his knuckles turned white in his fists. No matter how Emeline felt for him, he would take it. Anything she would give him would be a gift, and if, when this was over, she wanted to leave, he would let her. He would not allow Imenda to color their time together

Yet, even as Imenda had said the words, he knew deep down that she was right.

Emeline was the most beautiful woman he had ever seen, but her beauty was only the tip of the iceberg to him. She was kind, smart, and strong-willed, even if she didn't quite believe in herself as he did. No one had been more selfless and passionate as she had been, and every time she showed even a sliver of her true self, he could feel his heart skip a beat. She had him twisted up inside, and he couldn't get enough. No one, not even Imenda, had looked upon him as Emeline had. With compassion, and de-sire, but also awe. For centuries, he had only ever been looked upon with hatred and fear, but with Emeline, it was different. She cared about him, re-gardless of his appearance.

He frowned. But one day, she wouldn't be able to stomach the sight of him. She'd grow to re-sent him for hiding away from the world, to hate be-ing stuck behind closed doors, because she loved people. Emeline was a curious mind, an intriguing soul who would need to be out in society, to wish for friends and family to be close by, while he wished to remain in the shadows, without judgment. To live a normal life, it had to be that way, and even with the light in Emeline's soul, his darkness would ruin her.

And if his anger ever got the better of him…

He scowled. He would rather die then join Imenda in Hell, but the demon was getting into his head, and he glowered at her. "What is this? Some kind of trick?"

"No, no trick," she said with a smile as she chewed on her thumbnail. "Perhaps a distraction from what I am truly doing, but the offer is very real, Jasper."

A soft cry, muffled by the distance, made him shoot his attention to the closed doors and he took off at a run, his heart pounding in his chest. *Emeline!*

Imenda laughed behind him, her laugh grating beneath his skin. "It's too late, Jasper. My brother Tucker has her by now, and I heard he was very intrigued by her back at the bar. I do wonder what he might do while we wait for your decision."

Jasper stopped at the doors and a dragon's growl laced his words. "When I come for you, and I will, your days are numbered."

"Sounds kinky," Imenda said with a wink before she vanished.

"Jasper," called Ana as she approached him. "He's got Emeline and Navi," she said from the top of the stairs. "Tucker took them both!"

Chapter 19

Emeline woke up with a start, her eyes darting around the cold, stone room. From the musty smell and the high, narrow windows along the top of the room, she could tell it was a cellar, the view across the ground dimmed by the gray clouds outside. Tingles ran down her arms from her hands bound above her head, and her feet were braced apart with cuffs that attached to the floor. A cloth gag with a knot in the middle was tied behind her head, holding her mouth wide open, but muffling her cries.

She heard a grunt from the side of the room, and her gaze darted across the darkness, yet she couldn't make anything out. Magic dimly surged through her, and her eyes glowed, lighting the room enough for her to see Navi bound to the wall by dungeon-like cuffs that held him flat to the cold stone. He was shivering even as he woke, rocking his head back and forth, and she gasped when she saw the bruise on his forehead, a trickle of blood dripping down his face.

She shrieked to get his attention and he jerked awake, his eyes bloodshot.

"Emeline!"

She pulled on her bindings, then gave a start when a door from above opened with a slam. Light spilled down onto the floor, making her squint, and it filtered down the stairs as whoever it was strode slowly down the steps, purposely prolonging his appearance. His boots clunked against the wooden stairs, the sound ominous in the thick, silent room.

Tucker stepped to the bottom step and smiled at her cruelly.

"You weren't kidding," he said behind him. "It really is her."

"I told you," Imenda said as she followed behind him, peering over him at Emeline. "And if she behaves, maybe we will return her to the elves with her father. After all, from what I've heard, that's all she wanted to do anyway."

Tucker came closer to her and she pulled on the ropes, fear charging through her, but he grabbed her cheeks anyway, puffing her lips out around the gag. His eyes roamed down her torn shirt and back to her with a grin. "Nicely built, I see."

"Let her go," Navi shouted, jerking against his cuffs.

Imenda slapped him hard enough to jerk his head to the side. "Shut up! You are only here as incentive, so don't test me."

Emeline's skin crawled as Tucker hooked a finger around the torn neckline, peeking inside her bra, and his finger flickered over her skin. "This is going to be very satisfying, little sister. Such an exquisite gift you have given to me."

Imenda leaned her arm on Tucker's shoulder and smiled at Emeline, her expression cruel. "This is my brother, though I suppose you already met him." She waved her hand as she spoke, tossing the introduction aside. "So here is the deal. Jasper is too obsessed with you to see reason, and I can't take him as my king with you in the way, but I can't really kill you either. Wouldn't win me points with the man that I love."

Tucker held her face hard, causing tears to spark in her eyes, and she cried out as her cheekbones threatened to break beneath his grip. "So you're going to share a kiss with me and we're going to send the images to Imenda's boyfriend." He tapped his head. "Mentally. Like a vision, only in photo form."

Emeline's eyes widened in horror and she gave a jerk, bumping her body into his.

Imenda laughed as Tucker's hand ran down her side. "Aw, she likes it." She looked back to Emeline, narrowing her eyes. "With his heart broken, he'll have to come to me for comfort. And oh, will I comfort him," she cooed. "I cannot wait to feel his hands on me again. That man is a *hell* of a lover, though I suppose you wouldn't know that. Then happily ever after. Power, love, and revenge, all in one neat little package!"

Tucker pulled the gag from her mouth, then traced her lips roughly with his thumb. "Beautiful lips. I wonder what someone could do with those lips."

"I would never kiss a traitorous snake like you," Emeline snapped, jerking her face away from him. "I would rather die!"

Imenda put a finger over her lips as she pretended to think it over, then she pointed to nothing in particular. "See, I think you would. Especially if it saved your dear old father from demonic torture."

She whipped a hand behind her and Navi writhed on the wall with a shout of pain, the screams becoming more intense with every clench of her fingers. He shouted again as his skin turned red, the blood vessels beginning to burst.

Emeline gasped, jerking from Tucker's grasp and yanked on her bindings once more, desperate to get free. "Stop! Please, stop!"

Tucker shrugged. "You know what you have to do to stop his pain." He leaned close and she barely stopped herself from gagging at the smell of death on his breath. "Let's start with that kiss."

Tears filled her eyes but she looked between Tucker and Navi. Imenda clenched her fingers again and she heard a sickening pop echo through the room, followed by a tortured scream of agony.

Desperate, she squeezed her eyes shut, willing her consciousness to go away, and pushed her lips against Tucker's. Bile rose in her mouth as she let him invade her mouth, his tongue rolling against hers, and Navi's screams stopped.

A flash of magic made her stomach churn, and Tucker grabbed her braid, throwing her harder into the kiss as though she were enjoying it.

Emeline, came a pained, masculine mental roar of anguish.

She glared at Tucker as he took his time pulling away, and barely restrained her sobs from escaping her throat. "Satisfied?"

"In time," he said, running his filthy gaze down her. "But for now, that will do just fine."

Imenda smiled as she scanned the ceiling. "He's already pushing through my magic in his search for you. I forgot how powerful dragon magic is, but no matter." She pulled the pictures from her mind with her fingers, the image transparent, and they vanished in her fingers before Emeline could stop her. "We will simply expedite the plan."

Emeline watched them go and, once the door shut, she turned herself towards Navi, who was slumped in his bindings. There wasn't enough time or magic to free both of them. Imenda must have dampened her powers somehow, or perhaps the cellar itself was holding her magic back.

But why would she feel so much weaker, if the cellar was responsible?

Her eyes widened and she stiffened. Tucker's kiss. It had to be how she had weakened, but was he taking her powers? Ice seemed to flow through her veins as she imagined what he could do with her magic, and her hands began to tremble. She had to warn Jasper, and she had to save him from Imenda before anyone else could get hurt.

She looked out the window and saw clouds wafting around the grass, and relief sank into her heart. If they were still in Dragon City, then one of them could reach Jasper, tell him Imenda's horrible plan, and stop her.

One look at her agony-ridden father, and she knew what she had to do.

"You have to go tell Jasper what is happening," she whispered.

Navi struggled to catch his breath, sweat soaked into his shirt and pants, as he shakily pulled himself up. "What?"

"Tucker wasn't kissing me just for images," she said weakly, her strength waning. "He was draining my magic. He's got to be a siphon, though I thought they didn't exist until I weakened after his kiss."

His eyes widened. "How long do you think you have?"

"My elven side is already healing me," she said with a huff. "But it will take too much time. You have to go, your magic will heal you faster."

"I will not leave you here," Navi said firmly. "Not with those monsters."

"I will be fine," she insisted. "I can't leave you here, they will kill you but they need me. They won't kill me, not yet. I have just enough power to free you, but you will have to be careful not to run into them."

Magic surged through her weakened cells and she grit her teeth to hide a cry of pain. His cuffs clicked open, and he fell with a thud to the floor. Shaking his head, he rushed to the small window and found a flathead screwdriver on the sill, likely from the current or previous owners of the house. He worked to pull the screws free, then ripped the window open, letting in a burst of warm air in the otherwise cold interior. Once he was clear, he looked fiercely into the window. "I will come back for you, and the cavalry will be with me, Emeline."

"There isn't time," she said, her eyes drooping. "Just go...get Jasper...."

Jasper stared at the images before him, floating in the air like a taunting sign, and his eyes glowed red in anger, as he started punching at the walls of the entrance room, cracking the stone beneath his fists. Rage tore through him, grown from hurt, and he wanted to break anything, everything in his path. How could she do that to him? Their connection, the way she had writhed in his arms, and she threw it away for *him*?

Ana scoffed at him as she leaned on one of the pillars and rolled her eyes. "Oh, please. Tell me you aren't buying into this nonsense."

"She doesn't look as though she is fighting it very hard, now does she," he snarled. "How can I fall for the same trickery twice? How could I be so stupid?"

Ana stormed over to him and slapped him hard, the sound echoing against the dome ceiling above them. "Cut it out! Emeline would never hurt you like that, and you know it. Imenda doesn't want you back anyway, there has to be something else, something we're missing. She is working far too hard at this to simply want to rekindle a lost love interest."

He waved a hand at the images fading in the air before him as though the evidence should be enough for her. "Look at this!"

She blew fire from her lips to incinerate it, each image burning even as it shimmered. "I see it, idiot! But instead of letting your small ego rule your head, you should be angered that Imenda would force her into this! You should be out there, raging at *her*, and saving your woman, for crying out loud!"

"Then why take Navi," he growled. "There is no reason to take the old elf, he is no threat to anyone!"

"He is if he can be used as leverage," she hedged.

Jasper paused, his anger fading as Ana's logic seeped through the haze of hatred and hurt clouding his mind. With a grunt, he ran his hand through the longer strands of hair on the top of his head and shut his eyes, denying what Ana was saying even as he heard the truth in it. "What if the scene at the bar was trickery? What if Tucker and Emeline planned this from the start, and Imenda was simply retrieving her?"

"They didn't," she said simply. "Stop thinking what if and start thinking about how we're going to save your girl."

His hands fisted in his hair, and his dragon quieted, leaving him feeling empty and sore inside. "She isn't mine."

"Of course, she is," Ana said firmly. "And she is in big trouble." She held out a hand with the pictures newly formed and pointed to Emeline's hair. "Look at how tight her hair is around her ear there, the redness. And there," she said, pointing sharply, "that slight bit of skin there, that is his arm. The wrinkles by her lip, a sign of her trying to hold back vomit, and her eyes have a shimmer to them, probably restrained tears. The odds are that Imenda and Tucker hurt Navi, and Emeline, being Emeline, agreed to kiss Tucker to stop them. She is in big trouble, she needs you, and you are ready to turn her into another Imenda."

Guilt hit Jasper's gut hard and he swore under his breath. He should have known, should have seen what Ana saw, but instead, he had foolishly chosen to believe that Emeline had tricked him.

What an idiot he was becoming.

He blew a sigh of defeat and shook his head. "Where does Tucker live?"

Wynter burst through the doors, a stumbling and beaten Navi under his arm, and Wynter bellowed, "Jasper!"

Jasper lunged forward, catching Navi when he tumbled forward, and the elder elf grabbed the king's arms, staring desperately into the Jasper's eyes. His fingers dug harshly into Jasper's arm enough to make him flinch, but his anger only rose at how maltreated Navi was.

"Jasper...I...help her," he gasped, out of breath. "Save her, please save her! She sent me to get you, you have to save her!"

Jasper's gaze sharpened with determination and anger. If Navi was hurt, Emeline...

"Wynter, take him to the healers and join me at the gates." He pulled out his sword and heard Ana unsheathe hers as he said fiercely, "We're going on a demon hunt."

Chapter 20

Emeline woke with a start and her gaze darted around the room as she oriented herself. Looking up at the bindings above her, she pulled at her chains, but they held strong, unwilling to release her. She tried to find something to help her pick the lock but the room was bare, save for an old wooden table to the side.

She bit into the replaced gag as she cried out in anguish, and called on her dragon, begging her other half to rise against the threat to her as Ana had instructed. *Please, dragon,* she pleaded. *I know we haven't known one another, but I have to get free. We cannot allow these monsters to take the magic bestowed on us to wreak havoc on the world above and below us. Help me, please!*

For a long while, nothing happened, and she cursed Ana. Perhaps her dragon side was dormant, unable to rise with her elven side to save her. Nausea rose as a tear moved down her cheek. Tucker was going to take her, she knew it, and were it not for the gag, she might have thrown up at the thought of his disgusting hands on her.

With one last push, she reached deep inside of her, and mentally grit out, *If you don't come out, we'll die in here. Jasper and his people will die out there. Is that what you want?*

To her relief, magic suddenly rose through her and when her eyes opened again, they glowed gold. Pure power charged her as though she had been struck by lightning, and she felt something strong twist and rise within her, a roar ringing through her ears. Her fingers twisted as they lit and she tried to remember how locks worked from when her father tried his hand at being a locksmith. Once he had learned his trade, he had taught her, but it had been years since she had done it.

A soft click made her gasp before she fell to the floor, rubbing her sore wrists before she tore the gag from her mouth and tried to sit up, her muscles still aching. She knew that despite her magic surging through her just a moment before, it wouldn't be enough to get her out, but at least she was freed.

To get out, she would need to do things the old fashion way.

Footsteps above her made her jump and she scrambled to her feet as she stared at the beams above her. The old hardwood creaked at what she was sure were boots stomping across the floor angrily. Quickly, she bolted to the window her father had climbed out of, but it was shut and sealed with a magic that zapped her hands when she touched it.

Imenda must have seen he was gone when she re-placed the gag on Emeline and ensured the elf wouldn't escape, too.

Taking a deep breath, she slowly turned and looked up at the door as though it were a monster, waiting to attack her. Indeed, what lie beyond the door was much more terrifying, but it was her only chance.

Quietly, she made her way up the steps and listened at the door for voices.

"He should have given up by now," Imenda said with a scoff. "He sure gave up on me pretty fast without allowing for an explanation. It's like he is truly blind to what is right in front of him, the stupid man!"

Tucker's voice came next, chuckling and a glass hit the table hard enough to make Emeline give a start. "Maybe we should go a step further with the girl, then. Really get him motivated to rekindle things."

Silence met this proclamation.

He snorted. "Don't give me that look."

"You will not sleep with the wretch that stole my love from me," she snarled.

"You are no fun at all," he muttered. "Not even a little touching? Bet we could send more pic-tures, really sell the idea that she gave up the ugly bastard for a more attractive bloke like me."

Emeline's hands flamed dimly as she felt rage run to the surface, the new beast within her giving a threatening growl. *No one in their right mind would choose a masochistic bastard like you over my Jasper!*

"We should check on her," Imenda said in blatant annoyance, ignoring her brother's desires. "You never know when she might try to free herself and cause trouble."

Her eyes widened and she hurried quietly, but swiftly, down the steps, ducking below them into the darkness. The door opened and the siblings strode down the stairs, the pair confident with every step. Once they had cleared them, and made their way to where Emeline's bindings were, she carefully rounded and hurried up the stairs, then slammed the door shut with a grunt, locking it before she took off for the nearest exit. It wouldn't be long before Imenda and Tucker breached the door and came for her.

Emeline raced through the kitchen to the front door and reached for it, freedom from the lunatics so close at hand. But before she had a chance to open it, she heard shouting, then thudding against the basement door as the siblings began to slam into it for their freedom. She jumped with a surprised cry, eyes wide, and panic raced through her like wildfire, making her motions jerky. The basement suddenly jerked open, the door slamming against the wall be-side it, and she struggled to turn the knob for the front door, the lock holding with magic.

Tucker was on her before she could get away and slammed her into the door with his hand on her throat, his gaze menacing as he came nose to nose with her.

"You should have known it wouldn't be that simple."

"No but this is," she said angrily, her panic reaching her dragon enough to enrage it.

Her knee came up and connected with his manhood with a satisfying thud, sending Tucker back a step with a howl.

She gathered her magic and slammed her hands against the door behind her. As though hit by an explosion, it flew out into the street and she took off at a run, her bare feet scraping harshly against the cobblestone road. She had to get to Jasper, had to feel him near her, promising to keep her safe like he al-ways did.

Just as she turned a corner toward the palace, Imenda appeared in a puff of smoke, and Emeline bounced off her, stumbling back in surprise with a gasp.

The demon frowned at her, arms crossed, and her blackened eyes turned red with hatred. "Did you really think you could beat both of us?"

Tucker came up behind Emeline, his run awkward, and Imenda smiled, but no amusement reached her gaze.

"Lose her, did you?"

"Yeah," he snapped.

Emeline shook her head, desperation hitting home. There was no way could she stomach the thought of being brought back with them, not after she had tried to escape their house of horrors!

"You don't need me," she tried, reasoning with them.

"Oh, but I will need a refill," Tucker said crudely as he stepped closer, his fists clenched at his sides. "And I think I know just how I'm going to get it this time."

A loud roar drew their attention upward and Imenda smiled as she cried out in joy, "Here comes my love!" She looked to her brother, her smile fading as she demanded, "Hide her. Put her where Jasper can't find her."

Emeline opened her mouth to scream out to Jasper but Tucker slapped his hand over her mouth, lacing his arm through her elbows from behind to hold her hostage as he pushed her into the dark alley-way beside them, out of sight.

Jasper slammed to the ground in front of Imelda, his fist punching the stone hard enough to crack it. Wynter and Ana landed behind him as he stood slowly, his glare terrifying, and the gold glowing around his eyes. His hood was behind his head, showing him as the man he truly was to any onlookers, regardless of their reaction.

"Where is she," he demanded.

"I don't know what you are talking about," Imenda said, studying her fingernails.

Ana put her hands on her sword, glowering at her. "Cut the crap. Where is Emeline?"

"Oh, did she run away already? That's too bad."

Emeline jerked and struggled in Tucker's hold, making it hard for him to hold her as the dragons fell out of sight for them. She tried to scream for Jasper, to yank free, but was no use, as Tucker's strength far surpassed hers.

Tucker kicked his knee under hers and she gasped as she started to fall, then he spun and pressed her into the wall. "If you want your idiot king to see you as the whore you are, by all means keep struggling against me. Give me a reason, Emeline."

She froze, eyes wide and a tear slid down her cheek. This was happening, and there wouldn't be a thing she could do about it. It would break Jasper's heart that she had been right under his nose, yet he didn't know it until it was too late.

He smiled, looking her over again like a trophy. "I should just take you right now. Imenda never has to know it, and I'll be quick."

She jerked in his grasp and he groaned when her hand hit his stomach. "Just a little lower, sweetheart."

Her heart reached out for Jasper, wishing for his arms around her, his fierce protection, his warmth.

Jasper, she sobbed, reaching for him in her mind. *Help me.*

Jasper came up from the basement of Tucker's home and slammed the door to it as he exited the small house, nearly shaking the house in his anger. "No sign of her."

"I told you so," Imenda bragged. "I said he was gone."

He narrowed his gaze on her and knew from the over-confident look in her eye that she was lying. She knew where Emeline was, but she was keeping her hidden somewhere. If Tucker touched her…

A sharp connection breached through his mind, the fear nearly destabilizing him, and he stiffened, scanning the new connection in his mind for possible threats.

Jasper, help me. Please, came a soft cry along the connection.

An ache filled his heart and rage turned his blood into pure fire. He lifted his sword and put it to Imenda's throat, bearing his teeth at her. "Tell me where she is and I will end you quickly, if she is unharmed."

Ana's ear twitched, and she shifted her gaze to an alleyway as though searching for the source of the noise. At the smallest hint of movement, she nodded toward it and said softly, "Jasper, over there."

He shifted his gaze and when he saw a flicker of movement, he pulled his sword from Imenda, shoving her to Wynter. "Kill her if she does anything stupid."

Wynter grabbed Imenda's wrists, holding them tighter than he needed to, and gave a confirmed nod. "Gladly."

Jasper stepped closer to Ana and followed her to the alley she had indicated. "Are you sure?"

"Yeah," Ana said, her voice low.

At the far end of it, Tucker was fumbling with his jeans as Emeline stood pinned to the side wall with his hand around her throat, and tears on her face.

Jasper threw his sword with all of his strength, his rage uncontrollable, and it cut clean through Tucker's side and into the wall behind him, leaving him hanging there with a grunt of pain.

Ana drew closer to the demon and bared her teeth at him as blood trickled from his mouth, his breath jerky. "Don't worry. Your sister will be locked up right beside you soon enough."

His body slumped, eyes frozen open, but he didn't move as his final breath escaped.

Emeline turned and ran for Jasper's arms. "Jasper," she whispered in relief. "I tried to escape, I-I tried to be brave so I could find you, but he drained my magic and-"

Streams of white wafted from Tucker to Emeline and she gasped, back arching as she froze just inches from him.

Jasper's eyes widened in alarm as he held her in his arms and looked to Ana. "What is this? What is happening to her?"

"Her magic," Ana said grimly as she studied the streams. "Most of it, from the looks of it. Must have been from that forced kiss of his," she added sharply, giving him a dirty look for disbelieving her.

"A siphon," Jasper said in annoyance. "I didn't think they existed anymore."

The streams ended and Emeline gasped as her stiffened body relaxed into his arms, and she looked at her hands as the scrapes there healed. "Well, that will save me healing time later."

He held his hand out behind her for his sword and Tucker's body gave a jerk before falling with a thud to the ground, his sword dislodged as it flew through the air to his hand once more.

A scream made them turn toward Wynter as he held a crying, struggling Imenda upright as she screamed again over the loss of her brother.

Emeline tucked her head beneath Jasper's chin, her eyelids drooping. "I-I think I'm going to…"

Her eyes suddenly closed, and she fell limp in his embrace. Jasper swung her up into his arms gingerly and nodded to Ana. "Send the body to Lucifer and inform him of Imenda's actions. I want them both punished for this offense by nightfall, even if it means threatening a war to do it. No demon harms one of ours and lives."

Ana shook her head adamantly. "No way!"

"Take Wynter with you," he said firmly. "He won't let anyone take you back for good, you have my word."

Ana hesitated, then gave a nod. "Fine. But if I am not back in two hours, send someone to get us. Oh," she added sarcastically, "and you owe me big time!"

Jasper gave a nod and extended his wings as he pushed off the ground, leaving Imenda and her terrible brother behind him.

Chapter 21

Emeline, freshly cleaned and dressed by her father, lay quietly, asleep in her bed. Her white, flannel nightgown warmed her skin, and the neckline outlined the swell of her breasts under the blankets as her chest moved calmly up and down with her breaths.

If not for the trauma she had just endured, she would look like a peaceful angel, asleep and safe, but Jasper knew better. She wasn't safe, not yet, not until word of Imenda's punishment reached the palace from the devil himself.

He sank onto the bed beside her, tucking her hair behind her ear. His hand lingered, his thumb stroking her cheek. If not for Jasper, her life could have been different. He could have defeated the demons without her seeing him in the mortal world, and placed the elves back in the immortal realm, where they could hide better, but instead, he had foolishly brought her here.

Had foolishly begun falling for her, the woman he could never have, but wanted the most

"You don't have to keep pulling away from her, you know," Navi said from the doorway.

Jasper turned back to the elf and frowned, the pang in his chest making him rub the spot there. "She deserves better than me, and she will be better off without me putting her in danger like this. A woman like Emeline deserves extravagance and grace, adoration even, from the people she lives around. That's nothing I can offer her," he muttered.

Navi sighed. "You are too hard on yourself, son."

"Not nearly hard enough."

Navi smiled and shook his head. "You care about her, and that's enough for both of us."

Navi pushed off the wall and braced his feet shoulder width apart. "Even though, she isn't a fighter like the other women in this realm. She never has been, even when I tried to teach her some fighting moves her mother taught me, but I think her dragon is. Otherwise, she would not have been able to escape. How is that possible?"

"Dragons can gain the knowledge learned by their parents," he said softly, returning his gaze to Emeline. "If her dragon can fight, it learned it from her mother, perhaps even while in the womb."

Navi scoffed. "It must have, indeed. But what are dragons, really?" He sat on Emeline's other side, kissing her cheek, as he held her hand. "An extension of you and your kind, Jasper. It is a set of magical qualities that make us who we are. And I should have told her about them long ago," he murmured.

Jasper shrugged. "I understand why you wouldn't."

Navi looked up in surprise.

Jasper almost chuckled at the expression but suppressed the smile. "I feel the need to protect her, too. I am sure as a child, she was much harder to protect due to her curious nature, but you did what you had to do."

Navi smiled. "Thank you. I appreciate that."

"I remember Sarafine," Jasper said softly. "She was kind to me, even after my return from the war. I have no idea how any demon could slay such a mighty warrior, but if there is anything I can do to help find justice for your family, let me know."

"I appreciate that," Navi said, tears in his eyes. "But it was a long time ago. I am not interested in vengeance anymore. She wouldn't have wanted that for me, or her child." He sniffed, blinking back tears, then managed a small smile. "Can you help her?" At Jasper's sideways glare, Navi quickly said, "If she could learn to fight as Sarafine did, maybe hone the skill, she could protect herself from here on out. Perhaps that would put your mind as ease as well," he added gently.

Jasper paused long enough to come to a decision, then gave a nod. "I will do what I can. The dragon in her likely remembers the moves she learned. It is simply her allowing the dragon to be-come a natural part of who she is."

Emeline stirred and Jasper stood, staring down at her as he knew one would look upon an angel. "I will leave you two."

"Nonsense," Navi said with a sniff and he placed his hands on his knees to help him stand up. "She will want to see you when she wakes."

Jasper's brow furrowed as Navi made his way to the door. Why would Emeline wish to see him, after everything Imenda had done to her?

Navi winked with a grin. "She cares deeply for you, Jasper. Give yourself, and her, a chance to see if something could come from it. Don't decide what she wants before she does, either. She is a grown woman," he said fondly, watching her start to rub her eyes. "She knows what she wants and it appears to be you." He smiled, patting the side of the door jamb as he shut the door. "

"How thankful I am for that," the old elf said before it shut.

Jasper's brow furrowed.

Navi certainly was a strange, if ominous, one.

A soft sigh pulled him from his musings and back to the woman who so entranced him since the moment they had met. For just a minute, a small passing of time, he considered Navi's words. Could Emeline care for him as he cared for her?

He imagined a life with her, of their children and a family where kindness and passion were a way of life, not a wish that would never be granted. In that moment, he knew that he would give her anything she desired. Surprise struck hard as he realized that he would open the palace to his subjects, if it made her happy. Even if it meant hiding in his own home, it would have been worth it to see her smile and laugh with his beloved people.

He would have moved the sun and stars for her, if she only just wished for it to be so.

Emeline smiled when she saw him, eyes bright with joy as she turned onto her side with her hand under her head, and the warmth in her gaze nearly undid him.

He leaned on his hand beside her, careful not to touch her, lest he should be tempted to touch her again, to feel her soft skin beneath his fingertips, and hear her passionate sounds of pleasure.

"Hey," he said tentatively.

"Hey yourself."

She toyed with a loose thread in the blanket, her finger entrancing him as it twisted in the string like it was a toy.

"How are you feeling?"

"Still a little shaky," she said, her smile dimming. "But I think I will be fine."

He let loose the breath he hadn't realized he was holding and met her gaze again, forcing himself to focus. "Imenda is imprisoned in our dungeons. She won't be causing any more problems ever again for you. She is awaiting to hear of Lucifer's punishment for her, but I promise you, it will be a fierce one."

Emeline's free hand slipped over his, her trembling fingers threading through his. "I don't want to talk about Imenda or her terrible brother," she said softly. "But thank you for saving me. I really thought he was going to…"

She trailed off with a shudder, and the color drained from her cheeks.

Instantly his hand moved to her cheek stroking the soft skin there. "Never. Don't even think it," he said firmly. "I would never allow such a thing to happen to you. Especially you," he murmured.

She sucked her lip into her mouth and smiled slightly, releasing it as she whispered, "Why especially me?"

His strokes slowed and he tugged his hand free of hers as he frowned. "I think you know why."

Her frown mocked his and she sighed. "Why do you fight it? I know you feel the connection between us, even now."

"There is no connection," he insisted.

Her lips parted as she gaped at him. "Of course there is."

He turned away, leaning with his elbows on his knees. Even if he wanted to give them a chance, she would be safer without him. He knew one day, she would grow to hate him for hiding away from the world, for keeping the shame of being tricked by a woman he thought he loved in the shadows while she thrived in the light. No matter what he wanted, her needs had to come first.

And she needed someone else, someone better.

Anger rose through him at the thought of another man touching her, of another man kissing her, loving her, building a family with her.

His dragon roared and thrashed in denial within him, *Mine! No one else's!*

She pushed herself up on her elbows, her dark hair cascading down her arm, and tempting him. "I do not fear you, Jasper."

"Perhaps not," he agreed softly. "But you will one day grow to resent me."

Her brow furrowed. "What makes you think that?"

"Your love for your people does. The fact that you love being at parties and being kind to everyone you meet tells me that." His gaze found the wall behind her, unable to see the hurt in her eyes anymore. "I cannot give you the chance to live among my people. I cannot go out into the town without fear or condemnation following me, and it would follow you, too." His gaze finally fell to take her own, losing himself in the warmth of her golden gaze. "You would learn to hate my existence."

She sat up and he jerked back only to inch closer, to feel her breath on his lips, and he felt hot and hardened all over again as he had been at the arena the day before.

"I could not ever hate you," she murmured. "I think I could help you, if you wished."

Her hand rose and she traced the largest scar on his face, from his brow to his jaw. The old wound burned and itched, causing him to flinch but her gaze held his, reassured him, as she said. "Trust me. Please."

Trust. Such a simple word when it came to Emeline, and the way her gaze beseeched him, begged him to trust her, made him nod. He endured the burning ache her magic caused, wanting to trust her more than he had anyone else.

When her fingertips met the bottom of the scar, she smiled at him with pride. "There. Now go to the mirror."

He tilted his head curiously and she laughed. "Go on then."

He gave one last odd look, the sound of her joy breaking a smile from his lips, then stood and made his way to the dresser, leaning his tall frame to look at what she had done.

The scar had vanished.

His eyes widened as he touched his newly healed skin. He glanced at her in awe, and she gave a small laugh, her smile brilliant. For him? For his joy?

Another missed heartbeat, a beat he had taken from his life to give to her as he hadn't for anyone else before.

She gave a soft chuckle, toying with one long strand of her hair. "While I was…out, I gave thought to what Wynter had told me."

He stiffened and turned, arms crossed arrogantly over his chest. Wynter was trouble, and anything he said needed careful consideration. "What did he tell you?"

Her cheeks flushed. "He told me what Imenda did, and how much it hurt you. He said the elves tried to heal you but they couldn't get the scars to go away. Then Ana said-"

"Her, too," he seethed, grinding his teeth together. Neither of them had the right to share his life with anyone, especially Emeline. "The both of them will be punished for this."

She shook her head but smiled. "If they hadn't told me what they did, I never would have figured out how to heal you."

He gave that some thought, then waved his hand for her to continue.

"Ana told me that the dragon lived within me and was a part of me. It occurred to me that perhaps elven magic and dragon power could combine to heal your wounds fully, as they should have been healed when you were first injured."

"You figured this out on your own?"

"For you," she said shyly.

He strode to the bed and sat down, holding out his wrists with the scars that wrapped around them like constant reminders of his torment. If she could heal him, he needed to feel a part of himself disappear, healed by the only woman who could do it.

"Try again."

She leaned back on the pillows and splayed her fingers wide with her middle finger slightly below the others. Tracing her middle fingers around the scars, Jasper's eyes widened in amazement as they disappeared where she touched them. The ridges smoothed even as they burned and itched, vanishing before his eyes as though they had never been.

To be healed, to be able to go out to see his people without shame, without condemnation, meant he could have Emeline. If she so wished it, he could give her everything she wanted most.

He could finally get what he always wanted. Love, laughter, family.

Normalcy, in an abnormal world.

When she was done, he touched his wrists with an awed nod. "You can heal me," he insisted. "Please, do so, now."

She shook her head, leaning heavily on the pillows with a wince. "There are too many, and healing takes more energy than I have right now."

He frowned as guilt moved through him. How selfish of him, asking her to heal his scars when she had only just recovered from her ordeal. What she needed was rest, perhaps something to eat, not a king pushing her past her limits.

She ran her hand down the side of his newly healed face and smiled. "I wasn't trying to guilt you, only inform you. Elven magic is not limitless like many others are. We draw from the earth, only I think I could channel magic from my dragon but that will take time to learn how to do."

"There's your limitless supply," he quipped.

She laughed. "I guess you're right."

She dropped her hand and sat up further. "Jasper?"

His gaze met hers, a fiery look that struck them both. "Yes, Emeline."

She stared at his lips as she tucked her hair behind her ear. "I wish to kiss you."

He felt like a starving man being offered water as he fisted his hands to keep them to himself. Confusion seemed to be a way of life for him as he went back and forth on what he wanted to do next. Give her what she desired, or keep her safe from his enemies, from the life he led?

"You shouldn't, Emeline. You should seek out a better man than me," he added, his dragon growling beneath his words in denial.

She ran her hand over his, the tiny scars on his knuckles vanishing. "I don't want any other man," she said firmly. "I want you."

Chapter 22

Jasper's lips snapped shut and he stared at her. Dammit, if he hardened anymore, he would tear through his pants. Had any words ever been so hot, so desirable? If so, he didn't know them, but he wanted to hear them again and again.

Decision made. Emeline would be his, if only for a short time. Any time he got to have with her was time enough for him.

She shifted awkwardly. "What?"

He didn't answer, but instead slipped his hand over her cheek to hold her face as his lips descended onto hers.

The moment his lips touched hers, Jasper knew he wouldn't be able to stop. She was sweet, intoxicating, and it made him hunger for her. Carefully leashing what little control he had left, he deliberately took his time, savoring the moment before he came to his senses about what he was doing.

Eager to feel her body beneath his, he gingerly lowered her to the bed, tugging the blankets over him to keep her warm, though he doubted that with the fire raging through his body that cold was what she was feeling.

She mewled beneath him, wiggling, and he stiffened, his arousal pressing hard against the apex of her thighs. His control was holding on by inches, his beast roaring in his head, demanding that he take her, that he claim what was his. Without breaking the kiss, he moved his thigh between hers, and her moan vibrated against his lips, drawing a growl from deep in his chest.

Her legs opened for him, allowing him to fit between them, and he felt what was left of his control slip further from his grasp as he ran his hands up her thighs to the edge of her shirt. The second his fingers touched the skin of her belly, he knew the battle for control over his desire was lost, and his kisses grew with fervor.

She arched up to meet him and moaned, digging her fingers into his shoulders, and he inwardly cursed their clothing for keeping him from what he desired most. The feel of her silken heat around him, to know that she was his, and only his, for as long as she would allow him.

He tugged her nightgown over her head and kissed down her throat. The skin there vibrated beneath his mouth as she moaned. Her hands moved to his head, burrowing into his hair, and he quickly held her wrists above her head, causing her back to arch and her breasts to brush against his chest.

The rosy buds beckoned to him, and he was helpless to resist dipping his head and encircling them one at a time with his lips to draw on her. She cried out and pushed toward him, pushing her thighs together to relieve the pressure he knew would be building there.

With his free hand, he traced her curves, her soft skin like a drug to his fingertips, and she trembled beneath his touch. He paused when his hands curved around her bottom, and she squirmed, her pupils dilating with desire. The lace of her panties pressed into his palms as he edged his finger beneath the seam of them, moving up, up, up, until he met with her damp center.

A choking sound escaped from her throat and she threw her head back, grinding against him as though she were eager to feel him slipping inside of her.

In one fluid motion, he tore the panties from her and buried his face in her hair with a deep breath. Her rosy scent filled his nostrils, and he groaned, rubbing his face into the strands before he pressed his lips to hers again.

"Emeline," he murmured against her, his hips moving of their own accord against her own.

"Jasper," she pleaded, wiggling against his fingers.

His lips curved against hers, and he finally gave her what she wanted the most, thrusting his finger inside of her.

She cried out brokenly, moving with the motion of his fingers and driving them deeper as she wrapped her thighs around his hand.

He trailed his lips down her throat, and moved down her belly, the muscles there fluttering beneath him. Her breath hitched, and he continued lower, never breaking his moves below. A roar echoed throughout his mind and he grit his teeth, grinding his hips against the mattress for relief, but he knew none would be forthcoming.

Not when what he wanted most was writhing beneath him, her whispers ringing in his ears.

He pressed a hot kiss on the inside of her hip, then down her thigh, causing her to writhe beneath him once more, as he sought to drive her as mad as she was making him. He paused with his mouth poised above her, and intentionally let her feel his ragged breaths against her damp folds.

Her eyes closed and her lips parted as her chest rose and fell with her anticipated breaths. Finally, when he was sure she couldn't wait any longer, he flicked his tongue out and licked the bundle of nerves above his thrusting fingers before taking it into his mouth to suckle on.

She screamed and arched into his mouth. He moved his tongue between his fingers to dip inside for a taste, and his teeth pressed into the nub above them instead. She shattered against him, moving her hips away from him, but he pulled her back and rode out the spasms as she came against him.

He barely allowed her to come down before he was growling and shedding his clothes as he moved over her, aligning his body with her own. Newly freed from his grasp, she caught his face in her hands and pulled his lips to hers, hungry for the taste of him once more. Her fingers brushed against the scars on his cheeks and he bit back a moan, the sensations of her fingers touching him almost too much for him to bear.

He positioned himself between her thighs, then paused in realization, straining as his arousal hardened almost painfully at his desire to be inside of her. He twitched against her, touching her as though kissed by her center, and his vision narrowed, his dragon fighting him to keep going.

"Have you been with anyone else," he grit out.

Red hot anger shot through him like a bullet, and, for a brief moment, he felt like he couldn't breathe at the thought of another touching his woman.

Mine, he thought involuntarily.

Realization struck hard like a knife to his heart and he stared down into her golden gaze, losing himself in her. He wanted this woman as his own.

Now, forever, and always, he wanted her in his life, no matter what came between them.

Her gaze skittered away and she bit her lip, as though she were afraid of his judgment, and he wanted to break something, anything.

"N-No," she said at last. "Am I doing something wrong?"

He groaned and pushed at her entrance, unable to hold back his anticipation any longer. "No, nothing at all, Emeline. I just didn't want to hurt you."

She moaned as he rubbed against her, wrapping her arms around him as he slowly pushed inside of her, stretching her around him deliciously, until he felt the barrier against the tip of him. With one powerful thrust, he broke it and though he knew that she had felt the tear, she gasped with pleasure. He filled her perfectly, their souls seeming to unite for the first time, two halves of the same heart.

He lost the leash on what little hold he had had left on his control, and he started thrusting, in and out, groaning as the exquisite feeling of her, of the dampness she had left on him each time he pulled from her. She writhed and clawed at his back, as desperate for him as he was for her.

His lips locked on hers, his tongue exploring and tasting as though he could never have enough, and his hands roughly grasped her breasts, kneading and circling to drive her even wilder. His hands grasped her ass and he drove deeper into her, his movements frenzied as he drew closer, closer still to his edge.

She screamed her release into his mouth, wrapping her legs around his hips to draw him deeper and, when he felt himself slide into her as far as he could go, he roared his. The dragon's roar vibrated through her mouth, dragging out her own release. Every nerve in his body seemed to scream with pleasure as he erupted inside of her.

For a long while, Jasper held her to his side, her cheek in his hand as he kissed her over and over, while they came down from their high.

Reluctantly, he pulled away from her, and he rested his forehead on hers as his thumb stroked her cheek, and she grasped his wrist with an adoring smile up at him.

He shut his eyes, unwilling to move away from her again, and before he could stop himself, said softly, "Don't ever leave me, Emeline."

She raised her hand to his cheek, turning his gaze to her own as she said with a smile, "I won't, Jasper. I swear, I will always be by your side for as long as you will have me."

He groaned, pressing hot kisses into the center of her palm. "Forever."

She chuckled and he turned with her in his arms. Once she had turned so her back was to his front, he thrust inside her again, drawing a surprised gasp from her. He chuckled, kissing the back of her shoulder, and knew that no matter how many times he had her, it would never be enough.

"I never want to be without you," she murmured, eyes drifting closed with pleasure.

His arms tightened around her, pulling her against his body as tight as possible, and groaned against her shoulder.

"You never will be," he promised.

Ana smiled from outside the door, arms crossed over his chest in triumph.

Finally!

Footsteps sounded behind her but she ignored them, listening to the silence that now reigned in the room. Oh, what pleasure he had brought her! And she, him!

She nearly clasped her hands together with glee, but refrained, settling for smiling again. It was about time!

Wynter scowled as he rounded the corner. "Eavesdropping? Do you want me to tell the king you know his personal life?"

She pulled away from the door to give him a look full of false innocence. "I was walking to my room and heard a cry. I didn't know until I listened what the cry was for."

He snorted, shaking his head in disbelief. "Don't give me that. You knew exactly what it was from."

"Sex," she said with a shrug, modesty forgotten. "He deserves it."

"Yeah, well, we have another problem to face now," he said grimly.

She rolled her eyes. "Of course we do. Why would we get a day off as dragons?"

He narrowed his eyes at her sarcasm, his strong arms crossing over his chest. "You don't get a day off until your earn your reprieve. Think you know that by now."

She sighed dramatically. "What's the problem?"

"Tucker is missing."

Ana laughed as she stepped away from the door and urged him down the hallway with a hand on his arm. "Tucker is dead, I watched Jasper kill him myself."

"As did I," Wynter said firmly. "But his body is unaccounted for."

"What do we care," she said with a shrug. "A missing dead demon never does anyone any good, not even for their powers. It's just a husk."

"Something isn't right," he insisted. "Tucker should have ashed when he died, yet his body remained intact. The laws agreed upon by Lucifer and the angels clearly state that any purely evil acts will result in the transfer of a soul to Hell. Demons ash style."

Ana's brow furrowed. "So?"

"So the minute he assaulted Emeline, he would have become a demon. Or at least had demon blood in his system."

"Which is why he would have ashed," she finished in astonishment. Her wide eyes met his icy blue ones. "We need to warn Jasper."

"So far as we know, it is just a missing body," he said softly. "Nothing we will need to inform the king about just yet. We will interrogate Imenda on our own and leave the king to his business."

"*Sexy* business," Ana said with a snicker.

"Don't say that," he groaned.

Emeline's eyes fluttered open a couple hours later and she stretched her deliciously sore body with a catlike smile. Today would be a good day, and she knew exactly who to thank for it starting out that way.

A soft growl in her ear, and kiss on the back of her shoulder, made her relax into him and smile with her eyes closed.

"Good morning," she said dreamily.

He chuckled. "Morning. How did you sleep?"

She shrugged as he continued his lazy kisses up the curve of her neck to her ear, gently sucking on the lobe there.

"I slept great," she breathed.

She felt his smile against her cheek as he continued to trail kisses over her. "I haven't felt like this in a very long time," he admitted softly. His hand raised from her waist to turn her face toward his, his lips taking hers in a soulful kiss that she felt straight down to her toes.

When he pulled away, she smiled, biting her lip absently. His hair, short though it was, was mussed, his golden eyes amused for the first time since she had met him. It was like a light shone through him that hadn't ever been there before, and it sent warmth sailing through her like a wildfire.

I did that, she thought proudly.

He traced the edge of her lip with his thumb as she released it slowly. She knew she had him hypnotized by it every time she did it, and the twitch of him against her bottom only cemented her belief.

"I may never leave this room again," he murmured, stealing another kiss.

"Me either."

Chapter 23

*J*asper, Ana said in his mind.

Just the sound of his name make him stiffen in alert as he waited for her to continue. Lord knew she would never shut up until he let her speak anyway, not when the witch wanted something.

When she finally did speak, he wished she hadn't. *We have a problem. Wynter and I have been interrogating Imenda all night, to some high amount of pleasure, I might add. Seriously, that girl can scream like a banshee when we-*

Ana, he snapped, his kiss to the curve of Emeline's neck frozen in place.

Emeline turned onto her back, bringing the sheet with her to cover herself. "What is it?"

He shook his head, planting a quick kiss on her lips regretfully. "Nothing you need to worry yourself about," he said. "A king's duty is never done, it seems."

She gave an unsure nod. "Oh. Okay. I should probably go check on my father anyway, so we will meet up later?"

I'd rather not leave at all, he thought to himself. Out loud, he said, "Yes, we will."

Anyway, Ana continued in annoyance, *Putting aside the lovey dovey thing you have going on there, she won't tell us where Tucker is. And believe me, it isn't for lack of trying.*

His brow furrowed as he watched Emeline stand, her bare bottom causing him to feel hard all over again, before she covered up.

Dammit, he cursed inwardly. He could already feel that bottom in his hands, the skin of her back against his mouth as he-

Ana's words suddenly registered and he scowled.

Tucker is dead.

When she bent to pick up her clothes, giving him a full view of herself, he groaned, wishing more than ever to have her before he had to deal with more demons.

And demonic charges, he grumbled to himself.

Emeline flashed him a smile and he pulled the blankets from him, standing to pull her against his hardened arousal, her bottom against him. She wiggled her hips with a soft mew and he sank deep, groaning as she clenched around him instantly, issuing a cry of her own.

"What do you do to me," he ground out, his fingers digging into her hips as he held himself as deep within her as he could.

She gasped when he turned them, nearly making her stumble, and laid her over the edge of the bed as he moved inside her, unable to get enough. Her dampness clung to him with every thrust, cooling him, only to make him hot all over again when he sank inside solidly.

Leaning forward, he toyed with her nipples, knowing how sensitive she was there, and within minutes, she was orgasming around him, moaning his name in pleasure, and matching his thrusts for her own.

When his heart stopped pounding in his ears, he leaned over her, barely holding himself up with his arms, and buried himself so deep inside her, he wasn't sure where she ended and he began. He grasped her hair in his fist and pulled her upright gently, holding her up by the waist as he turned her for his kiss.

Emeline opened her lips willingly, letting him taste her at his leisure, and moaned into his lips as he strummed her favorite spot, the nub growing harder as he touched it. She grasped his hips as he thrust in her again and again, pulling another orgasm from her, and she screamed in pleasure.

The feel of her squeezing him, holding him inside her like a vise, was too much, and he grit his teeth as he growled his own release, pounding into her with the powerful waves that seemed to crash over him.

Jasper?

He grunted and pulled away from Emeline reluctantly, patting her bottom playfully.

"Don't forget about me," he warned.

She smiled, leaning up for one more kiss. "Never."

His arms came around her, holding her to him, as he gave her what she wanted and pressed his lips to hers. "When I get back, we are going to work on speaking telepathically. There has to be a link so I can always find you, no matter where you are."

She nodded and pulled the sheet around her as he reluctantly released her. It had to be the hardest thing he had ever done, and he cursed Ana in every way that he knew how for taking him from her.

She kissed his cheek, then moved to the bathroom off the bedroom.

Jasper bent to tug up his pants and fisted his hands when he heard the water turn on in the bathroom. All those droplets, making her beautiful body glisten in the light…

This had better be good, Ana. Imenda was not to be touched, spoken to, or bothered for eternity, as per my orders.

Tucker's body is missing, Ana said coldly. *Wynter pointed out that Tucker broke the laws and when he did that, he should have become a demon and ashed when you killed him.*

Jasper's chin lifted and he stared hard at the window with a curse. *Where is it?*

We don't know, she said in frustration. *We were hoping you could get her to talk. But Jasper,* she added gravely, *we don't know that Emeline is safe. Tucker may not actually be dead. Especially if we can't find the body. He may have found a way to evade death, and the only one who would know how he could have done that is Imenda.*

I will be there. Send Wynter up to guard Emeline and Navi, he ordered.

A pause met his decree and he nearly smiled. He imagined the last thing the ice dragon wanted to do was baby sit.

He is on his way but he is grumbly, she said in amusement.

Oh well, Jasper replied.

Steam wafted from the partially open door, attracting his attention, and he stopped midway to the door, staring toward the sound.

Maybe if he just went in for a minute…

He shook his head. Her safety had to come first above all else, and he could only guarantee that by getting information from Imenda.

No matter what it took to get it.

As he descended the stairs, Jasper pulled the hood of his cape up, the torn edges brushing his legs as he stormed down the steps. His shoulders felt tense and hard, his dragon roaring in protest over leaving Emeline to speak with the she-devil herself.

No matter, he told himself. It needed to be done.

Ana leaned on the bars of the demon's cell, twisting her fingers through the air as a red mist surrounded them, and watched in amusement as Imenda writhed and cried out from her torment.

"Enough," Jasper said firmly.

Ana rolled her eyes but did as he commanded, snapping her fingers, and Imenda slumped in her bindings. "I was just having a little fun. Since she isn't going to talk to us about anything of use anyway."

Between one blink and the next, Imenda shot to her feet, glistening with sweat, and glared into Ana's face. Her fangs dripped venomously, and her knuckles were white as she wrapped her hands around the bars. "I will get my revenge against you," she spat out, her teeth clenched together and bared, "and there will be nothing that can be done to stop it."

Ana smiled, leaning a hand on the bar as she leaned closer, her eyes glowing dangerous red despite the amusement that curved her lips. "Oh, would I ever love to see you try."

Imenda sneered at the ex-demon as she stalked away.

Jasper approached her cage, his hands tightly behind his back. "I will only ask you this once, Imenda. Where is your brother?"

She spun to look at him in surprise, as though only just realizing he was there, and her gaze softened. "I knew you would come to save me," she murmured, leaning on the cage bars once more. "I knew you would come to your senses and leave the brat-"

His hand shot out before she could react, easily fitting between the bars, and grabbed her throat like a vise, the slap echoing seconds after he made contact. He tightened his grip when she opened her mouth to speak, until her eyes were bulged in panic, her hands on his hand in a vain attempt to loosen his hold, but she was no match for his strength.

His pupils narrowed as his dragon rose up, demanding blood, and his sharp fangs pointed between his lips as the beast threatened to emerge from within him. As he spoke, the growl of a dragon echoed behind his voice. "I will never choose you, you traitorous bitch. She is everything you could never hope to become, everything I could ever want in a woman, and it will always be her over all else."

Ana's gaze fell to the floor behind him, but he barely acknowledged it as Imenda struggled to breathe beneath his grip. The sound of her choking, the feeling of her pulse in his palm, gave him a thrill, gave his dragon a thrill, and he watched her struggle and plead with him, waiting for her final breath.

It would be so simple to let her die, to end all of the chaos before it started again, and to further draw Tucker out, if, indeed, he had survived somehow, but something inside of him stopped him, forcing him to drop her in a heap on the floor.

She choked and sputtered, a hand to her throat, and her gaze locked onto the floor as she tried to calm her breathing again. Silence reigned around them as she gasped and then started laughing, the sound grating on Jasper's nerves. "I don't care what you say. You still love me, and denial won't make it any better."

He grunted.

She stood, her eyes studying him and her lips parted in astonishment, her gaze narrowed with disgust. "Your scar, my favorite one that framed your face!" She reached for him but he jerked back out of her reach. "It is gone. How," she hissed.

Ana snorted. "Like he would answer your questions when you won't answer his."

"Shut up, bitch," Imenda snapped, drawing her hand back inside the cage as though he had burned it.

Perhaps he should have, he thought.

Realization lit her eyes and she burst out laughing, wrapping her arms around her middle. "Is that why you have fallen for the elf? Because she has the power to heal you as no one else has ever had? How pathetic," she taunted. "How truly sickening, to keep someone around just to use them! I wonder if your little pet knows you keep her around as your personal nurse. I wonder, do you pay her? Perhaps with something more valuable than dragon coins or jewels, my love?"

He narrowed his eyes.

Her lips parted in mock surprise and she smiled again. "You screwed her, didn't you?"

Jasper remained silent, glowering at her, as he contemplated pulling her ribs out, one by one, to see how quickly they would grow back.

"Oh this is just too good," she said, dancing in the small confines of the cage. "What happens when your scars are gone, hmm? Does she get tossed out, finally? Or maybe your use for her will be over and she will burn in hell for eternity, the same damnation you put on me centuries ago."

She traced the bars of the cage, her expression thoughtful. "I could do some fun things with a beautiful elf in hell. I have some friends who have always wanted to breed with one, and with her beauty, I could fetch a pretty penny for her."

Ana stepped in front of Jasper before he could launch himself at Imenda, her hands on his chest, and her eyes circled with red. "Listen to me," she urged softly so Imenda wouldn't overhear and bringing his attention to her. Not an easy feat when his dragon was clawing at his insides, desperate to feel the demon's skin shredded beneath his claws. "She is baiting you. Instead, you need to rule the conversation from here on out. Don't let her get in your head and cause you to do something you'll regret."

"I'm already there," Imenda said in a taunting melodious voice. "He knows what happened to Tucker, he doesn't need me to tell him."

"He's alive," Jasper said stiffly. "What does he want?"

"At the moment, your elf," Imenda mock whispered. "And boy, does he have plans for her when he gets his hands on her."

His outrage boiled over and scales broke out along his skin, his dragon releasing a mighty roar as he pushed Ana out of the way and blew fire into the cage.

Imenda alternated between screaming and laughing as she burned, the smell of hot flesh scenting the air. No matter how hot he burned her, she continued to scream and laugh as he charred her, willing his fire to finally end her.

"Jasper," Ana said urgently, placing a hand on his shoulder.

His eyes glowed as his fire turned white, the heat of his fire rising, and he ignored her, bumping her hand from him.

"Jasper," Wynter's voice boomed from the stairs.

Jasper froze when the dragon's voice penetrated his rage-filled mind, the fire from his mouth ending. Imenda's blackened exterior began to heal itself even as she chuckled to herself and though he was aware of it, it was the pair of horrified golden eyes that caught his own that stopped his heart in his chest.

His lips moved but no sound would emerge as a tear slid down her face, the same face that had been laughing with him only hours before.

"Emeline," he said softly.

She turned and took off up the stairs, the skirt of her purple summer dress that he had found for her bunched in her hands, as she disappeared around the corner of the stairs.

"And now she knows who you really are," Imenda said with an evil smile, her chest heaving as her lungs healed. "No beauty could ever love a monster who would burn his ex-alive the way you would."

Ana shut her eyes as though in pain and rubbed the bridge of her nose.

Jasper grit his teeth together to calm the rage within him, and took off after Emeline, pushing by Wynter with a rushed order. "Make it hurt."

Wynter gave a nod and slowly approached Imenda, who shrank against the wall behind her, fear rising within her eyes. He just stared at her, his face expressionless, when within, he wanted to mock her, to revel in the fear he knew only he brought to those of her kind, as he said, "You know dragon's fire can only harm, not kill demons. Yet you led that girl to believe that she will end up like you."

Imenda swallowed hard but lifted her chin defiantly. "Jasper needs to know who he really is, and so does she."

Ice shot from his hand as he whipped it toward her and her shrieks died in her throat as she was encased in pure ice that filled the cage from end to end. Mist fell from the edges of the cage, and Imenda stood frozen, her mouth open in an unending scream of torment.

Ana turned back to Wynter, arms crossed and frowned. "We need to fix this."

"I'm not sure that we can," he said sadly.

Jasper caught her as she marched through the front doors, tears in her eyes, and turned her to face him, his hand on her arm.

"Emeline-"

"Is that why there was a break in your carefully erected shield," she said shakily, her body trembling beneath his grasp.

His heart broke in his chest, pounding away in distress. "No. No, Emeline," he insisted, brushing her hair from her face to hold her cheeks in his hands. His eyes beseeched her, desperate to ease her pain, but nothing could stop the way she saw him now.

Chapter 24

"Why is she here," she asked, sniffling as she held his wrists in her hands away from her.

She wanted to believe him, of that he was certain, but with what she had just seen, he knew it wouldn't be so simple.

"Emeline," he reasoned. "She is here so we can make sure that you are safe, that your father is safe. She has the answers we seek now, and without her, there are dangers to both of you that we cannot hope to stop."

She pushed his hands from her and his heart shattered in his chest as she swiped at the moisture in her eyes. She shook her head, dodging his grasp once more. "I don't want to hear this. I can't… Please, just leave me alone, Jasper."

He grasped her arms in his hands, holding her in place. "Emeline, listen to me-"

"Is that where I'm going to end up," she shouted. "Am I going to end up like her?" She ended on a whisper, her fist moving to her mouth as a sob broke through her lips. Terror filled her eyes and she twisted in his hands as though she meant to flee.

She feared he would burn her, as he had burned Imenda, he realized, and he frowned.

He shook his head, pulling her back when she tried to step away from him again. "No. Never, Emeline. I swear to you, no harm will ever come to you, and *never* from my hand. I would never hurt you, I promise you."

"Did you tell her that too," she hissed. "Did you promise her a life with you? That she was someone you cared for more than any other?"

"Imenda is a traitor and she caused the death of many of my people," he growled, absently tracing a scar on his thumb over her arm. "You have no idea the lengths to which she would go to serve herself."

"No," she said in disappointment. "But I know the lengths you would go to get your revenge against her now. And I know what you are willing to let your dragon to do people, even those as low as Imenda!"

Shocked, he loosened his grip and she took the opportunity to turn away from him, disappearing through the doors before he could stop her.

Wynter came up from the dungeon stairs and folded his hands behind his back. "It will be several days before Imenda thaws out, unless I wish it to be otherwise. Do you want me to follow her? Tucker is out there, from what Imenda says, and he wants Emeline. It's too dangerous for her to be alone right now."

"No," Jasper said. "You will act as king until I return. Tell Navi to-"

"I heard the commotion, I will go after my daughter," Navi said stiffly as he entered the room. "If you wish to follow us for protection, so be it. But do not interfere while I speak with her."

Jasper gave a curt nod and Navi took off out the door after Emeline.

Emeline ran through the courtyards of the palace, the plants all but dead from neglect, and ducked into the tree line behind it. Clouds wafted through the trees and for just a moment, she let herself marvel at the nature around her. Green leaves and shrubs surrounded her feet, the trees stretching high into the sky as though they stood on the ground instead of on top of a fluffy white cloud.

She sank to the ground behind some bushes and buried her face in her knees, heartbroken. The dragon she had just seen torturing Imenda could not be the same man who kissed her with such sweetness, her heart had stopped beating just to prolong the moment. The same man who had been so gentle, so passionate with her just a short while before could not have viciously burned a demon and ignored her horrible screams of agony.

It didn't even seem possible.

Imenda had accused him of becoming involved with her for her magic, and he had said nothing, had not offered protest. No proclamations that he cared for her, or that she was something more to him than someone he could use and dispose of.

That she was a tool for him to use had been the first cut into her heart.

What happened when he was finished with her?

She sobbed harder, her heart breaking apart, but the tears wouldn't stop, the pain in her chest too great for her to bear.

"Emeline," Navi said from behind her, his voice sad, as he approached her.

She crossed her arms over her knees and buried her face in them. "Go away."

"Emeline," he said again firmly. "This has to be a misunderstanding, you have to know what kind of man Jasper is by now."

"No," she whispered. "I heard Imenda's cries when I came to find you. I should have known he wouldn't love me. The moment I revealed what I could do for him, I should have known that that would be why he pretended to be in love with me."

He sank beside her with his arms around her and pressed a kiss into her hair. "Love you? Does that mean-?"

She snorted, gasping in sobs even as his embrace calmed her more with every moment. "I-I think I fell in love with him. I'm such a fool!"

"You are no fool," he said gruffly, tugging her up until she looked at him with red-rimmed eyes. "Jasper is exactly the man you think he is. He is ruthless and relentless, and yes, vengeful. But honey," he said as she leaned into his chest, "he is also afraid."

Her brow furrowed. "What would Jasper have to be afraid of?"

"You," Navi chuckled. "You are beautiful, untouchable. From what I've gathered among the whispers of the palace, no woman besides Imenda has ever cared for him. He is afraid to fall too hard for you, because he does not want to be hurt again. But he does care about you," he insisted. "Not just for your magic or your ability to heal him, though I imagine he likes that too, but because of who you are. Of your kindness and your ability to see passed the scars and the pain he has endured to the man he really is."

"I don't want to be discarded or burned like Imenda," she admitted.

"Are you Imenda," he quipped.

"No," she said, rubbing her nose.

He smiled, brushing scar hair from her face. "Then I don't think you have anything to worry about. We aren't traitors, we are loyal. Especially to those we care the most about," he added, looking behind them at something over her head.

Jasper stared hard, his fists clenched as he hid himself among the bushes, watching as Emeline spoke with her father.

She loves me.

He felt something twist hard in his gut and he ducked his head, the joy of it wafting through him. *She loved him.* No one had ever loved him before, not even Imenda, and it felt like a flood of longing washed over him. Yet, he frowned. She feared him because of what he had done, and that was not something he had ever wanted for her.

He wanted her to smile and be happy with him, to know that she was safer than anyone else, but sometimes there was horrific things that needed to be done to ensure the safety of not only her, but of his people. Luke had entrusted him with the crown, with the well-being of the dragons, and he wasn't going to let him or Fate down.

And right then, there was a psychotic demon-dragon on the loose who could likely heal himself-

Jasper's eyes widened and he turned away from Emeline and Navi, unable to look at them anymore. *He's channeling the powers of the fallen elves,* he said to Ana. *That is how he's avoided death. He must've concentrated the magic on himself before he fully died, and begun the healing process, which would have made it appear as though he had truly died.*

Which means he is in the city, Ana replied with a growl.

Jasper took one final look at the pair in front of him, then turned away again, sadness creating ice in his heart. If she feared him, then she would not want him near her, and he refused to frighten her further.

But she couldn't be left alone either.

You will watch Emeline, he said fiercely. *Wynter and I will go on the hunt for Tucker and end this, once and for all.*

No, Ana said firmly. *I'm not going to let you run away from her again. Besides, you have more power and strength and it may take both to take his bastard down when he comes after her again. You are the best chance we have at catching Tucker when he comes for what he wants, and we both know that he will. Wynter and I will notify you if we find him first, and I promise you, he will pay for all that he has done.*

Jasper finally gave a nod, his gaze straying back to Emeline. *Very well.*

Emeline sniffled one last time, the last of her tears shed, and leaned onto her father's chest, his familiar, pine-scent calming her.

Suddenly, a sinking feeling crawled into her stomach, making her feel as though it were full of lead, and she stiffened, looking around at the foliage surrounding them in alarm.

Navi's brow furrowed as he took note of her stiffened body. "What is it?"

"Something isn't right."

He stood, scanning their surroundings, and his expression became serious. "What do you mean?"

"I don't know, it's just a feeling that I have."

She backed away from the edge of the cloud, and Navi followed her. "Emeline?"

"He's alive," Emeline said in shock, her chest tightening, and her lungs burning for air as though she had lost every bit she had had. "Tucker is here. I can feel him, but why can I feel him?"

"Because he put his mark on you," said a demon who emerged from the cloud. "Which makes it that much easier to find you for us."

Her eyes widened and they turned to run but another demon landed behind them with a thud, hissing. "Oooh, she is a beautiful little abomination, isn't she?"

She stumbled over a branch and whipped around to look in horror at the demons that came from the ends of the cloud.

Tucker emerged from the tops of the trees, his wings hovering him down gracefully, with his fists clenched, and smiled down at her. He knelt and put a finger over his lips. "We've come to destroy the dragons and collect some bounty." He ran a hand down her cheek, a sickening smile on his face as she flinched away. "And you aren't going to get in our way, are you?"

"Don't you dare touch her," Navi snapped.

"As if you had a say in the matter," Tucker sneered. "Shut him up."

"No," she cried. "Leave him alone!"

The demons ignored her, grabbing Navi's arms and tying him to a tree despite his attempts to struggle, then gagged him with a cloth. He grunted and shouted, pulling on the bindings as though he could out muscle two young demons.

She reached for him, but Tucker grabbed her face, turning her to him. "I'm going to need you to scream for me, princess."

A loud thud behind Tucker made the ground shake, and a mighty roar filled the air just before three of Tucker's ten demons screamed in agony.

He released her and turned to find three piles of ash behind his demons. The bow in his free hand hit against the ground and twitched as he scoured the landscape for the source of the noise and deaths.

Emeline looked the opposite way and caught sight of a midnight blue, scaled tail as it swung out to snap the necks of two more.

Their bodies ashed before they hit the ground.

She smiled with satisfaction, then met Tucker's gaze. "You are going to be very sorry you touched me."

Another roar filled the air and Tucker looked upward, standing with an arrow strung and ready to fire. "Come out, you coward!"

A snap filled the momentary silence, and Navi pulled his hands free of the broken ropes, glaring at Tucker. "Didn't figure I would be tied up long." He looked toward his daughter and offered his hand, helping her up as he leaned in close to speak softly.

"Listen to me, baby girl," he said firmly. "You need to remember your mother now. Imagine her as a fierce, and wonderfully golden dragon, her powers surging through her as she showed you who she truly was. Her eyes would glow, and her strength would pour off of her like the sunshine. Think of it now."

Images flashed in front of her mind and she put her fists to her forehead as a pain began there. "What are you doing?"

"Trust me," Navi said, looking around as another demon behind Tucker was dragged by a set of clawed feet into the brush. "Look at me," he urged over the screams, pulling her eyes from the carnage building around her. "Your mother had an incredible amount of power that she channeled using her anger toward the demons. Her fear would bring it out to protect her as it has with you, but her anger toward those things and everything they stand for was what empowered her to be the warrior that she was. You have to be a warrior now, you have to trigger your memories of her to learn."

Memories of fight training flooded her and she gasped as it overwhelmed her, teaching her what her mother had learned. Skills her grandmother had taught Sarafine and on up the line as though she had lived each and every moment her ancestors had.

But how?

She opened her eyes when it cleared and they glowed white as she felt the two halves of her soul meld together, becoming one powerful being. For the first time in her life, she felt whole and full, the limitless supply of magic Jasper had told her about making her feel stronger than ever before.

She wasn't a dragon or an elf, she was something in between, and she was ready to end Tucker once and for all.

Tucker roared, his dragon echoing through the sky as he and two final demons searched for Jasper, their eyes glowing an angry red. Claws clicked together in anticipation, and fangs dripped into the ground, creating the scent of burnt foliage around them.

Navi looked to her and gave a nod of encouragement.

She lifted a white, enflamed, and trembling hand and one of the demons shot into the air with a shriek, his sword falling to the ground.

Tucker whipped his attention to her and snarled. "Why you little-"

It was the opening Jasper needed, and he dove from the treetops, tackling Tucker to the ground in a tangle of claws and fangs.

Emeline stored her shock for his size and ferocity away for later as the giant dragon mauled Tucker seconds before the demon turned into his dragon, his scales red and angry. Roars filled the air as they rose higher into the skies.

The final demon ran for her and she smiled, her hand still up and glowing. She eyed the demon above her, then raised an eyebrow at the other. "I wouldn't do that if I were you."

A shriek made the demon look up, and the one she had thrown into the air previously slammed into him, reducing them both to ash.

Navi cheered. "That's my girl!"

She turned back to Jasper and Tucker, and, waving her hands, she started ripping off his reddened scales, baring his flesh to Jasper's assault. Blood fell over the leaves of the trees and soaked the ground as Jasper dug his claws deep into the demon's flesh.

Angered, Tucker roared and threw Jasper off him into several trees. The trunks broke and snapped, sending the trees crashing, until the beast finally fell to the ground, unmoving. Slowly, it morphed back into Jasper, unconscious on the ground, his wings bent at odd angles, and his arms splayed to his sides.

Emeline's confidence fell and her glow vanished as she gasped, running with Navi close behind toward Jasper. With every step, she saw more bruises, blood, and cuts over his body and her heart stopped in her chest.

Chapter 25

Tucker bound after them, his wings thundering behind them, and roared as he blew fire at them, the heat made them sweat more than their running was.

Emeline fell to her knees beside Jasper and hesitated to touch him, too afraid anywhere she touched might hurt. She pressed her ear to his chest to listen for a heartbeat and shook him, panicked when she couldn't hear anything over the chaos around them. "Jasper! Wake up, please! Please be okay, please!"

"Emeline," Navi shouted over the roar of the fire and the slamming of Tucker's feet as the demon landed. "We have to go! Now!"

She shut her eyes and willed her mind to push out into what she hoped was the mind she needed. *Ana! Wynter, please! Help! Tucker is at the palace, Jasper is injured!*

Ana's voice came through clear and strong. *Hang on. We're coming.*

"Ana and Wynter are coming!"

"There's no time," Navi snapped. "We have to go now or we are going to be cooked!"

He grabbed Jasper's arm and threw it over his shoulder, faltering beneath the weight of the dragon king. "You're going to have to help me, Emeline!"

She immediately ducked under Jasper's arm and together, they dragged and struggled to run from Tucker's hot flames with Jasper on their arms.

Emeline heaved, her chest feeling as though all the air had been sucked out of it as she stumbled again, her muscles burning. "Father, it's too much. He's too heavy!"

"Here," Navi shouted, urging them behind a fallen tree, the large base towering high above their heads. "We can't stay here for long, but we should get a moment to catch our breaths."

Emeline helped to ease Jasper against the base of the tree, then peeked around it, eyes wide at the sudden silence that reigned through the trees. Where had Tucker gone? Had he given up?

Fear clenched the airtight in her chest, and she looked at Navi, eyes wide. "What do we do," she whispered.

He looked around himself, then held her shoulders as he whispered back, "Reach for Ana. She and Wynter are the fiercest warriors I've ever seen aside from Jasper, they can help you defeat him."

Tears swelled in Emeline's eyes, which widened impossibly more. "I can't defeat that thing!"

"You can," he said firmly. "You will."

"He's trying to take me. I can't even imagine what he'll do if he catches me," she added with a shudder.

Jasper groaned and she dropped to her knees to quiet him, her hands tracing his face as she tried to soothe him.

"Reach, Emeline," Navi instructed. "Reach your mind out, find Ana."

She shut her eyes and tried to concentrate, but every sound made her jump and panic. "I can't."

"Emeline," he snapped.

She looked at Jasper, hoping against the odds that he would wake but by the knot growing on the back of his head, she doubted it. Even if he had woken up, she wasn't sure how much more of a beating he could take before Tucker caused permanent damage, or worse. Leaning forward, she rested her ear on his chest and shut her eyes.

If she was going to die, the sound of his heartbeat would be the last thing she heard, no matter what. The thunder of it made hers jump with delight, and she breathed in his fiery scent, wishing to remember it in whatever life came after this one.

Her mind reached out as she calmed and she felt Ana's urgency flood her.

Ana, she said in relief.

Don't worry, Ana sent back. *We are coming, but you need to move. Now. I can sense Tucker nearby, and his anger radiates off the trees like wildfire. Run!*

Emeline shifted as Navi kept looking out, bending her legs beneath her so the top half of her body laid on Jasper's chest. *We can't. Jasper is too heavy for us to carry, and we won't leave him.*

You have to, Ana insisted. *We will find him but Tucker is after you and if he finds you, he finds Jasper. If you do not leave Jasper behind, he is as good as dead.*

Emeline bit her lip and shook her head even though she knew Ana couldn't see it.

Her mind found Jasper's and the familiar warmth seeped through her, calming her and assuring her.

Jasper, please wake up, she sobbed into his mind. *I need you. We need you. Just please, please be okay!*

A branch snapped to their right and Emeline sat up straight, eyes wide.

"Father," she said shakily.

"Be still," Navi whispered back.

A big, strong dragon herself, and, even with her mother's memories, she didn't know what to do to save them. It was enough to send her into a fit of tears all over again. Instead, she traced her hands over Jasper's face, her eyes lit, and focused on what she could do. She might be a dragon, but she was raised an elf, and elves had a special place all their own in the world.

Without hesitation, she put her hands to his wound and white magic began to glow around her fingers, surging into him to heal him.

Navi jerked and snapped to attention. "Emeline, no! He'll sense your-"

A clawed hand reached around the tree and grabbed her hair, jerking her back and she let out a bloodcurdling scream as she was pulled through the leaves and dirt, the thorns in the shrubs cutting her skin.

"I knew you would miss me," Tucker said as he pulled her to her feet in front of him, several yards away from her father and Jasper. "You know, with Jasper out of the way, you are just a helpless little nobody. Wonder if Imenda would mind me taking the time to get to know you."

His clawed finger trailed down her cheek, her throat, down to the swell of her breasts and she smacked his hand away, trying to pull her hair from his grasp. He smiled and pulled her against his chest, easily trapping both her wrists at the base of her spine. "I love fighters. They scream the best after they have lost, and the struggle is gloriously arousing."

Something large moved out of the corner of her eye and before she could scream in fright, something cold slammed hard into Tucker, sending them both to the ground, and leaving a trail of frost in his wake. His hold on her loosened and she bolted, racing for the tree where Navi and Jasper were.

No one was there.

Her heart raced in her chest and she leaned against the dirt and roots, fear keeping her in place. She tried taking deep breaths but nothing stopped the ebb and flow of her rapidly racing heartbeat.

If Tucker had taken Jasper away, had stolen her father away from her, she had no one to blame but herself, and already, she could feel the pain of loss slicing through her.

Warmth wrapped around her, making her close her eyes and she felt as though she were hypnotized, being led away from the fray happening behind her. Moving almost robotically, she followed where it seemed to be coming from and found herself in front of a nearby crack in a cliff, the cavern dark but warm.

Jasper emerged, his muscles bulging as the shadows ran from him, his power chasing them away from him as though light were coming from him instead of the skies above.

Relief poured into her heart and she ran for him, jumping into his arms, and sobbed into his neck. "Jasper! Thank heaven you're alright!"

His arms tightened around her and he turned them, gently pushing her toward the entrance. "I want you and Navi to hide here while I go help Wynter and Ana. Tucker will not survive this night."

Emeline gaped at him. "No! Jasper, he almost killed you."

"You would have me hide like a coward then, and let my friends die in my place?"

She jerked back as though she had been struck. "No but-"

"Then you will stay put," he ordered. "Or I will restrain you myself."

"Emeline," Navi said cautiously. "Let him go."

"Is that what you think of me," Emeline snapped. "That I am a coward?"

He snapped his mouth shut and, with a helpless look toward Navi, remained silent.

She stomped over to him. "Tucker is a powerful dragon, one who takes pleasure in killing and hurting people. I cannot beat a dragon as an elf."

"You will not try as a dragon either," he grumbled.

"You would have me hide," she mocked. "Like a coward?"

Navi grasped her shoulder firmly, his expression grim. "Emeline, enough."

"I just saved your life," she said angrily. "Do not disrespect me by calling me a coward again."

Jasper glowered at her. "Enough time has been wasted. It is time to go. Please," he added. with a deep breath, closing his eyes in exasperation. "Just listen to me."

He took off into the woods before she could answer, and Emeline huffed, crossing her arms over her chest indignantly.

Navi chuckled. "Fear does not make you a coward, but it can hold you back on who you truly are if you cannot face it."

She looked back to her father in frustration. "So what should I do?"

"Follow your gut. What does it say?"

She turned back to Jasper, who had disappeared in the foliage, and knew deep in her heart, what it was she was meant to do.

Even if it meant further angering Jasper.

Ana slammed the butt of her staff into Tucker's temple just as Jasper emerged from the bushes, sending him to the ground with one powerful hit. Tucker fell with a thud, but he didn't move.

Wynter spat on him, the saliva turning to ice against Tucker's cheek. "Put up a hell of a fight but nothing two of the strongest warriors in existence couldn't handle."

Jasper sighed. "He can heal himself."

Wynter's brow furrowed and he stepped forward as though challenging the news. "What?"

Ana shut her eyes, holding her staff on the ground with the end down. "He can channel the powers of hell."

"How," Wynter demanded.

She bit her lip, nibbling on it. "I don't know. I thought only Lucifer could do it but there lies proof otherwise."

Jasper frowned. "He wants Emeline."

"From what I saw," Wynter said, nudging Tucker in the side with his boot as though testing how unconscious he was, "he doesn't just want her magic. He wants her body for himself, too."

Jasper growled. "He may try. She is mine and mine alone."

Ana stopped chewing her thumbnail and heaved a sigh. "Have you two connected yet?"

Jasper's brow furrowed, his arms crossing as he narrowed his eyes. "What business is it of yours?"

"I don't care if you've screwed," Ana scoffed. She put her hand on her hip and pretended to buff her fingernails. "But if you *did* screw, then your souls, if they were meant to be, would have melded together."

"What?"

She rolled her eyes, muttering something that sounded suspiciously like, "Men are so dumb."

"If you two had sex, then your souls would have torn," she said aloud. "With the strength of your dragons, you may not have even noticed but there would have been a moment where it felt as though you were one. Perhaps like not knowing where one ended and the other began."

He blinked. "What would be the significance of that in this?"

"Well, if you two are soulmates, you could heal yourself from injury."

"I could heal my scars," he said in disbelief.

"Well, no." She shifted from one foot to the other. "Emeline has the blood of an elf, she is an elf. You would access her powers, but only she could combine them with that of a dragon, so only she can heal your scars. Though if I do say so myself," she added with a snicker, "I say keep them. They make you sexy."

Wynter rolled his eyes. "Oh, how amusing your little crush on the king is," he retorted. "But we have bigger problems."

Jasper gave a curt nod, forcing his mind to put a halt on his thoughts.

A rustle of leaves made the trio look downward in astonishment.

Tucker was gone.

Jasper looked around for any sign of him but the dragon was long gone.

"How many powers have they collected, for crying out loud," Ana objected, her hands rising and falling to her sides in disbelief.

Wynter lifted his gaze to his king, his expression grim and angry. "Where is Emeline?"

Emeline leaned on the side of the rock and blew a sigh, arms crossed over her chest as she stared up at the jagged ceiling. The crack in the rock was almond shape, barely big enough for her to squeeze through, let alone Jasper.

Navi paced inside with firewood and approached the fire brewing in the center of the cave, tossing his bounty on top to keep the flame heating the cold interior of the cave.

"He should have been back by now," Navi grumbled. "We are sitting ducks if Tucker or his psychotic sister get loose of the dragons."

She shut her eyes, crossing her arms at the wrists behind her on the wall. For a moment, she let go of her anger toward Jasper and imagined him there, holding her arms behind her back as he ravaged her, his hands intertwined with hers. He would look into her eyes before ducking his head to put his mouth on her own, demanding, pressing, devouring her as though he would never be able to stop. Her back would arch, offering him more, and as her body pushed toward him, his would press against hers, his heat seeping into her skin…

"Emeline," Navi said softly. "Are you alright?"

She jolted out of her musings and realized her lips had parted, her back arching just slightly and her legs trembled as though threatening to give out at any moment

She felt heat rush into her cheeks and met his gaze. "Yes. Daydreaming to pass the time."

"About the dragon?"

With a sigh, she nodded, looking out into the foliage.

He stopped pacing and approached her. "You have to learn to trust him."

"I can't," she murmured, unable to meet her father's gaze. "I saw what happened to Imenda. If I am just a means to an end, he will never love me. He will never see me as his mate, and I don't want just a passing thing with him." Her head turned against the rocks as she finally looked to her father. "I want love. And I want someone who loves me for being me as much as I love him for himself."

"He cares deeply about you, Emeline," he said encouragingly. "If it is love, he may not even know it yet. Give him time to discover it for himself."

She shook her head, watching as the sunlight began to wane in the distance. "I want to go home. I want to forget we ever came here and I want to for-get-" She stopped, her lips refusing to say his name next to forgetting.

It was going to be impossible to forget Jasper Rogue.

Navi watched her for several minutes, then blew out a sigh. "If that is what you wish, then we will leave once Tucker and Imenda are dealt with. But I think it is a decision you will learn to regret."

Emeline frowned and looked out over the trees in silence. She already knew she would regret the decision, knew how much her heart would long for him, day and night. No man would ever come close to him, and she knew it meant a life without love.

But how could she continue to remain there with the dragons, when she would never know whether he loved her, or simply wanted to use her?

Chapter 26

"We need to move," Jasper said harshly, as he approached sometime later and landed behind Emeline and Navi. "Tucker disappeared, and we don't know how many powers he has now."

"Where is Wynter and Ana," she asked cautiously.

"Heading back to check on the castle."

She straightened, then looked to Navi. "We are going home."

"No," Jasper snapped, shaking his head. "You will come with me. Tucker will not give up on his search for you. I can protect you here."

"I don't want your protection, Jasper. I want to go home."

"What you want and what you need are two different things, Emeline."

Navi stepped between them. "Emeline, we will go to the castle to discuss this. It will be dark soon and there is no telling what Tucker has planned for us. We can't stay here, or he will find us."

She raised her chin, ignoring the tremble in her bottom lip, but his gaze locked on the motion, the only betrayal of her façade. "I will walk back carefully, then."

Jasper turned his attention to Navi, his golden eyes warm, and said gently, "Give us a moment, won't you?"

She looked ready to protest but Navi merely nodded and moved back into the cave, tossing a worried expression over his shoulder

She shook her head. "Jasper, I can't be with you. I can't trust that you aren't only interested in me for my abilities. We…" She hesitated and swallowed hard as she looked away from him. "We have to be done."

He stepped forward, his hands twitching to resist the desire to grasp her face in his hands and kiss her untrue words away. She couldn't mean it, she just couldn't. Not after everything they had been through, not with everything she brought out in him.

"We are not done," he ground out.

"Yes, we are," she forced herself to tell him, her voice strained. "I need someone who cares about me for something beyond my powers. Imenda might be right about us. We-"

He gave in to his growing anger with a roar, and put his hands on her cheeks, pulling her into his kiss. At first she resisted but with every heated press of his lips, she relaxed more until she was pushing back, her hands on his sides. Her lips parted for him, and he slid his tongue between them, demanding, taking everything from her.

He slid one hand into her hair, and the other to the small of her back, making her feel the hardness of him against her soft body. Almost absently, she rubbed against him, mewling against his lips, and confirmed what he already knew.

She wanted him.

"Does this feel like someone who wants to use you," he demanded of her, nibbling along her jawline until she was melting against him. "Don't heal me, don't trust me, I don't care, but don't you ever leave me."

She moaned, her knees buckling beneath her until she leaned against his chest, her forehead on his shoulder as she shook her head from side to side. He continued his intoxicating kisses down the side of her throat to her shoulders, and growled, "I have to have you. Now, here."

Her nipples brushed through her dress to his chest, the points hardened, and she shuddered in his arms, tracing her fingers over the skin of his back. A breeze made her shiver, and his fingers twitched, itching to touch her, to see how wet she was for him. Instead, his fingers tangled into her hair, and his other hand cupped her bottom, bringing her hips to his, and he *rocked* against her

"Jasper," she breathed, lifting her head to whisper it into his ear.

He lifted his head, staring down into her eyes and warmth spread throughout his body swirling through and consuming him just from the heat lying in her eyes. There was no choice. She had to be his, had to remain with him forever or he would surely perish. If she did, indeed, leave, he knew he would never recover, and it was about time that she knew it too.

She closed her eyes when his hand moved up to her jaw, tilting her up for another kiss.

Somehow he managed to break away from her, but his arms remained locked around her, too afraid of letting her go. His forehead came down to meet hers as he breathed in her rosy scent, her breath meeting with his to heat the air between them. Her gaze moved up to his own, and he was lost in what he found there.

She loved him. She truly, fully, and completely loved him, and he wanted to kick himself for not noticing before.

"I care nothing for your power, Emeline. I only care for you, I swear it."

"But Imenda-"

"Is a liar," he growled. "She caused several of those that I loved to die and she did this to me," he added grimly, looking at the scars on the tips of his fingers as she traced them with her own. "She gave you to her monster of a brother for sport, and I cannot handle the thought of what he might have done to you had you not found the courage to try to escape."

He expected her to continue to fight him, or to reject his proclamation, but to his surprise, she shushed him soothingly, her fingers raising from his to trace the scar over his lip. "Nothing happened to me. I'm safe right here, with you."

He tightened his arm around her, air hissing between his teeth when she wiggled against him, and he grew impossibly harder for her. "I promise."

Navi cleared his throat but instead of amusement at their moment, he was looking around in alarm. "It is almost dark. We must leave before we are at a disadvantage."

Jasper wanted to roar high into the heavens in frustration at the interruption, but he knew that the elder elf was right. Most dragons could see in the dark, but elves could not, and if he missed something, anything that was out of place, it could mean their deaths.

And that, he would not allow.

"Get on my back."

"There has to be a place where we can escape Tucker and his sister," Navi said firmly. "Where can we go?"

Jasper frowned, crossing his arms over his chest. "My castle is plenty safe."

"Not without the extensive guards you once had."

"I still have an army," the dragon king fired back. "They have been out of commission for a long while, but I could bring them out of hiding easily."

Before the old elf could respond, and further insight his dragon, Jasper pulled Emeline up into his arms, then turned his back to Navi. Taking the hint, Navi wrapped his hands around the base of Jasper's wings and braced himself for the flight.

"Why don't we just tell Lucifer what is going on," Emeline asked suddenly as Jasper crouched for added momentum. His body stiffened and his eyes flashed gold. For a moment, she even thought she felt scales against her back, as though his dragon reared its head in protest over the idea of Lucifer's involvement.

"No," Jasper said firmly. "Lucifer is nothing but pure evil. If we ask for his help, he will demand something worse in return."

Navi shrugged. "Can't be worse than this."

"It can."

With the finality of his tone, Emeline closed her mouth but she knew she couldn't live with the fear any longer. The running, the terror of what would happen if they ever stopped trying to hide from the monsters stalking them, it was no way to live. And she knew, deep down, that the siblings weren't going to give up quite so easily. And for every moment that she and Jasper spent trying to be together, that fear would always hold them back.

Yet Jasper refused to do the one thing that would end it, that would ensure that the deranged maniacs after them would be put away forever.

Emeline had been foolish to have even thought for a moment that Jasper hadn't cared for her, that he was only interested in her for her powers to heal. His passion, the way he had spoken to her before, had put to rest every fear that she had been silly enough to have because of a demonic brat, one that Emeline should have known better than to believe.

She frowned and sighed as Jasper pushed off into the sky. *Well, if Jasper isn't going to do anything to stop them, I guess I'm on my own.*

Ana leaned on the wall of the dungeon, watching as Imenda thawed across the room. The bitch's eyes could blink and she stared with hatred at the dragon. Ana would have been lying if she had said that she didn't find amusement in the demon's agony. Because despite the silence that seemed to ring through the room, Imenda still looked as though she were ready to scream.

And oh, how glorious of a sound that would be!

Ana just smiled back at Imenda in triumph, her small fangs peeking out. "Can't say as though I am surprised you ended up iced. Wynter will be back any time to reinforce the ice that you have managed to melt, and oh, how it will hurt and burn! I should know," she added softly as she twisted the edge of her dagger against her index finger. "Being half-demon myself, I can't touch him. It burns and festers like an open sore. I can only imagine how much ice hurts you as an ice cube."

Imenda's eyes narrowed.

Ana shrugged. "You know, I'm glad we have this time to talk. Let's begin with something emotionally painful, just to take your mind off your physical pain." She leaned towards Imenda with a wicked smile. "Jasper will never choose you over Emeline. She is everything he needs, everything he wants, and though I suspect he does not know it yet, she is his soulmate. I sensed elven magic in his system the last time we spoke, which screams of their connection, but that is something he and Emeline will need to discover on their own." She pushed off the wall and strode confidently to the bars of Imenda's cage, wrapping her hand around one to lean in closer. "I know your brother can heal himself, but I have to wonder, can you?"

Imenda continued to glare.

"Oh, this is horribly boring," Ana said on a sigh as she rolled her eyes and twisted her blade between her fingers. "How about we speed up the process?"

Fire shot from the fingers of her free hand, melting the ice around Imenda's head. The demon drew in gulps of air, her relief obvious.

Ana stopped flicking the dagger and held it by the hilt as she gestured with the blade toward Imenda. "Try anything stupid and we'll see if your head grows back, too."

"We'll see how big and bad you are when Tucker comes to my rescue," she spat. "He will rip your head from your neck for harming his baby sister!"

Ana shrugged, unperturbed. "Many have tried, none have succeeded." She leaned forward, glaring inside the cage. "Imagine what I could do to you in the meantime. Healing or not, I can do things that would make you wish you were dead for good."

Imenda laughed with a shake of her head. "You think I care? Emeline will leave Jasper after what he did to me. She knows he will dump her on her high and mighty rump when he is finished with her and find a way to put her in hell. Even now, she fears him. I saw it the moment she entered the room while he burned me. She fears that the monster inside of him is too much for her to control, that she will be the next one to scream and burn."

"That is what you think," Ana said simply. "But what you did against this kingdom put you in hell. Jasper simply put you were you belonged."

"Belonged," Imenda mocked with a false laugh. "He condemned me to a fate worse than death. For decades, I have been cut, torn, violated, impregnated-"

"Tortured, raped, insulted," Ana finished for her. "Try it for five centuries."

For the first time since they had met, Imenda blinked in surprise. "You?"

"And my sister, yes," Ana said with a hint of sadness.

"Then why are you helping him," Imenda snapped venomously. "Why not kill him and all the souls who were spared our torment?"

"I never desired to be evil. Selfish, sure, but never evil. When I died, I wanted to join my father in Afterlife. Instead, I took the place of my mother alongside my own baby sister, without knowing it. Well, twin sister but younger by ten minutes," she added with a grin. "She is just as ruthless as you are but she, at least, has standards. Morals that keep her from being holy evil, despite our wrongful time in Hell."

"Where is the fun in that," Imenda quipped.

"We get to escape hell, that's what," Ana snapped. "Which is more than I can say for you. Now, where is your brother?"

"Bite me," Imenda snapped.

Ana sighed as she traced the edge of the cage with her eyes. "I was once in here. My arms were bound above my head, my legs confined to the floor below me and a gag over my mouth to keep me from reciting spells. Not that I needed them," she added quickly. "I am more powerful now than I have ever been. A flick of my fingers, a blink of my beautiful eyes, and wonderful, sometimes horrible things can happen."

"This is touching," Imenda said drolly. "But I'd rather my head be frozen."

"I was given an offer," she continued, as though the demon hadn't spoken. "I was told that if I helped to stop a great evil, I would be granted access to this world. A chance to earn my place in Afterlife."

"I am not interested in Afterlife," Imenda said with a groan. "I just want my love and my kingdom. Power and romance, all wrapped in one beautifully scarred, dragon-size bow."

"He does not want you."

"He will, soon. Emeline is too soft, too trusting, and too naïve to know it, but his dark side will learn to hate her. Her light will never outshine the monster that he is and he will never feel like he measures up to her, but he does to me."

"Way to lower your standards."

"Ycah, wcll," Imenda looked down at her encased body. "Not like I have the skin of snow or the body of a dragon. I am no fool. I know she is more beautiful than I, but her beauty will not surpass his needs for me."

"Keep telling yourself that," Ana said with a snort. "Maybe one day someone will believe you."

"Bitch," Imenda snapped.

"Sometimes. Where is Tucker?"

Imenda's lips snapped shut.

"What are his powers?"

Again, silence.

Ana shrugged as she toyed with the tip of her blade again and sighed, as though dealing with a child. "Did you know Wynter has many powers? Well, they are all ice related, obviously, but the things he can do with it..." She shivered, smiling when fear flickered over Imenda's eyes. "God, it's hot to even think about."

"Oh, so a crush on both dragons then," Imenda said with a roll of her eyes. "How droll."

"Just one, but I'll never tell you which one. I am no fool."

"Yet, you tell me of how you became a dragon."

"It isn't something that you could use against me," Ana said confidently. She began to circle the cage, her high-heel boots clicking on the floor as she walked, her fingers running over the bars. "He can push ice through your skin and into your blood, your muscles, even your brain. Demon blood will burn and react, but with the amount of power in him, it will never be enough to burn him out of you."

Imenda lifted her chin but her lip quivered.

"So I can call him in here and tell him it is his turn, or you can answer me, since I asked so nicely." She stood in front of Imenda, her dagger clenched in her hand. "What powers have you acquired and how do you access them? Where does Tucker hide?"

Imenda's eyes watered but she said nothing.

Ana sighed. "I wish demons had more brain, less brawn or false bravado. Wynter," she called over her shoulder as she stood.

Wynter descended the stairs, his gaze murderous.

Imenda shook her head in denial at the frost in his eyes. "We have the powers of all from our level," she blurted out. "Tucker found out how Lucifer channeled the powers of hell, and we used the same method, only concentrated on our level."

Ana put her hand up and Wynter stopped just behind her, his expression full of terrifying promises, as frost misted from his wings to the floor.

"Lucifer *is* hell," Ana said in confusion. "It's an extension of him, a lifeline, if you will. No one can channel the powers except for him, and nobody knows how to cut the connection to him."

Imenda glowered at them. "When I am free, I'll show you just how wrong you are with the powers from our level."

"You cannot create your own level of hell," Ana said firmly. "No demon can."

"A demon who was once a witch, combined with the magic of a demon who became a dragon? With demons who wanted their own land, free of torment? Easily done," Imenda snapped.

Wynter and Ana exchanged a look.

Imenda smiled. "Everyone knew I had power and lots of it, enough to create my own realm within Lucifer's, undetected. Well, until you and your band of misfits decided it was time to out me."

Wynter's deep voice finally boomed through the room, echoing off the walls. "We did not out you. We would never align ourselves with Lucifer."

"Yet your little elf and king used enough power to alert him to our level."

Ana shook her head.

Imenda giggled, the sound high pitched and foreign in the dark room. "Don't believe me? How many demons were with Tucker when he came to get his prize?"

"Jasper counted ten, maybe a couple more," Wynter said.

"Then he only brought ten of a thousand. And when he comes, there will be nothing left of this rock but chaos, pain, and torment. Everything I endured in hell for looking out for myself will rain down on the heads of those people who are here and my revenge will be completed. The realm of Dragons will end and be reborn as my city." Her arm wiggled and her eyes began to glow red. "I want Jasper by my side and I will go to any lengths to see that it is done." The dungeon began to shake and tumble, making the dragons look around in alarm. Still Imenda seemed calm. "If I can't have him, if nothing I do changes his mind, then I will make him watch as I rip his precious plaything to pieces before I do the same to him."

Wynter lunged forward, ice tumbling from his lips as fire had from other dragons. A bloodcurdling scream echoed as his ice misted around her, the ice slamming into her skin and further, freezing her alive.

Ana turned away, unaffected by the pain of the demon, and looked worriedly at Wynter behind her. "If Tucker brings demons to the realm of Dragons, many dragons will be killed. Lucifer would gain more power in his war against the angels, even if the terror twins don't succeed."

"Unless Imenda and Tucker plan to hide them away in their level," Wynter said gravely. "Which would only add to their collection of powers. They could easily take down Lucifer if they had the powers of the dragons on top of their own, and the ability to heal from their elven souls."

Ana frowned. "I know he is busy, but Jasper needs to know about this."

Wynter gave a curt nod of agreement and together, they strode up the steps toward their king and his charge, Imenda's gaze glaring at their retreat.

Chapter 27

"But if we tell Lucifer-"

"No," Jasper said firmly.

"He will want to know someone is using his realm, stealing power from him!"

"I don't care," he snapped, running his hand over his short hair.

Only moments had passed since Jasper had landed on the front steps of the palace and carried them inside, their weight like air to him. One look at the king had convinced Navi to leave them to their talk with a parting, "I'll notify Ana and Wynter of the coming dangers so we can ready the army."

Sometime later, their argument had begun.

Emeline put her hands on her hips, glaring at him. "If you won't tell him, then I will."

He stepped toward her, fists clenched and smoke wafted from his nose as his eyes glowed angrily. "You will do no such thing."

"I will," she insisted. "There is nothing you could do to stop me."

His knuckles turned white as though he restrained himself from grabbing her, but he said nothing. She threw her hands up with a scoff, and stormed to the window, crossing her arms as she looked out in angered silence.

He took deep breaths, trying not to let his temper get the better of him even as his dragon rose up once more, clawing at him. But he knew what Lucifer would do. He would demand a deal and what he would want in return was never pleasant. If the devil himself put his hands on Jasper's love…

He blinked.

He couldn't love her. He had to let her go when this was over. She deserved more than what he could offer. Yet the idea of her with another man set him aflame all over again, and he felt the urge to punch his fist through a wall.

"Why do you not fear my wrath when you fear everyone else's," he demanded.

She scowled at him. "I do not fear anyone other than Tucker and Imenda. Something about him terrifies me." Her gaze softened on him. "I know you would never hurt me. At least, I don't think you would."

"I wouldn't," he said firmly.

Just like that, his anger evaporated and the only urge he felt was to pull her into his arms, to kiss the argument from her mouth so they could return to where they were before Imenda had interfered. But he knew that if he took her into his arms again, he wouldn't ever be able to let her go.

He shut his eyes. *Dammit, I do love her.*

No matter how hard he had tried not to, he knew it was true. She may not be a fierce warrior like him, but she was soft, kind, and strong in her own way. She cared for people, cared for *him*, despite everything he had done.

His scars didn't frighten her, either, but in fact, seemed to draw her in more.

For the first time since Imenda bestowed the wretched things onto his flesh, he wondered if he should heal them, return to the man he once was.

Would Emeline see him differently?

He sighed. "I am trying to protect you, Emeline."

She nibbled her full bottom lip, making him feel the full tightness in his pants as his arousal twitched and hardened.

"I know," she said barely above a whisper. "But I also need you to at least consider what I have said. Lucifer could end all of this, end both of them, and it wouldn't matter the price. We could pay it, so long as we can get peace."

He shook his head but contrary to his motion, he said almost painfully, "If I promise to think about it, can we end this discussion?"

She seemed to mull it over before finally giving a nod. "Very well."

He shifted from one foot to the other. "Imenda is not right, Emeline. The moment I discovered her betrayal, I realized I never loved her." *Not like I do you*, he wanted to add, but he didn't, too afraid to cement what he already knew he might have to give up. "She is nothing more than a means to an end. A demon with information we could use right now. When we are done with her, she will be returned to hell and not the level she is in now, but a deeper one."

"A level that she created herself," Ana said from behind him.

He turned to her and frowned. "Demons can't create levels of Hell."

"Witches can," she said glumly. "Witches who were dragon shifters and now demons? Almost certainly can."

"Where is Wynter," Emeline asked hesitantly.

"With Navi, getting the army ready."

"What did you find out," Jasper demanded, his tone harsh.

Ana conveyed all they found from Imenda, sparing no detail, and when she was finished, Jasper's face was one of pure rage.

"She thinks to steal not only my kingdom, but my mate from me? We will see just how powerful she is when Michael takes her powers from her."

Emeline's eyes widened. "*Archangel* Michael? He exists?"

Ana raised an eyebrow in amusement at the elf. "You should brush up on your Afterlife history. Maybe visit the library while we deal with this?"

Jasper shifted his attention to Emeline once more, drinking in the sight of her. If Imenda truly was able to concentrate enough power to create a level in Hell that Lucifer himself wasn't aware of, Jasper knew what he had to do.

But it didn't mean he had to like it.

"I will be right back once I have checked with Navi. And Emeline," he added softly, "we will speak with Lucifer, but I wish for you to stay here. You are not to be part of any bargain the devil will make."

She nodded, understanding and something else he couldn't quite name flickering over her gaze. "I will."

The words rang in his ears, and it took all of his strength not to cross the room to gather her into his arms again, to kiss her for agreeing to his terms instead of fighting him on them. Willing himself to brace for the upcoming mission, he fisted his hands and something primal narrowed his vision.

His dragon growled in anticipation as he followed Ana down the hallway, and he gave a subtle nod to his dragon.

Soon, he promised.

Left alone, Emeline waited until their footsteps had faded before taking off out the door and down the path Wynter had shown her to the dungeons. She knew Jasper wouldn't be very happy about what she was about to do, but she *had* promised to stay at the palace, and Emeline needed answers, answers she knew that wasn't going to get from Jasper.

If she was to miss out on speaking to Lucifer, then she was going to do some discovering for herself.

Once she reached the open doorway to the dungeons, she checked for any sign of dragons, or her father, but the room was empty, cold, and silent.

Her gaze locked on the cage in the center of the room and she gasped when she saw Imenda, frozen solid like a statue. She hurried to the cage and reached in through the bars to touch Imenda's blue-hued skin. It was rock solid and she pulled her arm back against the cold, damp bars. It was as though the bars had been encased in ice once, but now the ice only surrounded the demon in front of her.

How can I get answers from a frozen woman?

Her eyes widened and she swallowed hard with a hand to her throat. Jasper had breathed fire, a power most dragons were rumored to have. Did that mean she could access that kind of power too?

Would it hurt?

Closing her eyes, she searched her new memories from her mother for a way to breathe fire as Jasper had. When it came, she gasped, and her hand around her neck tensed. She saw Sarafine as she fought with a dragon Emeline didn't know. His red eyes glowed as he held a mighty sword, his dark hair blowing in the wind as his muscles bulged.

Luke, she realized, blinking, but the images continued.

"You must connect with your dragon," his voice thundered. "Remember its strength, its heat. Let it build inside of you, burning until there isn't a choice but to release it. A dragon's flame is the most powerful magic we have, and one that can save our lives."

She shook her head to will the vision away, then took a deep breath, reaching for the beast within her. The dragon seemed to stretch and growl at having been woken, but when it rose, Emeline could feel her strength pouring into her, as though filling every cell in her body and making her feel even more alive.

She smiled, comforted by her new companion, and closed her eyes. *We can do this.*

Reaching deep within her, she imagined heat enveloping her, rising to meet her needs, and fulfilling her desires. It wasn't long before the dragon roared in her mind, ready for the battle ahead and giving her the courage she wasn't sure she could feel.

Heat curled into her chest and she blew, the blistering heat pushing up her throat and through her mouth without burning her. Within minutes, Imenda let out a cry and collapsed, thawed out by the heat of Emeline's dragon flame.

Instinctively, she stepped back and watched the demon sputter and try to gather herself together.

Imenda jumped forward, reaching through the bars as she slammed into them, and Emeline jolted backward, eyes wide.

When recognition finally hit, Imenda dropped her arms, rolled her eyes, and paced back to the cot behind her, fluffing the pillow. "So what? The dragons couldn't break me, so they sent the fragile little damsel in distress?"

Emeline's hands clenched at her sides and she grit her teeth. "I am *not* a damsel in distress, and nobody sent me."

"Then why are you here," Imenda asked in a bored tone. She sank onto the stale mattress, raising an eyebrow after a long pause. "Well?"

"Why can't you just let Jasper go?"

Imenda smiled. "Jealous? Do you not realize that he is using you as a plaything, something to replace me?"

"That's not true," Emeline said softly in denial.

"But it is," Imenda insisted with a wider smile. Her fangs peeked out over her bottom lip, fairly dripping with intent. "I know Jasper better than you ever will. Did you know he is best friends with Luke? Or that he was once in love with the former king's wife?"

"So what," Emeline challenged. "From what I heard, Luke and his wife are together and happy."

"And dead," Imenda added. "Jasper let them die on the battlefield, fighting Fate's evil stepmother, Dawn Grey. She turned into a demon, too, only she was a lowlife who served Lucifer like a faithless bitch. I serve no one," she added with a snarl.

Emeline hesitated. "What do you mean, he let them die?"

"I was there," Imenda whispered. "He knew their plan, knew they wanted to die to save the world, and he let them do it. The woman he fancied, and he let her die because she chose Luke over him." She stood, her eyes laughing at the elf. "What do you think he will do when you choose to go home, instead of remaining with him?"

Emeline lifted her chin but her bottom lip quivered. "Jasper would never hurt me and any choice Fate made was her own. He would *never* allow harm to come to anyone that he cares about." She stepped forward, the courage from her dragon side filling her as she leaned into Imenda's face. "If you think I would choose to leave him then you are sorely mistaken. If I choose to leave, he will come with me."

"So you can heal him right," Imenda snapped. "Fix him? What an ungrateful little bitch you are," she sneered. "You have a beautiful warrior before you, and yet you decide to steal away his scars."

"Scars *you* gave him," Emeline snapped. "Scars that remind him of the terrible things that you did to him."

Imenda laughed and shook her head. "Oh, you truly are as naïve as they say, aren't you? I had no choice, dear, not if I wanted to save him."

Emeline reared back as though the demon had slapped her. "What are you talking about?"

"I tried to explain it to him years ago, but he wouldn't listen," she said in a bored tone of voice. "Lucifer offered me a deal." She paced away, then back, true sadness in her eyes. "If I joined his side, he would let Jasper live, but only if he came back more damaged then he was before."

Emeline's lips parted in disgust. "Why didn't you reject the deal? Why did you take it?"

Imenda gave a short blurt of a chuckle, but it lacked any humor. "Because if I refused, Lucifer was going to steal his soul and put him in the first level of hell. Along with myself, of course. The worst of the worst live there, and his scars would have been the least of his problems."

Emeline's gaze fell to the floor and wondered if she would have taken the same deal. She shook her head. Jasper was a powerful and capable warrior, he would not have lost even all those years ago, and she knew she would never have been able to do as Imenda had done. "You didn't have to do so much damage. You could have told him what was going on, let him help you get out of it."

Imenda pulled down the top of her shirt, revealing a burned scar over her heart. "There was a tattoo above my heart, engraved by Lucifer that allowed him to hear and see everything I did. When I saw Jasper locked in the dungeons of Lucifer's castle, I couldn't bring myself to do it. So Lucifer cut down his throat, told me that either I could do it or he would." She shut her eyes. "I knew he wouldn't survive torture by Lucifer. I had no choice."

"You had a choice to free him, to *trust* him," Emeline said sharply. "You didn't do it."

"No, but I will get him back and I will fix it."

Emeline's eyes glowed as her dragon growled in challenge. "No, you won't."

Imenda snapped her attention to Emeline. "Jasper is and always will be mine. We bonded, a feat only true soulmates can do. I am a stain on his soul but I am there as he is here." She pointed to her heart and glowered at Emeline. "You will never bond with him now. Not so long as he is connected to me."

Emeline turned her back on the demon, tears stinging her eyes as her dragon thrashed inside of her, begging to be let loose on Imenda, if only for a moment. "It is not true. I will remove any traces of you, I swear it."

"Impossible," Imenda said with a snicker. "Once bonded, there is no way out. He will see you for the cowardly little brat that you are eventually and remember my strength in the face of it. I can fight by his side, keep his people safe from harm, and I can make his enemies bow to him, as every being should have by now. Soon enough, you will be a forgotten memory, a stupid little plaything he will regret for the rest of eternity."

Emeline whirled on her. "He will not!"

"He will."

Her nails dug into her palms as she glared at the demon. Imenda was getting under her skin, and Emeline knew it, but she couldn't seem to stop her.

Instead, she demanded, "Why does Tucker keep coming after me?"

"An oracle was brought down into our level several weeks ago. She told us that you and Tucker will end up together and even if you resist at first, you will come to accept your fate. She claimed it was a romance for the ages, and that you would belong to him."

"Never," Emeline snapped. "I belong to Jasper. I always will."

"We will see," Imenda said with a laugh.

"I can see why Jasper wants you dead," Emeline said softly. "You play with people's minds and make them believe in whatever you do." She slashed her hand in the air. "No more. I will prove you wrong. If Jasper loves me like I love him and, if he will have me, then I will stay with him, and I promise you, I will keep him safe from you."

Imenda's laughter echoed off the walls as she threw her head back. "What power could you possibly have to stop me?"

"Well, if she doesn't have the power to defeat you, I certainly do," Ana's voice said from behind Emeline. "Being incredibly awesome and all, I mean."

Chapter 28

Emeline froze, her back stiffening as she sensed the girl approach.

Much to her surprise, Ana smiled proudly at her. "I knew there was a dragon spirit somewhere within you."

The tension drain from her shoulders and she felt her magic surge to her hands, her dragon's way of pushing Emeline to end Imenda once and for all.

Imenda snorted, sitting on her cot once again with her knee raised, her elbow on her knee as she stared out the other end of the dungeon. "When my brother comes for me, and he will," she added venomously, "you will all answer for what you have done to me."

Ana snorted. "Not likely." She crossed her arms one over the other and leaned on one foot as she looked almost sideways at Emeline. "Your man is wondering where you are. Has even threatened to tear the entire city apart just to find you." She smiled wickedly at the demon in the cage. "Sound like a man pining for you?"

"In the worst way," Imenda half-whispered.

Ana chuckled and gave a jerk of her head. "Come on."

Emeline reluctantly followed Ana up the steps with only one last glance back at the cocky look Imenda was shooting to her.

"I thought Jasper was going to speak with Lucifer," Emeline said hesitantly.

"He sent Wynter instead," Ana answered breezily. "He is needed here."

She slowed at the doorway at the top of the steps and began toying with her fingers nervously. "I-I don't think Jasper should know I was down there."

"Duh." Ana looked over her shoulder as Emeline stayed in the doorway and stopped walking, brow furrowed. "What is it?"

"Did Jasper let Fate kill herself in a war against her stepmother?"

Ana's usually humorous expression darkened. "There are many things about that that you wouldn't understand."

Emeline pulled her pinky finger outwards slightly, the tip of her index finger against her fingernail. "Please tell me. I've made the mistake of falling for Imenda's tricks before, and I don't want to again."

Ana studied her for so long that Emeline wasn't sure she would answer. Finally, she blew a sigh and rolled her eyes. "Fate and Luke were lovers over six hundred years ago. The evil stepmother that

Imenda no doubt told you all about was, regrettably, my flesh and blood. We treated Fate terribly when she was alive, which is how we ended up in Hell."

"Wc?"

"I have a twin sister," Ana said with a shrug. "We don't talk much these days. It's complicated. Anyway, we had learned to be like Dawn, and when my mother found out about Lydia," she hesitated, correcting herself, "*Fate's* tryst with the new king, she grew furious. She made Luke kill Lydia in a fit of rage with her magic. For centuries, they never found one another because Lydia had become Fate, never staying in one place longer than it took to decide if someone should live or die, and Luke became the king of the dragon shifters, sworn to protect his people and the innocents in the living realm."

She leaned on the wall, pausing to assess Emeline.

Emeline gave a nod of encouragement.

"After they found each other, they were overjoyed, as I'm sure you can imagine, but the Afterlife law created by the angels and the fallen at the dawn of time forbade them from being together. If Fate was distracted by love, people would suffer and if Luke was distracted, he would be unable to perform his duties as king."

She hesitated, crossing her arms as her wings twitched in agitation. "Dawn, my mother, kept interfering and causing danger to everyone around her, forcing them to work together. Luke, like any stubborn dragon around here, wouldn't give up on their happily ever after. And when Jasper met her, she was the first woman who hadn't shied away from him for his scars. She didn't even flinch at his appearance, she simply accepted him as he was. He fell for that, but her heart would belonged to Luke, always. So when the great battle broke out, they made a plan that Jasper had no idea about until afterward."

Emeline leaned forward, eyes wide and eager.

"Fate would use every drop of her power to kill Dawn. Luke was to disappear and join her, but Dawn killed him. Sword to the gut," she said softly, a single, small tear dripping down her cheek. "I regretted everything we had done to Fate and when the battle was won, I wanted to right my wrongs. She gave me the chance to redeem myself, to purify my soul so that I could join my father in Afterlife, despite everything we had done. I couldn't save her, but she left behind a way to save me."

"Jasper didn't let her die," Emeline said softly. "And you had no idea they were going to do it."

"No," Ana said on a whisper. "No one did. But there is a secret that you can never share, not even to your father."

Emeline hesitated, then nodded in agreement. "I promise."

"Fate and Luke are rumored to be hidden away in Afterlife. From what I've heard, they had a beautiful and healthy baby girl who adores him, and he visits often. It was against the rules to do so, so the angels cannot find out, but especially *demons* can't find out. It would be too dangerous for them. Only you, Jasper, and I know where they are, and it will stay that way," she added firmly.

Emeline nodded. "I promised and so it will be." She smiled softly as she said fondly, "He helped to save them, to give them the happily ever after they couldn't have."

"In a way," Ana said with a shake of her head. "Yeah."

Emeline smiled to herself and lightly held her hands together in front of her.

A thunderous crash made Emeline jump, and Ana shifted her gaze to the ceiling, then snickered. "He's about to start ripping the palace apart looking for you, so if you don't want to get caught sneaking out of the very place he didn't want you to go, I suggest you follow me quickly."

Emeline followed her through a series of hallways, always peeking around the corner before turning it. What would Jasper do to her, if he knew she had gone against his wishes to speak with Imenda?

"Does Jasper…act like he cares about me to you," Emeline asked cautiously.

Ana stopped, causing Emeline to stumble into her. The ex-demon smiled over her shoulder and shook her head. "You are a foolish girl. What else has Imenda tried to convince you?"

"She said Jasper was going to get bored with me. That he was only using me as a plaything and for my healing abilities."

"Oh, I'm sure he enjoys your *powers* too," Ana said with a wink as she continued moving with Emeline close behind. "But I've never seen him so twisted up into knots before. It's baffling and adorable, all in one. And I never thought I would ever call the brooding, powerful king himself adorable," she added with a laugh.

Emeline smiled. Perhaps she had misjudged the sarcastic, witty dragon. Sure she was selfish, but she had a good heart.

She stopped when Ana turned into a massive study, and Emeline could only stand and gawk in awe. A cherry wood desk sat in the back with a lamp and an exquisite high back chair behind it. The fifty foot tall walls curved around huge windows and along each, bookshelves were filled with several assortments of books from encyclopedias to romance novels.

Emeline gaped in astonishment, her hands raising to her open mouth.

Ana leaned her back on the wall, her wings parting to accommodate for the corner. "Everything you could ever want to know about Afterlife and its realms, plus some of their residents, can be found here, among other things."

"This is fantastic," Emeline rasped out.

"Well, enjoy it now, because Jasper is on his way and he is not happy that we took him on a wild goose chase." She flinched and her hand rose to rub her forehead. "He's also not thrilled that I wouldn't answer him, so there may be some fighting involved."

Emeline climbed up one of the ladders that hung on the wall until she reached the beginning of a series of books. She tugged a book from the shelf, an encyclopedia of the who's who of Afterlife.

Ana rolled her eyes. "Why are you so thrilled with books, anyway? I mean, I can read better than most people of my generation, but I find it incredibly dull."

"Not when it can provide insight about who you are or where you came from," Emeline murmured, speed reading the pages. So many people had come here, looking for the same answers as she had, and each had left their mark on the pages, the dog-eared edges and smudges speaking to the amount of souls looking for whatever they needed to know.

Ana gave another eye roll. "I know where I came from. I didn't like it."

"To each their own," Emeline said absently.

Several seconds passed in silence as Emeline studied her book. Ana seemed to wait for her to toss the book aside to find something more fun to do.

When she didn't, Ana scoffed. "Alright well, I can feel his anger radiating from here so I'm going to make myself scarce, but you let me know how this whole book scavenger thing goes. Nobody comes in here anymore, so I guess the room is yours to do with as you please."

Emeline looked up from her page, touched. "Thank you."

Ana gave a nod and swung out of the open doorway, disappearing from sight as quickly as she had come.

Emeline stared at the pages in fascination, reading about the dragon realm.

Heavy, vengeful footsteps drew her attention, nearly making her jump from the ladder and drop the book she held. She quickly sat at the top of the ladder, pretending to read when she really wanted to rush into his arms, and assure him that she was safe, that she wasn't going to leave him as Luke and Fate had.

Like everyone seemed to have.

He turned into the library and stopped, his hooded gaze scanning for her. When he didn't see her at floor level, he looked up and she felt his heated gaze burn into her, causing an involuntary shiver to slither up her spine.

"Emeline."

His caressing tone was relieved. She nearly dropped the book and jump into his arms at the sound of it.

She looked down at him with adoration and smiled. "Hello, Jasper."

"When you weren't in our room, I thought…"

His voice trailed off, breaking her heart at even the smallest amount of suffering. How she hated to lie to him, but she didn't know what he would do if he found out. How angry and hurt he would be.

"I wanted to learn more about your people, your world."

"*Our* world," he muttered. "You aren't leaving me, ever."

Unable to quench the urge any longer, she marked her page, shut the book, and scurried down to him. Once he pulled her roughly into his arms, she leaned her head on his chest and shut her eyes, listening to the thundering of his heartbeat.

"Never. I swear it."

His brow furrowed even as he stroked her back soothingly. "Not that I want to return to it, but I thought you were angered with me."

"I've been enlightened," she said with a smile. "I never should have listened to Imenda. You were doing what you did to protect this city." She turned her face up to him, gazing into his eyes as her heart swelled in her chest. "To protect me."

"Always," he murmured, ducking his head to hers.

Her eyes drifted closed, savoring his gentle, sweet kisses as he gave them to her, and dug her fingers into the book she held, the pages cutting into her fingers before finally succumbing to her grasp.

Happy tears filled her eyes as she raised her arms around his neck, never wishing to let him go again, and the book fell to the end table behind him. Her arms wrapped around his neck and she let him take her to the heavens with his sweet kiss.

Chapter 29

Jasper felt something wet touch his cheek, and reluctantly pulled away, touching his cheek. His fingers came back with tears that were not his own, and concern filled him as he looked down at her in astonishment. "What is it?"

If someone had hurt her, if anyone had caused her pain, he would tear them apart. No one and nothing would be able to stop the pain that would befall the monster who had hurt Emeline. Lucifer himself would be put to shame, he was certain of that.

"I love you," she said with a watery smile.

His lips parted in surprise and he automatically searched her eyes for any sign that she was lying. Pure, radiant love shone back to him, and he tightened his grasp on her, wishing to hear it again, to assure himself it hadn't been his imagination.

His heart swelled and heated, the beat faster than normal, at hearing the words he had longed to know coming from her delicate mouth. Joy pushed through him with every beat and he wanted to shout to the heavens with it.

"Emeline-"

"I understand if you don't feel the same," she rushed out, "but I think I've always loved you, ever since the first time I saw you. I know I'm not a war-rior, I know I'm not courageous or fearless but-"

He silenced her with a kiss, his growl vibrating into her mouth. Pulling away, he rested his forehead against hers, eyes closed. "I shouldn't love you, Emeline. I should push you away and save you from living the same isolated life that I lead." He raised his hand to her cheek, stroking her bottom lip until it parted from the top one, opening invitingly. "I am dangerous and I have a temper, but I swear to you, when I love, I love with everything I have." She kissed his thumb, flickered her tongue over the scars there and he pressed against her, the action arousing him further than he thought possible. "Emeline, I love you with everything inside of me. I shouldn't, but I do and no matter what happens, you will always be mine."

She looked up as a single tear moved down her cheek and she licked it when it touched her lip. "Do you mean that?"

"Yes," he said eagerly. "I've never felt this way about anyone. This passionate, this intense desire that I have is for you, only you." He hesitated, glancing away before he gave a firm nod. "I do not wish you to heal my scars."

She looked up in surprise, eyes wide. "Are you sure?"

"If you are not repulsed by them, I will keep them as badges of honor," he said tentatively. "Whatever will bring you happiness is what I wish."

Emeline smiled and tears glistened in her eyes again. "You are the most handsome, fierce man and dragon I have ever met, and I have never been bothered by your scars. Especially this one," she added, tracing her finger down the scar on his bottom lip. "I love this one."

His lips parted to pull her finger into his mouth and her breath caught as his tongue swirled around the tip. "I think I could learn to love it too, then," he said, his eyes heated on her own.

She tugged her finger free and cupped his cheek. "Imenda told me that she was certain you would be bored with me, that you would throw me away when you were done, but I never believed her. Not for a second."

He stiffened, his eyes hard on hers, and he frowned. "When did you speak with Imenda?"

She froze, eyes downcast.

"Emeline," he demanded. "Why did you go down to speak with her? Is that why Ana wouldn't answer me when I asked her to find you?"

"I-I wanted to ask her questions. Questions I wasn't sure you would answer."

He jerked away from her, leaving her cold and empty, her arms raised from where he had been.

"What could you have possibly wanted to know that you didn't think I would tell you, Emeline?"

She bit her lip, dropping her arms to toy with the edge of her fingers. "I wanted to know the story of what happened between you two. I wanted to know why she thought she could win you from me."

"I could have told you all of that," he said softly, hurt in his eyes.

She stepped forward. "I'm sorry, I-"

"Enough, Emeline."

Her brow furrowed in anger. "No," she ground out. "I am not one of your subjects, I am not someone you can order around! I went to Imenda and do you know what I found out? I found out about Fate and Luke. She said you left them to die, that you did nothing to stop it when she knew you could have."

"And you would believe the ramblings of a psychotic, unstable demon?"

"Would you have told me?"

He snapped his lips shut.

"Ana did," she said softly. "She trusts me with secrets. She knows she can trust me not to over-react or to hate you for what has happened. Luke and Fate were selfish to leave everyone behind for the sake of love, especially without telling you. They left you here alone to be together, but it is the one time I can understand being that selfish."

His lips parted but no words came out.

"I didn't believe Imenda," she said shakily, her tears flowing freely. "I trusted in you, which is why I asked Ana for the truth." She grabbed her book from the table, and strode past him with a parting, "Because I knew that you wouldn't have told me."

She turned the corner out the door.

Jasper shut his eyes, a mix of emotions flooding him.

Anger that she had gone down to see the she-demon without him, putting herself at risk without anyone with controllable powers with her.

Sadness, that she had been right. He wouldn't have told her about Fate and Luke, but he also wouldn't have wanted her view of him to be tainted by Imenda's history with him. What kind of monster must she have thought him to be, that he would have allowed it to happen if he had known?

Hurt that she hadn't trusted him to tell her what she wanted to know. But could he blame her? She had known what would happen if she had asked, and she took actions to get the answers she had needed. Ones he should have been able to give her.

Turning on his heel, resolute in his decision, and he strode after her, easily catching up to her as she clutched her book, but never broke stride.

"Imenda tortured me for Lucifer so that he could try to overrun the dragons and rule the realm for himself."

She froze, nearly causing him to topple over her. "What?"

"Imenda was a demon first, given to Lucifer for her evil doings on Earth, which I didn't know until long after what had happened. She was granted access to the dragon shifters, allowed to take the time to redeem herself, but the act of torturing an innocent man for the devil himself was an evil act." He sighed, crossing his arms over his chest, and bracing his feet shoulder-width apart. "She told me, while she was cutting me, that Lucifer had given her no choice, that he had threatened my life."

"She could have chosen not to take the deal, to believe in you," she said softly.

"When I finally freed myself from her torture, I brought her straight into hell. It was out of anger," he added admittedly. "But it was also the divine punishment. She was placed on the first level, the worst of the worst. She had caused many deaths by reporting to Lucifer, and she cost herself her redemption by giving me these scars."

Tears filled her eyes anew. "I didn't know."

"Of course you didn't. I should have been the one to tell you," he said glumly.

"Yes, you should have."

His head tilted forward as he rubbed the bridge of his nose. She cupped his face in her hands to pull his gaze to her.

"But I understand why you couldn't."

"Fate and Luke have a baby girl now," he said softly. "Anabelle."

She smiled as he swiped her tears away with his thumbs. "It's a beautiful name."

"Someday, I'll take you there to meet them," he vowed. "Fate may interrogate you a bit, but they will adore you."

"I hope so. From what Ana tells me, they mean a great deal to you."

"They are my family," he said firmly.

She lifted her lashes to look up at him. "Then I look forward to it."

He gave a nod, determined. "We will deal with Tucker and Imenda, and then we will visit them."

"I think Ana should see them too."

He frowned. "How do you know she hasn't already?"

She shrugged. "She sounded wistful when she spoke of how she missed them, as though she knew they are somewhere but not where and wished to see them."

He gave a nod. "I know where they are. Myself and an angel of death, who has kept their secret as well as I have."

"Why would he do that," she inquired, brow furrowed. "Doesn't that go against his code or the rules?"

His eyebrows raised.

She flushed and indicated the book clutched in her arms. "I read about them in this book," she said. "They are sworn to loyalty for the angelic counsel. So why would he keep them a secret?"

"He is friends with Fate."

"Oh."

She looked at her book, then back up to him, and cleared her throat. "Why didn't you tell me sooner?"

"It was never my secret to tell. And I thought you might view me differently, and I guess I liked that pedestal you had me on."

His brooding gaze met hers and she laughed. "I think it is honorable of you to let them have their happily ever after." Her laughter slowly died and she shifted from one foot to the other nervously. "Do you think we could have a happily ever after?"

"I will make sure of it," he decreed, wings twitching in anticipation.

Her smile returned, filling him with pride. "Very well."

Jasper, Wynter's voice boomed in his mind. *Imenda is gone.*

Jasper stiffened.

Emeline's expression melted to concern. "What is it?"

"Imenda is gone," he growled.

Ana, Wynter, Jasper, Navi, and Emeline stood around a large, circular table in the center of a dimly lit room. A single light shone down on the table, illuminating the image of the world imprinted on the marble top. Golden streams of light emanated from it, giving off a power all its own, as the lights danced and moved.

Emeline gaped in amazement. "It's beautiful."

"It's a view of the Afterlife realm over every world," Jasper explained. "And those lights are the good souls of the world."

"Lights Imenda wants to put out," Wynter seethed.

"So what do we do," Ana asked. "This castle has been infiltrated. Tucker has to have gotten inside somehow to release Imenda, it's the only thing that makes sense."

"No it isn't," Navi said firmly. "Imenda might have planned this all along. Perhaps she wanted to get caught."

Emeline stared at the world as they chatted around her, but it felt as though they spoke from a distance. Imenda hadn't stolen anything, of that she was sure. She certainly hadn't succeeded in breaking up Emeline and Jasper.

So if she had wanted to get caught, it had to have been for another reason.

Emeline's eyes widened when she realized what it could have been. "Redemption," she said quietly.

Despite the volume of her voice, the silence around her became heavy as everyone paused to stare at her.

From across the table, Jasper's brow furrowed and he leaned forward with his arms on the table. "What?"

"Redemption," Emeline repeated, looking toward Ana. She licked her lips to brace for what she was about to suggest. "What if Imenda was never the one pulling the strings? What if that was just how it was meant to look?"

Navi looked thoughtful. "It would explain why Tucker seems more powerful then she is and why the demon listens to him."

Wynter gave a nod. "So then, why would she come here?"

"Redemption," Jasper muttered with his eyes closed in acute pain. "It is likely what Emeline said.

Imenda was hoping to share her side of the story for redemption, while Tucker used the distraction to gain some ground in tracking Emeline down."

Emeline stared down at the souls in the world. "Or she was distracting him." Her gaze lifted to Jasper. "For you. To keep you safe."

Jasper shook his head. "It matters not. She is a traitor."

"Even so," she insisted, "she came here to explain herself. Perhaps gain penance for what she has done. Tucker won't appreciate that too much, if that's the case."

Navi rubbed the bridge of his nose. "She let you escape from the basement."

"By using magic so we could track you," Ana finished with a sigh. "She wanted to get caught."

Wynter snorted. "What could she possibly hope to gain? No one here was going to grant her entry into the realm of Dragons."

"She has been in the first level of hell for decades," Emeline said, toying with her fingers as she always had when she was nervous. "Perhaps she lost herself down there, forgot her sanity?"

"I was stuck down there for five hundred years," Ana snapped. "I think I'm perfectly sane."

All eyes swung to the dragon witch in disbelief, and she challenged every gaze. "What?"

Jasper and Wynter shook their heads in disgust and rolled their eyes.

Navi hid a chuckle behind his hand.

Emeline smiled and winked at her.

"So what do we do?"

Emeline bit her lip. "What if we turned her to our side the same way Fate turned Ana?"

"No."

"No way, not going to happen."

"I'd rip out her liver and feed it to her with my witchy powers out of boredom first."

Jasper was the last to respond, and he swung his gaze to the icy dragon to his left. "There may be another way to move her to our side."

Wynter glowered at his king, arms crossed. "I'm not going to like this, am I?"

Chapter 30

The trio of dragons and two elves stood in a semi-circle in the front hall, waiting.

Ana had her arms crossed, her manicured fingernails digging into her bicep to still her trembling. "This is *so* stupid."

Wynter stepped closer to her, placing a hand on her shoulder, and she shivered. "He will not take you or harm you. He has little interest in you anyway, at this point."

Jasper peeked out from beneath his hood. "Lucifer may show upon the news of an imminent threat and challenge of his authority, but he will not take my charge from me."

Emeline circled to the front of him and pushed the hood from his head, gently settling it between his wings. "Let him see you for the fierce, sexy warrior that you are."

He bent his head for a kiss. "Very well."

Navi smiled behind his hand.

A small tornado of black smoke circled in front of them, knocking out the lights provided by the candles on the wall sconces. The smell of death and sulfur rose with the wind that swirled around them, and darkness filled the castle despite the early evening light outside.

Jasper folded his hands behind him, glaring at the smoke. "Steady," he told the others. Wynter stood stiff as stone, but Ana shifted from one foot to the other, uneasy. Navi's eyes widened in fright and surprise as he stumbled back, and Emeline joined Jasper's side, her hand brushing his own in comfort.

For him or herself, he wasn't sure.

Finally, it sank into the floor, revealing a man with blackened wings, his hands folded in front of him. He wore a dark gray suit with a red tie, and black dress shirt beneath his blazer. His eyes were charcoal black, his mid-length black hair tugged back into a neat, business-like ponytail.

Though he appeared as normal as any dark angel could be, it felt as though the air had been sucked out of the room. Death, pain, and sorrow clung to this man like a second skin, causing everyone around him to cringe and shy away.

All except Jasper. "Lucifer."

"Jasper Rogue," he said, his voice neutral. "You would do well to address me with respect instead of distain, especially if you plan on asking for my help. Now, why have you summoned me here?"

Jasper frowned. "Imenda and Tucker have created a level, where they have stored elven and demonic souls to channel the same magic that you, yourself, have syphoned. They seek to overthrow you."

"And why come to me," Lucifer asked, his voice deceptively calm. "Why should I help my enemies, after you and your dragons cost me a levels' worth of demons?"

"You were trying to take over the Afterlife realm," Jasper said in a low voice. His dragon roared and fought for freedom within him, but instead of wishing to fight the danger around him, Jasper could feel the dragon urging him to run, to hide away from the king of Hell so that they wouldn't be next.

He mentally shushed the beast, folding his arms across his chest. *It has to be done.*

Lucifer waved a hand as though it were of no consequence to him. "Obviously, I didn't succeed at my plan, but that does not make us any less enemies. Didn't my demon take the lives of your friends? What were their names?"

Jasper narrowed his eyes in challenge. "I wouldn't go there, if I were you."

"Why should I help you with the two demonic brats? We are not allies, I owe you nothing, so it must be that you wish to make me a deal, perhaps?"

"No deals," Jasper said firmly. "We offer our services to help *you* keep the respect you so covet among those who have fallen into hell instead of losing it to your enemies. We are offering our help in defeating this new threat, and to keep you carefully perched on your throne. There are demons, thousands of them, who wish to overthrow you in favor of another, and even you do not have the ability to defeat them all on your own."

Lucifer's eyes changed to red, but he showed no other outward signs of being angry. "What do you mean? Who would dare challenge my authority?"

"The same ones who have created a level in your hell undetected, who now threaten the safety of my realm and those within it."

Lucifer's gaze snapped to Emeline, who gasped and instinctively stepped backward. His dark red eyes studied her as though she were an insect he wished to crush beneath his expensive shoes. "I feel the power radiating off her like heat off a flame. I will find a punishment that will be more suitable-"

Jasper stepped in front of her and felt her lean gratefully between his wings. "She is not up for discussion, and she is not the threat of which I speak."

Lucifer's gaze neutralized and he took in the weight of the group. He settled on Ana, smiling sadistically. "It's been a while."

She palmed her dagger. "Try it."

Jasper growled. "You will listen to me without making assumptions or threatening those who belong to me as king of this realm."

For the first time, Wynter looked upon him with respect, and it gave Jasper the strength he needed to straighten his shoulders.

If even Wynter was finally seeing him as a king, there may just be hope yet, he thought to himself

Lucifer's wings twitched, the only sign of his agitation. "Then hurry on with it, then. I have other business to get to."

"The seventieth layer of hell," Jasper all but growled.

"There is no such level," Lucifer informed him. "The layers only go down to ten."

"Then it was named seventy-six," Jasper shot back. "Imenda and Tucker Jones are the perpetrators, and they have robbed you of your souls, of the power you weld from them. Thousands, based on the information we got out of Imenda before her escape."

Lucifer smiled. "I remember her. Beautiful, naïve, strong." He breathed in a deep breath as though smelling her. "I have had much fun with her."

Jasper tried to feign indifference, but he felt the slightest bit of guilt pool in his chest. Though he had wanted Imenda to suffer, he couldn't imagine what the devil had done to her, and he never wanted to.

It had to be done, dammit.

"Then help us defeat her, her brother, and the demon army they have constructed, and we will offer our help in return."

"No," Lucifer said simply.

Jasper stiffened. "Excuse me?"

"No," Lucifer said with a lift of his shoulders. "It is not my problem. She poses no threat to me, only you."

"And me," Emeline said behind Jasper, stepping out with her hands glowing. "You would allow your demons to see you with a challenger? Imenda and Tucker could take over hell and you will sit idly by and watch?"

"I care not until they make a choice to go against me."

"If they have an army of dragons at their disposal," Ana chimed in, "what makes you think they would not? Dragons have been hunting demons for centuries, maybe even millennia, so how long do you think it would take to tear through the ranks to get to you?"

A muscle ticked under Lucifer's eyes. "They wouldn't dare."

"But they would," Wynter said firmly. "They have already infiltrated this world, attempting to destroy it for more power. With the elven souls they have collected, they can heal themselves. How much more power will they have if they get ahold of dragons souls? Angelic souls?"

Lucifer glowered at the group, his gaze narrowing as he paused, silent for several minutes, before he said at last, "Very well. I will deal with the demonic siblings and help the dragons with their little problem."

Lucifer lifted a hand to disappear and Emeline hurriedly stepped forward just out of Jasper's reach, her hand up to stop the devil from escaping. "What would it take to free the souls of the elves trapped down there?"

Lucifer stilled, a smile curving his lips.

Jasper grabbed ahold of her arm, pulling her back into his chest as though to keep Lucifer from grabbing her, but she could feel the tension strumming through him like a guitar string.

Lucifer gave a small shrug. "I have no need for more elven souls. Enough evil elves have died for me to obtain the ability to heal over the centuries. Too many pure souls will cause an imbalance, and an attack that I am not yet ready for, but I will be. Soon," he added with promise. "For alerting me to this threat, you may have your elven souls. I supposed I will retrieve them, but do not expect me to be so gracious after this."

Emeline's brow furrowed but she simply said softly, "Thank you."

Lucifer chuckled, and something softened in his once harsh gaze. "Don't thank me just yet, love. I see great things for the two of us someday, and you will repay this favor, tenfold."

With that, he vanished.

Jasper whirled her around to face him. "Do you know what you have just done?"

"I freed the souls of hundreds of innocent people," she snapped. "Those elves can heal and be happy in Afterlife now."

Ana stepped forward before he could respond. "She has also weakened their front. If they can't heal, then they can be killed, which gives us the advantage"

Jasper's lips snapped shut.

Navi's eyes watered. "But the favor-"

"Will never come to pass," Jasper ground out between clenched teeth. "I will take her place if need be, but you," he growled to Emeline, "will never talk to Lucifer again."

Emeline lifted her chin defiantly. "If I am called upon to save my people, then I most certainly will."

"Are you that determined to die," Jasper growled. "What if he wishes for your soul in return?"

"I don't think he does," Emeline said, lost in thought. "I think he wishes for my healing ability."

Wynter raised in eyebrow in inquiry. "What makes you think that?"

"The look in his eyes. It seemed as though he had a specific favor in mind, and he rubbed his ring finger when he thought of it, almost as though a ring had once been there."

Ana nodded. "I saw that too."

Wynter chuckled. "The devil has a love? I look forward to hearing that story."

"If it is true," Jasper growled. "Enough of this. Wynter, ready the troops in the training room. Ana, alert the angelic counsel of the goings on. Navi, prepare your room for attack, and bind the room so that no one can enter, not even me. You and Emeline will be staying there for the upcoming battle."

She gaped at him. "No! Jasper, you can't just lock me up!"

He glared at her and caught her shoulders roughly in his hands. "I can and I will. You've gotten yourself into enough trouble. I won't have you getting into even more."

She leveled her own glare to match his own. "I saved people. I weakened the enemy and I convinced Lucifer to join us. I fail to see how I have gotten myself into trouble."

Navi eased Emeline from Jasper's grasp. "We will do as you ask."

Emeline gaped at her father next. "But-"

"Emeline," Navi said firmly. "No more words until everyone calms down, lest we should say something we regret," he added with a firm look at the king.

Jasper gave a curt nod. "I will create a strategy in case Lucifer is unsuccessful. Until then, move to your stations and brace for the worst."

Imenda paced the front room of the castle ruins in her level, her hair waving against the blade sheathed at her back. Agitation was making her twitchy, and she grumbled to herself incoherently, her thoughts scattered.

Tucker twisted the blade against his finger as he sat in the corner, waiting. "What is your problem?"

"I've explained myself," Imenda said in agitation. "Emeline should have told Jasper what I've said by now. He should have left her weak ass at the castle, and come running to my rescue, and this should all be over now."

He chuckled. "You really think it is that easy? If it were, I would have had Emeline in that alley, regardless of her protests, and you would be in the arms of your love. It looks like I will have to kill her and take her soul in order to have her now. All of the fun things I could do to her down here, free of fear for dragons."

Imenda sighed. "I should have been redeemed by now."

"Will you shut it? We are invincible. No one can touch us, why do we need the realm of the dragons for that?" He leaned back and set his sword beside him, his hands laced behind his head. "I say we keep stealing souls and building our power. Soon enough, not even Lucifer himself will be able to stop us from taking over hell, Afterlife, and the land of the living."

"I don't know if I want power," she said softly, looking out where a few bricks were broke and missing from the wall. "I just want Jasper."

"Then maybe you shouldn't have betrayed him by torturing him for Lucifer."

"I was trying to save his life," she snapped. "I couldn't stand to lose him. Lucifer-"

"Is nothing more than a has-been," Tucker said loudly. "Move on from the dragon, find someone new. There are plenty of sexy-looking demon men down here who would happily take his place, why do you not replace him with one of them?"

"There will never be anyone else."

"Then make hell your love," Tucker chuckled. "First the dragons, then hell, eventually the entire universe will bow at our feet. Then Jasper will be begging to be by your side or crying for mercy at the tip of your sword."

"Unfortunate that you should say such trivial things," came a dark, deep voice from all around them. It seemed as though the one responsible was coming from every direction, the power that seized the room paralyzing the twins for a moment.

Tucker shot out of his chair and drew his sword, looking for the source. "Who says they are trivial?"

"Why," Lucifer appeared in front of them, his eyes glowing a deep, terrifying red, "I do."

Imenda stepped back, eyes wide, and fear twisted her stomach into knots.

"Lucifer!"

The endless nights of torment, the days of pain, and hours of agony over the past few decades had honed her for his arrival, for the pure power that drove through her like a knife, reminding her of whom she was facing. No one terrified her quite like Lucifer, and as he stood with his fists clenched at his sides, his muscles bulged and ready for a fight, her heart seemed to stop in her chest.

Her every instinct screamed for her to run, to hide away so he could never find her, yet her feet remained rooted to the spot.

Tucker snorted, and held his arms out, bearing his chest. "Go ahead. Torture me, kill me. I'll just come back stronger than ever, and we'll start again."

"Not without your elven souls you won't," Lucifer said with venom. "I contacted an angel of death, who was very intrigued to hear about your little operation, and the pure souls are where they belong now. The very few evil souls you gathered are in the lowest levels of hell. Under my power," he added with a sneer. "So what power do you really have now against me?"

Tucker seemed to shrink in front of his sister's eyes, and he went pale. "I-I'm sorry, Lucifer! I swear, I-"

Lucifer slammed his fist into the dragon's chest with a sickening snap, grasping his heart in his chest. Tucker wheezed and his eyes bulged in shock as Lucifer squeezed. Imenda screamed, stepping back and away in horror. Red veins popped around Lucifer's arms, his eyes black as his fangs hissed at the former dragon, and blood ran down Tucker's chest onto Lucifer's arm, but the king of Hell didn't seem to care.

"No," Imenda screamed, hands over her mouth in denial. "Please, have mercy!"

Lucifer gave a cruel smile, sliding his gaze to Imenda. "Let this be a lesson to anyone who dares to oppose me as you two have."

Tucker gurgled, blood dripping from his lips as he tried to dislodge Lucifer's hand, but it didn't budge from his chest

"You and I," Lucifer hissed at Imenda. "We're going back to the top level and, for such treason, I will be sure to handle your punishment *personally*."

Tucker raised his sword shakily and Lucifer tore his heart out with a sickening pop. Tucker turned to ash and Lucifer smiled at Imenda, the veins disappearing. He beckoned to her with his finger and her feet moved without her, bringing her closer and closer to her tormentor with her hands raised in front of her.

"Hold this."

He slapped her brother's bloody heart into her trembling hands and tears spilled down her cheeks as she sobbed.

He put his hand on her shoulder and glared at her, his voice menacing as he spoke, "Remember this as you warn the other demons of the consequences of your actions."

Imenda glared back at him through her tears. "You are a monster."

"A beautiful, wonderful monster who is going to raise an army larger than this little band you once had. I will rule the universe on my own, on my terms, and in my own time."

"And Jasper?"

"He will die with the rest when his use is spent."

Imenda was released and she dropped Tucker's heart, watching it turn to ash with the rest of his body, but his blood remained on her hands.

The world trembled around her and more of the ruins crumbled with it.

"What's happening," she cried out.

Lucifer bent his tall frame to level with her, his face dangerously close to hers. "I am destroying this level and stripping you of your magic. I will not allow for this to happen again, should I decide to release you someday."

She lifted her hands and tried to blast him but nothing happened.

"No," she hissed, staring at her hands. "No, please!"

"Too late."

She fisted her hands at her sides and reached for what little magic remained as he drained it. "I still have enough magic to do this."

She disappeared without a trace, leaving Lucifer in the rubble as he continued to destroy the beautiful realm she had created.

Chapter 31

Jasper brought his hand up to Emeline's door, then hesitated, his shoulders tense.

It had been hours since Lucifer's visit, and his irritation still ebbed over how things had happened, but it had faded with the news Lucifer had sent to him.

They were free.

Imenda was in the wind, Tucker was dead, and their kingdom had been destroyed, the souls placed where they should be. Every elven soul had been placed in Afterlife with no memory of their time in Hell and healed by the angels themselves.

All was right with the realm.

He dropped his hand and blew a sigh before bringing himself to pound on the door, murmuring, "Emeline."

On the other side of the door, he heard shuffling and a sigh, then quiet, as though she were building up her courage. Perhaps she worried that he would lecture her over Lucifer or feared who would be on the other side of the door.

He frowned. That she might be afraid to see him was disappointing, and he had hoped they were passed that phase in their relationship. But she truly didn't know about his world, didn't know what danger she brought on herself by making a deal with the devil himself.

Finally, he heard her footsteps as she approached the door and opened it with a forced smile as she sighed. "Jasper."

His shoulders drained of tension as he looked at her, his relief considerable. "I'm sorry."

"No, I'm sorry," she insisted. "I should have heeded your warning. You were just trying to protect me from harm, and I should have appreciated that. I just don't want you to think of me as a liability or a damsel in distress."

Jasper stepped inside her bedroom, causing her to step backwards so he could shut the door behind him, his large frame dwarfing hers. "You have never been a burden or a damsel to me."

Her lips twitched in a fleeting smile, and she flickered her gaze away from him.

He lifted his hand to her cheek, gently turning her back. "I do not like it when you are angry with me."

"Then do something about it," she challenged with a laugh.

He bent his head and the heated press of his lips against hers undid him. He groaned and moved her over to the bed without ending their kisses. She wrapped her arms around his neck and her legs around his waist. He ground himself against her core, as hungry for her as she was for him, and her hands roved through his hair and over his shoulders.

He truly had waited too long to kiss her again.

"Finally," Emeline hissed, but her voice sounded echoed, as though two spoke in place of one and the sound set off red flags in his mind. He pulled away to furrow his brow at her and studied her as he stiffly held her up.

"What, my love," Emeline asked innocently.

Jasper jolted away from her as though she were on fire, the voice echoing over Emeline's and into one that he wished he didn't know. "What is this?"

Emeline blinked, brow furrowed at him. "What is it?"

"Imenda."

She opened her mouth, then blew out a sigh and rolled her eyes. "Oh, fine." Reluctantly, she shifted back into herself. "I so love dragon magic. So easy to siphon, and so useful in getting me what I want!"

"Where is Emeline," he demanded.

Imenda stood, toying with the sleeve of her half-shirt. "Forget about the elf. We could be happier than she could ever make you. We could have a family, a life. I don't care about the dragon realm or your crown, I just want you. I will even give you the baby you always wanted. A hundred, a thousand babies, however many will most please you."

He stepped away from her, eyes wide, and flinched. At one time, he would have jumped at the chance, desperate for love from anyone, even Imenda, but no more. He knew what love was, and he already had it with a beautiful, barefooted elf with the heart of gold.

"I would rather suffer a thousand deaths than create anything with you."

She shrugged. "It would be so fun to go that route, but I say we go the more fun way."

The doorknob turned behind him, and as it began to open, Imenda grabbed the back of his neck, pulling him against her and into the wall as she kissed him, wrapping her legs around his waist like a viper.

Emeline, reading a book, swung the door open and stuck her bookmark in place as she finished her sentence. Setting the book down on the table beside the door, she lifted her gaze only to gape in horror at Jasper, making out with Imenda against the wall.

In the same position he had first kissed her!

Imenda's legs were open, her skirt allowing him to sink against her and his hands were against the wall by her head. As if to add to the image,

Imenda moaned and squirmed against him, her legs locked around him.

He ripped away from her and wiped his mouth on the back of his hand, snarling. "How dare you-"

Emeline's wide, hurt eyes collided with his and guilt filled his golden gaze as he froze in place. "Emeline, this isn't what it-"

"She was right," Emeline whispered, tears in her eyes as her hands flew to her mouth, the other balling into her stomach. "You chose her."

"No, Emeline," he reached for her. "Let me explain."

"No," she cried, stepping away from him. "Ana told me this was over! She said you would never go back to her!"

Imenda smiled, pretending to fix her shirt. "I told you that he would choose me in the end, elf."

"Shut up," Jasper snapped. "I am not choosing you. I've never chosen you, and I never will."

"But you have," Emeline said softly, backing toward the door with her hand behind her. "I-I have to go."

With a twist of her hand, the door opened and she ran through it, disappearing into the hallway before he could stop her.

Emeline swiped at her tears as she strode to the front door, her heart in pieces, and her breathing was labored, but she couldn't stop. The image of them together, making out against the wall, was enough to send her into another fit of sobs.

He had chosen the demon, despite everything Imenda and her psychotic brother had done! Pain shredded through her chest, but she couldn't stop, wouldn't let herself go back to him, to plead with him that she hadn't seen what she had.

But she knew, in her broken heart, that this time, it was truly over.

And it was time to go home.

Jasper lunged forward, his panic rising harshly in his chest. "Emeline! Stop!"

"Don't bother with her, my love," Imenda said, trailing her fingers over his shoulders. "I have many plans to make up being naughty to you and I want to start it now."

Jasper's gaze narrowed and scales broke out over his skin seconds before his dragon overtook him, and Imenda screamed one final time before his claws dug into her throat, reducing her to ash in seconds.

He released a roar of anguish that radiated through his body, pulling even his dragon into his misery, and reached his mind for Ana's. The second his mind connected to hers, he felt the anger in it, the resolution to help Emeline and Navi, and he bolted for the door.

If you take her away from my castle, I will revoke your redemption!

Ana scowled. *You can do no such thing, snake. I vouched for you, I reassured her that you would never betray her, and you were about to screw the bitch who hurt her? You can go to Hell!*

Navi, seated by the front windows, saw Emeline, and stood, concern covering his face as he hurried to her. "Emeline, what-"

"I am going home with or without you," she sobbed.

Navi caught her hands in his, bending down to meet her gaze. "What has happened?"

"Please," she whispered. "The fight is over now, no one is after us anymore. Let's just go home. Please, Father."

A roar echoed through the halls and Emeline jumped in fright, her breath caught in her throat. She knew the roar, knew the anguish in it, and she looked pleadingly at her father. "I do not wish to see him! Please, I just want to go home!"

Navi glared behind her before giving her a reassuring nod. "So we shall."

"I will take you," Ana snarled from behind her. "I heard what happened from down the hall at my room. Let's move now, before he comes down to find you."

She blocked his mind from hers and gave Emeline a hug. "I'll take you home. Navi, grasp my wings."

"Are you sure you are stable enough?"

Ana scoffed. "I *have* been practicing, you know."

Just as Jasper raced down the steps from upstairs, they took off out the front door, the sound of Ana's wings nearly masking the sound of sobs that broke his heart. Emeline gave him one final, heartbroken glance before she was gone from sight.

Tears rolled down his face as he fell to his knees, watching them go and another angry, pained roar ripped from his throat as he threw his head back and let himself grieve.

Emeline, the only woman who had ever truly loved him, had just left him behind.

Alone.

Again.

Three Weeks Later...

Emeline sat in the valley of her homeland, absently toying with a white lily in its center, her thoughts a million miles away. The breeze was warm as it blew her newly shortened hair from her face, highlighting the sadness in her golden eyes. The short strands had been a snap decision, but one that hadn't helped her heartbreak in the least.

Her dress pooled over her feet, the dark blue color accenting her creamy skin even with the clouds looming overhead. The heart-shaped neckline of it outlined the swells of her breasts, hugging them to her snuggly.

It had drawn the attention of many men in the elven village, all of whom had politely tried to court her, but she had barely noticed beyond a rejection that was just as polite.

She was done with love. Her heart felt like it had been ripped from her chest, leaving an empty hole that no other would ever be able to fill. She couldn't stop the pain from radiating from it, couldn't stop wishing for the feel of Jasper's arms around her, his fiery scent enveloping her into his world as he murmured promises into her ear, his deep voice lulling her into a profound sense of calm.

But all the longing in the world wouldn't change what he had done. He had made his choice, and no matter how much she wished it to be otherwise, he was gone from her.

Her heart ached and she swiped at the tear on her cheek, cursing it. Her dragon hadn't risen since the roaring she had heard in her mind on that fateful day. It seemed as though the beast had sank deep into her soul, hiding away from the same pain that she had felt as deeply as Emeline had.

More tears joined the first and she braced herself for the coming sobs. Once they began, she knew they wouldn't stop until she had worn herself out, too tired to cry anymore.

Then the dreams would begin again as she slept, moving from his hands on her to his hands on Imenda, and the cycle would start over.

She shut her eyes and let herself cry.

It was just another day without him, and she knew she was going to have to get used to it.

Navi watched, his own heart breaking at the pain his daughter faced. How foolish they had been to ever leave the safety of the elven village. Perhaps then, she would have found love with another, one who would not have broken her heart so. Even then, he could see the pain he had once had long ago reflecting back at him in her eyes. She had connected, had mated with Jasper, and getting over him would not be easy, of that he was certain.

Her spirit had been drained and she'd barely spoken a word since she had come back to the cottage. Even then, she had only spoken to him and enough to give a polite, "No, thank you" to the elven men who had come, seeking to become a suitor for her.

He rocked in his chair on the covered porch, frowning as he watched her look up into the clouds. Her mind was on Jasper, there was no denying it, but

Navi could only follow her gaze and sigh with a shake of his head.

"Sarafine," he murmured, "Tell me what I must do. You would have known exactly what to say, how to ease her pain, were you here."

But there was nothing the old elf could do to heal her broken heart, which only caused his own heart to break for her all over again, and he could only watch as she lay in the flowers and cried herself to sleep.

Chapter 32

Ana turned as Jasper entered the dining room, her face a mask of anger as she glared at him. "Come to eat finally?"

He didn't respond as he paced through the room to the kitchen.

"Imenda got what she deserved, though I wish you had allowed me to see it for myself."

Again, nothing.

Ana threw her fork onto the table, the silver crashing against the porcelain plate hard enough to crack it. "Enough of this!"

Jasper stopped, his hand on the doorway, and tension radiated off of him as he turned, his face expressionless. "Enough of what?"

"Moping," she snapped, hands on her hips. "You have been floating around here like a ghost, barely sleeping or eating. You chose this path, you chose Imenda, and it cost you the best thing you had in your afterlife!"

"She attacked me," Jasper said softly. "I ripped out her throat right before *you* took Emeline from me. Based on what you thought you heard from outside the room, which wasn't the truth."

"Attacked you," Ana demanded. "What does that even mean? Emeline told me you were ready to screw the bitch when she walked in."

"Imenda saw the knob turning and grabbed me, shoving me against her into the wall so it would look that way."

Ana snorted, but one look at the sorrow in his eyes silenced her. "You're not lying, are you? She really staged it?"

"It doesn't matter now," he said without emotion. "It's over."

"Yes it matters, you dolt," she snapped. "I've been keeping an eye on her, and from what I've seen, she hasn't hardly spoken since she left and she is miserable without you! Not even the elven suitors of her village have made her smile or feel better! So why don't you just tell her the truth?"

"She wouldn't believe me."

"Well, she certainly isn't going to if you keep putting it off!"

He turned back to the door, hesitated, then pushed through without another word.

Emeline stared out into the night as the breeze blew over the valley, one arm over the other. Their wooden house hadn't changed in the years since they had left it, and she still have a stunning view of the valley behind the house, and the mountains covered in trees that seemed to glow in the wake of the moon-light.

A white nightgown with cap sleeves and a low neckline hugged her as she brushed her hair behind her ear only for the lock to slide back into place alongside her cheek. For a moment, only a moment, she allowed herself to pretend Jasper was behind her, waiting to take her into his arms so that he could see the moon beyond the glass of the window. His warmth would remove the chill that seemed to settle on her like a second skin, his lips against the curve of her neck as he would rock her and assure her that he would never let anything happen to her.

She sighed.

"Emeline."

She shut her eyes, the caressing sound of his voice slithering down her spine but she remained silent, wishing his voice were real. That after so many days away from her, he had come for her, some kind of explanation willing away what he had done.

"Emeline, look at me. Please," Jasper added softly.

She sniffed, her swollen and red eyes watering as she felt him, heard him, and her heart could only break more, shattering in her chest like glass that cut into her from the inside out.

"Just go away," she whispered.

"I want to show you something. The truth," he added gently.

Jasper's voice sounded pained and she pulled her bottom lip into her mouth to nibble on before she turned, hesitating before she met his darkened gaze. A lump formed in her throat and tears began to fill her eyes when she saw him, real, and broken, in the shadows of her room.

He stood, as brooding and hauntingly beautiful as she remembered, in the corner of her room, where the shadows encased him in darkness. His hood was over his head, leaving only his golden gaze to shine in the moonlight as he stared at her, unable to look away.

She bunched her hands into the skirt of her gown. "I saw the truth." Her voice shook and she felt her hands begin to tremble as she tried to speak through tears. "I don't want to see anymore."

Sadness seeped into the depths of his eyes. "If you do not wish to see me anymore after I have shown you the truth, I will never return to you again. You can move on with your life, and I will not haunt you, but I cannot live anymore with the knowledge of how pained you are. I cannot live without knowing that you know what really happened that day."

A tear slid down her cheek and his arm twitched as though he wished to touch her but refrained. And oh, how she wished he wouldn't, that he would rush to her and promise everything would be okay.

She licked the tear off her lip and gave in with a nod. "Very well. But you will leave when you are done?"

"Yes," he choked out.

She stepped closer, the pain in her heart intensifying with every step she took. Ana's red eyes glowed from in front of her and she gasped moments before Ana's hands curled around her own, jerking her into a vision.

She saw everything, every horrifying moment Imenda put him through. The kiss he had given her thinking it was Emeline, his mate. The vision closed on the doorknob as it turned and Imenda, jerking him into a kiss and jumping up to wrap her legs around him, making him catch himself on the wall before he toppled over.

The way he slashed through her throat the moment Emeline had left, his anger giving him claws as his dragon took out his revenge.

When it ended, she stumbled backward, reeling with shock, and pressed a hand to her heart.

Ana smiled sadly, her hands drifting to her sides. "He didn't choose her, Emeline," she said softly. "He chose you, always, and Imenda destroyed it in her selfishness."

Ana gave one last, sad smile before she turned and disappeared into the darkness.

Emeline met Jasper's apprehensive gaze, shock stealing the words from her parted, trembling lips as she realized how wrong she had been. How ready she had been to believe a demon over him, and she shook her head.

How could she have believed Imenda over Jasper!

He never would have hurt her that way, especially with Imenda, and it broke her heart anew to know how hurt Jasper had been.

Jasper bowed his head after several moments had passed. "As you have wished it, I will go and I will never bother you again, as I promised."

He turned and disappeared out the way Ana had, leaving her alone.

Emeline dropped to her knees, her tears flowing onto the floorboards as she put her fist to her chest and felt the fresh ache there.

Rage grew inside of her at what Imenda had done, and she struggled to breathe with through it. When her gaze shot up, her eyes were red, and she punched the floor once, twice, cracking the wood beneath her as though she punched paper. Her dragon roared with outrage, rising for the first time in days, and she hit harder, breaking more boards beneath her fist with the added strength of her dragon.

She kept hitting until her energy waned and her mind finally cleared.

Her lips parted, eyes going wide and she stood, running barefoot downstairs and out into the field as she looked desperately for Jasper, for any sign of him.

Even in the full moon light, he was nowhere in sight.

"Jasper," she shouted to the skies, her hands on her heart. "I don't want you to go away! I want you here, with me! Please, come back! I'm so sorry, Jasper! I never should have believed Imenda! Please," she whispered brokenly. "I love you!"

Silence answered her cries and she fell to her knees, her energy spent as she tried to yell but ended up whispering, "Please come back to me."

She watched her tears fall into the grass as she struggled to breathe. He was truly gone, disappeared as he had promised, and he had always kept his promises. She had made such a terrible mistake, and it didn't seem like she could ever repair it. If only she had listened, let him explain what had happened earlier, perhaps she could have saved them both the heartache.

"I should have trusted you," she murmured. "I should have known your love for me was true, and I never should have let Imenda trick me as she had. If she were here…" Her voice trailed off and a growl rippled through her. "I can't live without you," she whispered, her chin dropping to her chest. "I miss you, I have missed you so terribly over these last few weeks. So many nights, I dreamed of your arms around me, of your face waking me in the morning. I love you, I love you so much, and I need you in my life, please forgive me!"

Silence met her and she shut her eyes, rubbing her eyes with the heel of her hand.

A rustle behind her made her sit up straight, eyes wide, as she scanned over the bushes and trees for any sign of movement, for any hope that he had returned.

Strong arms suddenly banded around her waist, tugging her to her feet as he warmed her instantly and his soft, warm lips trailed down the side of her neck to her shoulder. She leaned into his strength in relief and clutched his hands around her, unwilling to let him go. Her breathing was choppy as she choked on fresh sobs, her finger tangling in his.

"There is nothing to forgive," he murmured as he turned her to face him. "But you have to be sure that this is what you want, Emeline," he said firmly. "Because I bear to lose you again. Ever."

She threw her arms around his neck and held tight, determined that she would not ever be able to let him go again. "I promise! I want this, I want you, always!"

His arms tightened around her and he rocked her gently, burying his face in her hair. "I do not like it when you cry."

She burst out a laugh and leaned back to face him, her tears happy ones. "I couldn't help it." He stroked her cheeks, wiping away the tears she had shed, and she leaned into his touch, starved for it after weeks without it. "I felt like my heart had been ripped from my chest when I thought you had…"

"Never," he said firmly. "Never, no one but you."

She leaned her head on his chest, listening to his heartbeat, and his hand moved to her cheek, pressing her into him as though he might never let go.

His fingers tangled in her hair and he frowned. "You cut your hair."

She stiffened, looking at him with uncertainty as she tugged on the strands. "Do you like it?"

He pulled her fingers free and kissed the tips of each, taking his time to enjoy the taste of each one. "I do."

She smiled.

He kissed over her face, every heated press of his lips making her want him even more. "I have missed you, Emeline."

"I've missed you too."

His lips finally met hers and she grasped his arms, pushing into the kiss that she had craved for so long.

"I love you," she murmured. "I will always love you, forever and always."

He chuckled, reluctantly pulling away from her. "I will always love you too."

Her brow furrowed after a moment. "But where can we live?"

"If we keep this house for your father, we could visit often," he suggested. "But right now, I only crave you. The rest can wait until tomorrow." His hands slid down her back to cup her bottom and he ground against her, making her feel damp and tight between her thighs. "It has been far too long since I have had you in my arms, connected with you in a way I have not connected with any other. And I need you now."

She kissed his nose, his jaw, all along his scars until he groaned, the sound vibrating against her lips as she moved down his throat. Her lips continued down to his collarbone, savoring the salty taste of his skin there, and she breathed him in, taking the scent of fire in with her, and knew that she would never tire of it.

He hissed in a breath when her lips reached the center of his chest and she flickered her tongue out, tasting him again.

"Emeline," he moaned.

She wiggled her hips against him, eager to feel him fill her, for his skin to touch her own. His fingers tightened on her bottom, cupping her there, and the ache building for him, always him, grew, making her lift her head to kiss his jaw.

She gasped when he picked her up and laid her down on the grass, taking his spot between her thighs so he could rub himself against her.

"I cannot wait any longer," he groaned.

She wiggled impatiently, lifting her hips to move against his. "Then don't."

He tugged his sweatpants over his thighs and moved his hand up between her legs to find her wet and waiting for him. With a growl, he slid his finger inside and her hips arched as a cry escaped her, her fingers digging into his shoulders to keep her grounded. Every touch and press of his lips sent her higher and higher until she forgot everything around her, everything but him and this moment.

He pulled his finger from her and moved over her, sinking deep with one powerful thrust that had them both crying out in pleasure. Immediately, she felt whole and connected to the other half of her soul. The void that had seemed to consume her just hours before had filled with her passion for him, for the simple act of loving this man who hid in the shadows.

For the hero who held her so delicately, and yet, was firm in his resolve to have her.

His lips found hers and he moved, unable to help himself as he thrust in and out of her, dragging moan after moan out of her, and a tear moved down her cheek at the beauty of it. As he moved, she felt herself driven higher and higher, her muscles tightening around him until she was throwing her head back and moaning uncontrollably.

Finally, she felt as though she had burst into flames, crying out his name in bliss as she grasped onto his arms and rode the waves. Every thrust made her spasm again and again, unable to stop as he built her up again, demanding her orgasm and coaxing his own. Her muscles clenched down on him, already moving toward another orgasm, and he pulled away from her mouth to kiss down her throat to her breasts, closing his mouth on each nipple in turn through her gown.

She moaned, meeting him thrust for thrust as she grew needy and desperate for their release.

"I will never get enough of you," she whispered to him.

He nipped her opposite breast in response and caught the other between his fingers, causing her to erupt around him once more. He twitched inside of her, his body tensing as he thrust deeper and slower than before, his own orgasm building to the breaking point.

Unable to hold back anymore, he roared into the night as he released into her, throwing his head back as he did, and for a moment, his pupils narrowed, glowing in the moonlight. She looked up as he grit his teeth and groaned, finally collapsing on top of her, spent from the events of the night.

For a while, they stayed like that, trying to catch their breath. She stroked his hair as he rested his head on her chest, listening to her heart pound as she had for him. When they had come down from their climaxes, she slid her hand up into his hair once more and trailed her fingers down his cheek.

"Will it always be like this with you?"

"Always," he murmured, nibbling her shoulder.

She laughed as he rolled to the side, staring up into the stars. As he peered up, he frowned and she traced the line, frowning with him. "What is it?"

"The counsel will want to meet with you. By now, they have been informed of the goings on, as they are careful to keep a close eye on Lucifer and his movements."

"And you fear that they will judge me?"

"Yes."

"But I have done nothing wrong," she protested.

"No," he agreed firmly. "But they will want to deal with Navi, as well as you, for the decision to have you. Such an act will not go unpunished."

She sat up fast, furious, and bumped him off her. "I will not allow them to prosecute my father for finding love."

"It is something beyond my power," Jasper said, rubbing his eyes in exasperation. "However, we can fight them if they choose to move down that route. I will not allow them to wrongfully punish you or your father."

"*Then* we can be together?"

He smiled. "Then we can get married."

She blinked. "Married? I didn't know we were engaged."

"I just assumed you would say yes," he said with a grin.

"Maybe," she teased.

He pretended to scowl. "I won't give you a choice."

She giggled.

His expression sobered. "They wish to see you and Navi tomorrow morning. Ana informed me of this only a few moments ago."

She toyed with the edge of her gown. "Does that mean you're going back to the palace?"

"It means *we* are going to the palace, yes."

"And Father?"

He blew out a sigh and turned his head to look at the darkened house in the distance. "Is he not asleep?"

"Well yes, but-"

"Then let him sleep. We can gather him in the morning."

She gave a reluctant nod, burrowing deeper into his arms to hide in his warmth from the chill of the night. "Very well."

Chapter 33

The counsel was more heavenly than Emeline had thought it would be.

The buildings were made mostly from clouds, with pillars made of stone around the outside and the clouds surrounding them looked endless. White pillars, much like those in Greek mythology, rose from the clouds to curved roofs several stories high. The hallways were open and angels with large, white wings moved from one end to the other, some moving through the pillars to other, smaller buildings.

Jasper urged her forward with his hand on the small of her back to follow Navi and her shoulder bumped into the guardian angel at her side. Jasper growled in response but she reached her hand behind her to lace with his to calm him. His dragon had been on the verge of emerging ever since they had arrived, as though fighting against being with the angels, but Emeline had learned that with a touch of her hand, he seemed to relax and remember himself.

The counsel's room was large with only a tall platform in the middle, and golden steps led up to the top. Twelve oval, white thrones with golden cushions were lined up with a taller, rectangular one in the center. All the angels on the counsel were seated with their heads held high, their hands adorned in rings and jewels. Their robes were white with golden trim and tall, golden crowns sat upon their heads. The men's crowns were tall and decorated with rubies and emeralds and the women's were smaller and decorated with sapphires.

The guardian angels left the massive, mostly empty room and shut the doors behind them with a loud thud that echoed through the massive room. Even from the bottom of the stairs, Emeline could feel their power and trembled with nerves. Beings that powerful could easily erase her from existence, if they so chose to do so, without flinching.

Jasper's voice filtered through her mind through their newly strengthened mind link, his warmth replacing the ice that had seemed to solidify in her veins.

Steady.

"Emeline Lilian," the tall man in the center bellowed. "I am Michael, the highest angel of the angelic court. We hear you are something we are to be concerned about, and so we deigned that it was time to see for ourselves."

She tucked her hair behind her ear and forced herself to lift her gaze to Michael's. "I am of no threat to you or your kind," she said softly.

"And yet you have hidden away from us all these years."

"I hid her away," Navi said firmly, as he stepped forward. "I did not want any wrath to befall her mother or I simply for building a family together."

"And going against our rules," Michael said with disapproval.

Emeline narrowed her eyes, her dragon giving a low growl. "Your rules can bend when true love is at stake."

"Our rules are there to protect the people of Afterlife," Michael countered. "Those same rules keep the living people from finding out about our world. A world that you are now a part of."

She flickered a gaze over her shoulder to Jasper for strength and back. If they thought to keep Jasper away from her…

"What of me then? If I chose one from this world, would I not be allowed to live in it? To keep my mate?"

"You are a complicated matter," he said stiffly. "One that will require specific rules."

"You will not take her from me," Jasper growled, joining her side with his fists clenched. Briefly, she thought she saw scales break out over his skin, but they were gone as quickly as she had seen them. "I will bring my army to fight and many angels will die to ensure she is mine," he added as he growled low.

"You would do well not to threaten the ones who can wipe her existence from time and space, Rogue," Michael said, as he stood. "You will allow us to speak before you disrespect us again."

Jasper remained quiet but his golden glare promised bloodshed.

Navi fisted his hands at his sides but said nothing.

Michael sat back into his seat, the picture of poise and calm despite his declaration only second before. "Sarafine was a beautiful warrior, and she earned her place in Afterlife with all the good that she caused. This will excuse her lovechild, but it will not forgive the rules that were broken."

"What will, then," Emeline asked pointedly.

"Nothing," Michael said softly. "Sarafine broke the rules and Navi helped her to do it. When she married you," he said to Navi, "she was entering a sacred union, one that even we could not break."

"You knew about us," Navi said in disbelief.

"Yes," Michael said. "But it was too late, you had already bonded."

"Bonded," Emeline's small voice said from behind her father. "What does that mean?"

"Two souls became one. They can channel each other's magic, and, in this case, cause one of the living to inherit a piece of the dragon."

She gaped at Navi, who had the nerve to look guilty. "That's how you knew about the dragons."

"I never used my dragon magic," he insisted to the counsel with his hand up. "But I drew on the memories of hers to enlighten my daughter of her heritage."

"We have already found a solution to this dilemma."

The trio waited while he gathered his thoughts.

"You are a beautiful creature, one who has chosen the side of good, so you are welcome to live unless there is such a time where you should choose to use your magic in a way befitting a monster. We cannot, however, allow you to live among the elves *and* the dragons, so you must choose which world you will live in. For no being of this world can live in the world of the living, or we risk exposure and endanger every soul on the other side."

Emeline looked between her father and Jasper. "But what about my father?"

"He too, has the choice."

Navi met her gaze and gave a nod of encouragement. "I will go wherever you wish, Emeline."

She turned back to Michael, concerned. "But what about my people? The elves? Will they be safe without us?"

"The elves are under the protection of the dragons, so long as their souls remain pure, but the living and the dead may not live amongst one another. You must choose which you wish to remain in, or we will choose for you."

Jasper stepped back, his hands hanging loosely at his side, and his brooding gaze darkened. She tugged him back with a hand in his and smiled reassuringly to him. "There is no choice for me, your grace. I choose Jasper, now and always. I choose the dragons, the protectors of the innocent."

Michael bowed his head. "Then is it done. For your service in rescuing the elven souls from Hell, we also wish to extend your life to match Jasper's so that you both shall live happily for however long you please."

"And my father?"

Michael grimaced. "Very well."

She smiled and hugged first Navi, then Jasper.

Michael lifted his chin and eyed Jasper. "A piece of advice, your highness."

Jasper released Emeline and stepped forward.

"You need your people behind you," he said slowly. "Which means you need to win them over. I believe your beautiful new bride will be able to aid you in this, but it must be done to avoid disaster.

Without your dragons behind you, the innocents of the worlds are left to fend for themselves."

"And so it will be," Jasper said firmly.

"Good," Michael said. "Then this session is over. Enjoy your Afterlife," he said with a wink at Emeline.

She smiled.

So, the stuffy angel had a sense of humor after all.

Emeline rested on Jasper's chest, fast asleep after the events of the previous few days and their numerous lovemaking sessions. After leaving the angelic counsel, Navi had been granted access to Afterlife, and sent word that he had happily reunited with Sarafine.

Emeline had been thrilled for him, but she wanted to move into the palace at once, which Jasper had assured her would be done. They had hardly left the bedroom since, and he hadn't been willing to let her go for longer than he had to.

In her sleep, she nuzzled her nose under his chin, breathing deep as though to catch his scent to calm herself from a nightmare, and he stroked her back to further soothe her. No nightmares would be allowed to plague her this night, he would make sure of it.

He smiled as he watched the fire in the fireplace across from his bed and tucked his opposite arm behind his head as he marveled at how everything had turned out.

In no time at all, a single elf had taken his life and flipped it upside down. He had been determined no one would ever love him, that nothing good would ever happen to him, and yet right then, he was certain he would never know any other life. That his heart could not be anymore full than it was right in that moment, with her peacefully sleeping beside him, the fire dancing over her skin.

He shifted his gaze down to her, watching the fire flicker over her face as she rested and kissed her forehead. Despite the peace, her eyes were still puffy from her tears the night before and he frowned, tugging his arm free from behind his head to stroke her cheek as though to wipe away the tears that no longer existed.

The pain she suffered, even emotional, tore his heart from his chest, and even knowing that the tears were over did not help ease the ache. He wanted to take every hurt, past or present, and obliterate them, to replace them with memories that would make her smile and laugh.

To give her memories that she deserved.

She stirred and he froze with his hand on her cheek.

Her lashes lifted and she smiled. "Hello."

He stared down at her, trapped in the weight of her gaze. "Hello yourself."

She rubbed her eyes sleepily. "Is something wrong?"

"No," he murmured, kissing her forehead.

Her lips parted in a yawn. "Are you sure?"

"Yes. For the first time in many years, everything is perfect." He turned to his side, resting his head in his hand once more. "I wish for you to meet Fate, Luke, and Anabelle."

She shrugged, causing the sheet wrapped around her to slip slightly. "Alright. When do we do that?"

"It isn't too late," he hedged. "We could go now."

She looked down first at herself, then at him. "I think we need some preparation time first. I don't even have anything to wear that isn't packed into a bag right now."

"Yes you do," he said with a chuckle.

Epilogue

Emeline toyed with the edge of her black tank, her knuckles brushing her gray sweatpants as she shuffled her bare feet on the cobblestone.

"I don't feel like comfort clothes is what I should be wearing."

"You look beautiful," he complimented. "And they are going to love you."

She blushed.

A girl with long, dark red hair opened the door, her smile wide even as her orange eyes looked first to Jasper, then to Emeline and lit with excitement. "Finally! I thought you would never bring the mystery girl around to meet the family!"

A tall, dark-haired man stepped up behind her, his arms around her waist, and gave a nod of approval, his red eyes scanning Emeline from head to toe. He rocked with the woman in his arms, his chin on the top of her head.

"She's a catch, Jasper," he teased.

Jasper scowled.

Fate elbowed Luke in the gut, causing him to grunt and rub the spot with a grin, and he stole a kiss on her cheek, amusement dancing in his eyes.

Emeline smiled. "I can already tell we're going to get along well."

A soft cry made both parents shoulders slump, and Fate sighed, shutting her eyes as though she were pained.

Jasper straightened, brightening more than Emeline had ever seen him. "I will get her," he offered proudly.

The couple's eyes widened, but both stepped aside to make way for the large warrior to stride through and disappear inside the warm house.

Emeline laughed at their dumbfounded expressions. "I heard all about Anabelle on the way here. It seems that your daughter has a solid hold on Jasper's heart that even I couldn't rival."

Fate stepped aside, sweeping her hand to invite the elf inside. "Make yourself at home. Well, not too much at home," she added with a dark look at her husband.

Luke smiled down at her, tucking his hand in her hair to tilt her mouth to his own. When he finally broke free, he murmured, "Only for you."

Emeline slid passed the two and found Jasper leaning over a bassinet in the living room, speaking soothingly to the child inside. His expression was soft as he gently rocked her with one hand, and Annabelle held his finger on the other, staring her luminous, red eyes up at him.

Her heart swelled when she looked upon Annabelle's sweet face and the way it melted Jasper's usually harsh exterior. From what he had told her, Fate and Luke had named him the godfather, and an official uncle. Somehow, she knew he would be a great one, and she foresaw toys and trinkets for the child in his future.

No doubt, he would spoil her rotten.

"She is beautiful," she said. "And I see she has you wrapped around her finger."

"Her Uncle Jase," he said with a proud, tender smile and he wiggled his finger when she grasped it to draw a giggle. His eyes twinkled when Annabelle brought his finger to her lips as though kissing it, and he leaned closer to kiss her forehead.

In that moment, Emeline knew she had made the right decision. She would miss her elven family, but nothing could have prepared her for the beauty of the moment. Tears filled her eyes as her heart filled with love for the kindhearted man before her. Determined, she knew that one day, she would give him this. She would bear him a child and give him everything she knew he had always wanted.

A home and a family who loved him beyond measure.

Because, heavens knew, she always would.

Dragon scars and all.